PRAISE FOR

EMMA CLINE

THE GUEST

NAMED A BEST BOOK OF THE YEAR BY
The New Yorker, Time, NPR, *The Washington Post,*
Financial Times, Harper's Bazaar, Elle, Vogue,
Newsweek, Good Housekeeping, Slate,
Chicago Public Library, Electric Lit

"Under [Emma] Cline's command, every sentence as sharp as a scalpel, a woman toeing the line between welcome and unwelcome guest becomes a fully destabilizing force."
—*The New York Times*

"Cline's writing at its very best—hypnotically propulsive, viscerally disquieting, and moving in the most unpredictable ways."
—*Financial Times*

"Sultry and engrossing, with a note of menace, [*The Guest* is a] gorgeously smart affair whose deceptive lightness conceals strange depths and an arresting originality."
—*The Guardian*

"Pitch-perfect . . . In *The Guest*, Cline has written a thriller about trying to get by, a summer read for the precariat."

—*The Nation*

"Cline weaves through settings and characters with intentional disorientation, shifting ever darker, ever more suspenseful. . . . Cline proves herself to be one of the boldest, most complicated writers working today."

—*San Francisco Chronicle*

"Cline puts her fearsome talents to work depicting the deeply destructive capacity of a lone mind that is utterly sick of itself. . . . The way [Cline's] writing is hospitable to the senses represents the highest form of thinking."

—*4Columns*

"A smoldering thriller that explores desire and deception."

—*The Washington Post*

"With her propulsive third book, Cline confirms her reputation as the literary prophet of women on the brink. . . . Dreamlike and disaffected, this charged study of class and gender lingers like a bad sunburn."   —*Esquire*

"Cline quietly continues to be one of the best and most discomfiting young writers working today."

—*Entertainment Weekly*

"A wonderfully suspenseful examination of luxury, delusion, class and fear." —Minneapolis *Star Tribune*

"Cline generates an impressive amount of intrigue. . . . The descriptions are frequently bracing and acute, sharpened to icepicks by a stance of amoral neutrality."
—*The Wall Street Journal*

"Emma Cline's *The Guest*—the must-read anxious-girl book of the season . . . offers a sharp, nuanced approach to an outwardly frothy premise, submerging her readers in an anxiety-ridden world where class struggle seethes under the surface."
—*Time*

"Enthralling . . . Who needs living when you've got *The Guest* in your bag?" —*Jezebel*

"Eerily captivating." —*Elle*

"Galvanizing and so utterly readable. The reader, who ingests the novel's sumptuous atmosphere and the thrill of trespass captured in Cline's sharp, tense prose, is implicated alongside the protagonist." —*The Millions*

"An intoxicating, sun-drunk work that tells the story of a hand-to-God grifter, one whose head you're both terrified of and want to bask in forever, until you wake up sunburnt to a crisp." —*NYLON*

DADDY

"When I read Emma Cline I think of Mary Gaitskill's psychological acuity and of Joy Williams's sardonic gravitas. And yet something about Cline's intimate tone, her talent for conjuring the feeling of being alive, is entirely and uniquely her own."　—RACHEL KUSHNER

THE GIRLS

"Spellbinding . . . A seductive and arresting coming-of-age story hinged on Charles Manson, told in sentences at times so finely wrought they could almost be worn as jewelry."   —*The New York Times Book Review*

"Debut novels like this are rare, indeed. . . . With the maturity of a writer twice her age, Cline has written a wise novel that's never showy: a quiet, seething confession of yearning and terror."   —*The Washington Post*

"Outstanding . . . Cline's novel is an astonishing work of imagination—remarkably atmospheric, preternaturally intelligent, and brutally feminist."   —*The Boston Globe*

BY
EMMA CLINE

The Girls

Daddy

The Guest

THE
GUEST

THE
GUEST

—

A Novel

—

EMMA
CLINE

RANDOM HOUSE · NEW YORK

Thank you to Bill Clegg and everyone at the Clegg Agency, and
to Kate Medina and the Random House team.

For early help, I'm grateful to Willing Davidson,
Hilary Cline, David Gilbert, Alexander Benaim, Sara Freeman,
Lexi Freiman, and Megan, Elsie, and Mayme Cline.

———

2024 Random House Trade Paperback Edition

Published in the United States by Random House, an imprint and
division of Penguin Random House LLC, New York.

RANDOM HOUSE and the HOUSE colophon are registered trademarks
of Penguin Random House LLC.

LIBRARY OF CONGRESS CATALOGING-IN-PUBLICATION DATA
NAMES: Cline, Emma, author.
TITLE: The guest: a novel / Emma Cline.
DESCRIPTION: First Edition. | New York: Random House, [2023]
IDENTIFIERS: LCCN 2022037681 (print) | LCCN 2022037682 (ebook) |
ISBN 9780812988031 (trade paperback) | ISBN 9780812998634 (ebook)
SUBJECTS: LCGFT: Novels. Classification: LCC PS3603.L547 G84
2023 (print) | LCC PS3603.L547 (ebook) | DDC 813/.6—dc23/eng/20220812

LC record available at https://lccn.loc.gov/2022037681

LC ebook record available at https://lccn.loc.gov/2022037682

Printed in the United States of America on acid-free paper

randomhousebooks.com

2 4 6 8 9 7 5 3

Book design by Barbara M. Bachman

For Hilary

THE
GUEST

1

THIS WAS AUGUST. The ocean was warm, and warmer every day.

Alex waited for a set to finish before making her way into the water, slogging through until it was deep enough to dive. A bout of strong swimming and she was out, beyond the break. The surface was calm.

From here, the sand was immaculate. The light—the famous light—made it all look honeyed and mild: the dark European green of the scrub trees, the dune grasses that moved in whispery unison. The cars in the parking lot. Even the seagulls swarming a trash can.

On the shore, the towels were occupied by placid beachgoers. A man tanned to the color of expensive luggage let out a yawn, a young mother watched her children run back and forth to the waterline.

What would they see if they looked at Alex?

In the water, she was just like everyone else. Nothing

strange about a young woman, swimming alone. No way to tell whether she belonged here or didn't.

WHEN SIMON HAD FIRST taken her to the beach, he'd kicked off his shoes at the entrance. Everyone did, apparently: there were shoes and sandals piled up by the low wood railing. No one takes them? Alex asked. Simon raised his eyebrows. Who would take someone's shoes?

But that had been Alex's immediate thought—how easy it would be to take things, out here. All sorts of things. The bikes leaning against the fence. The bags unattended on towels. The cars left unlocked, no one wanting to carry their keys on the beach. A system that existed only because everyone believed they were among people like themselves.

BEFORE ALEX LEFT FOR the beach, she had swallowed one of Simon's painkillers, a leftover from a long-ago back surgery, and already the familiar mental gauze had descended, the surrounding salt water another narcotic. Her heart beat pleasantly, noticeably, in her chest. Why did being in the ocean make you feel like such a good human? She floated on her back, her body moving a little in the push and pull, her eyes closed against the sun.

There was a party tonight, hosted by one of Simon's friends. Or a business friend—all his friends were business friends. Until then, hours to waste. Simon would be working the rest of the day, Alex left to her own devices, as she had been ever since they'd come out here—almost two weeks now. She hadn't minded. She'd gone to the beach nearly every day. Worked through Simon's painkiller stash at a steady but undetectable pace, or so she hoped. And ignored Dom's increasingly unhinged texts, which was easy enough to do. He had no idea where she was. She tried blocking his number, but he got through with new ones. She would change her number as soon as she got the chance. Dom had sent another jag that morning:

> Alex
> Alex
> Answer me

Even if the texts still caused a lurch in her stomach, she had only to look up from the phone and it all seemed manageable. She was in Simon's house, the windows open onto pure green. Dom was in another sphere, one she could pretend no longer quite existed.

STILL FLOATING ON HER BACK, Alex opened her eyes, disoriented by the quick hit of sun. She righted herself with a glance at the shore: she was farther out than she'd imagined. Much farther. How had that happened? She tried to head back in, toward the beach, but she wasn't seeming to get anywhere, her strokes eaten up by the water.

She took a breath, tried again. Her legs kicked hard. Her arms churned. It was impossible to gauge whether the shore was getting any closer. Another attempt to head straight back in, more useless swimming. The sun kept beating down, the horizon line wavered: it was all utterly indifferent.

The end—here it was.

This was punishment, she was certain of it.

Strange, though, how this terror didn't last. It only passed through her, appearing and disappearing almost instantly.

Something else took its place, a kind of reptile curiosity. She considered the distance, considered her heart rate, made a calm assessment of the elements in play. Hadn't she always been good at seeing things clearly?

Time to change course. She swam parallel to the shore. Her body took over, remembering the strokes. She didn't allow for any hesitation. At some point, the water started resisting her with less force, and then she was moving along, getting closer to shore, and then close enough that her feet touched the sand.

She was out of breath, yes. Her arms were sore, her heartbeat juddered out of sync. She was much farther down the beach.

But fine—she was fine.

The fear was already forgotten.

No one on the shore noticed her, or looked twice. A couple walked past, heads bent, studying the sand for shells. A man in waders assembled a fishing pole. Laughter floated over from a group under a sun tent. Surely, if Alex had been in any real danger, someone would have reacted, one of these people would have stepped in to help.

———

SIMON'S CAR WAS FUN to drive. Frighteningly responsive, frighteningly fast. Alex hadn't bothered to change out of her swimsuit, and the leather upholstery cooked her thighs. Even at a good speed, the car windows down, the air was thick and warm. What problem did Alex need to solve at this moment? Nothing. No variables to calculate, the painkiller still doing its good work. Compared to the city, this was heaven.

The city. She was not in the city, and thank god for that.

It was Dom, of course, but not only Dom. Even before Dom, something had soured. In March she had turned twenty-two without fanfare. She had a recurring stye that drooped her left eyelid unpleasantly. The makeup she applied to cover it only made it worse: she reinfected herself, the stye pulsing for months. Finally she'd gotten an antibiotic prescribed at a walk-in clinic. Every night she tugged on her lids and squeezed a line of medicated ointment straight into the socket. Involuntary tears streamed only from her left eye.

On the subway, or on the sidewalks, woolly with new snow, Alex had started to notice strangers giving her a certain look. Their gaze lingering. A woman in a plaid mohair coat studied Alex with unnerving focus, her expression twisted with what seemed like mounting concern. A man, his wrists white under the strain of many plastic bags, stared at Alex until she finally got off the train.

What were people seeing in her aura, what stink was emanating?

Maybe she was imagining it. But maybe not.

She'd been twenty when she first arrived in the city. Back when she still had the energy to use a fake name and still believed gestures like that had value, meant the things she was doing weren't actually happening in her real life. Back when she kept lists: The names of the places she went with the men. Restaurants that charged for bread and butter. Restaurants that refolded your napkin when you went to the bathroom. Restaurants that only served steak, pink but flavorless and thick as a hardcover book. Brunches at mid-range hotels, with unripe strawberries and too-sweet juice, slurry with pulp. But the appeal of the lists wore off quickly or something about them started to depress her, so she stopped.

Now Alex was no longer welcome in certain hotel bars, had to avoid certain restaurants. Whatever charm she had was losing its potency. Not fully, not totally, but enough that she began to understand it was a possibility. She'd seen it happen to others, the older girls she'd known since moving here. They defected for their hometowns, making a grab at a normal life, or else disappeared entirely.

In April: A manager had, in low tones, threatened to call the police after she'd tried to charge dinner to an old client's account. Too many of her usuals stopped reaching out, for whatever reason—ultimatums eked out of couples therapy and this new fad of radical honesty, or the first flushes of guilt precipitated by the birth of children, or just plain boredom. Her monthly cash flow fell precipitously. Alex considered breast augmentation. She rewrote her ad copy, paid an exorbitant fee to be featured in the first page of results. Dropped her rates, then dropped them again.

Six hundred roses, the ads said. Six hundred kisses. Things only very young girls would want six hundred of.

Alex got a series of laser treatments: flashes of blue light soaked her face while she looked out of tinted medical goggles like a somber spaceman. In the meantime, she had her photos redone by a twitchy art student who asked, mildly, whether she might consider a trade for services. He had a pet bunny that lurched around his makeshift studio, its eyes demonic pink.

May: One of her roommates wondered why their Klonopin was dwindling so rapidly. A gift card had gone missing, a favorite bracelet. A consensus that Alex had been the one to break the window unit. Had Alex broken the window unit? She had no memory of it, but it was possible. Things she touched started to seem doomed.

June: Desperation made her lax with her usual screening policies—she waived references, waived photo IDs, and she'd been ripped off more than once. A guy had Alex take a cab out to the JFK airport hotel, promising to reimburse her in person, and then stopped answering her calls, Alex on the sidewalk dialing again and again, the wind attacking her dress while the taxi drivers slowed to look.

And in July, after the roommates demanded that the back rent be paid in the next two weeks or else they would change the locks, Dom came back to town.

DOM HAD BEEN AWAY for almost a year, a self-imposed exile in the wake of some trouble she didn't want to know too much about. Better, with Dom, to never know too much. He said he'd been arrested—more than once—but never seemed to actually spend any time in jail, alluding vaguely to some variety of diplomatic immunity, some last-minute intervention on his behalf by high-ranking officials. Did he think anyone believed the things he said? He lied more than she did, lied for no reason. Alex had promised herself she wouldn't see Dom again. Then he texted—someone who actually wanted to spend time with her, maybe the only person who wanted to spend time with her. She couldn't quite conjure the reasons she'd ever been afraid of him. They had fun, didn't they? He liked her, didn't he?

He was staying in an apartment he said belonged to a friend. They drank room-temperature ginger ale. Dom walked around barefoot, lowering all the shades. There was a line of whipped cream containers covered in stickers along a windowsill, empty seltzer cans in a CVS bag on top of the trash. He kept checking his phone. When the apartment buzzer rang, and kept ringing, he ignored it, giggling, until it finally stopped. He made an omelet at four A.M. that neither of them touched. They watched a reality show: The older women on-screen sat on the sunny outdoor patio of a restaurant, sucking violently at glasses of iced tea. The women's conversations were heated, faces in a mask of drama. "I never said that," the dark-haired woman bleated.

"You seen this before?" Dom asked without looking away from the TV. He was cradling a stuffed penguin in his arms, worrying its shiny button eyes.

The woman on-screen stood up, knocking her chair over. "You're toxic," she screamed. "Toxic," the woman repeated, her finger fucking the air. She stalked away, breathing hard, a cameraman backing up out of frame when she came barreling past.

They watched another episode, and then another. Dom lay with his head on her knee, licking the drugs off his fingers. When he put his hand in her underwear, she didn't move it away. Still they kept watching. All the women in the show hated each other, hated each other so much, just so they could avoid hating their husbands. Only their little dogs, blinking from their laps, seemed real: they were the women's souls, Alex decided, tiny souls trotting behind them on a leash.

How long had Alex stayed there with Dom? At least two days.

And how soon, after she left, had Dom figured it out?

Almost immediately.

Dom called her four times in quick succession. He never called, only texted. So instantly Alex understood she had made a mistake. The texts came rapid-fire.

> Alex
> Are u fucking kidding me
> What the fuck
> Can you just
> fucking
> pick up

Alex had been on hour ten of a nice, swimmy run of benzos when he'd called: a warm compress cooling on the last dregs of the stye, takeout stinking up the room but blessedly out of sight. The texts from Dom had seemed funny.

But then Dom left a message the next day, almost crying, and he had been nice enough to her. Almost a friend, in his demented way.

She finally responded with a text:

I can't talk rn. But in a few days, ok?

Alex had assumed, at first, that some solution would turn up. It always did. So she kept putting Dom off. He checked in almost daily.

Alex?

Things escalated. Dom calling again. Dom leaving voicemails. Acting lighthearted, even jokey, as if this was a low-key misunderstanding. Then swinging wildly into aggression, his voice going to some eerie psycho register, and she was genuinely afraid. She remembered the time—last year. Or it must have been before that, before he left the city. When he woke her up with his hands on her throat. Her eyes locked onto his—his hands tightened. His expression was one of mild concentration. She didn't look away until he pressed hard enough that her eyes closed and she felt them roll back in her head.

Alex could change her number, but what about the ads she'd already paid for, ads that were linked to this phone number? She told herself Dom would get tired of this eventually. He'd require fresh blood.

But then, leaving her place one morning, she'd spotted Dom across the street. Dom lingering on the sidewalk, hands in his pockets. It was Dom, it had to be. Maybe not. Or was it just a coincidence? She hadn't given him her new address. She was suddenly paranoid. The stye was coming back. Her roommates no longer acknowledged her in the common areas. They changed the Wi-Fi password. The bathroom cabinet had been emptied of every medication, even ibuprofen.

Alex had the disorienting sense that she was infectious.

IT HAD BEEN A dead night, no takers.

Maybe Alex was giving off a spiky, desperate air—people could tell when you needed things, had an animal nose for failure. Alex kept checking her messages, waiting for a bite, but Dom was lighting up her phone, offering to call her a car, trying to get her to meet him at the subway stop near the park. Alex turned the phone over.

Alex was on her second seltzer in a rocks glass—better not to actually drink, just appear to be drinking—when a man sat down a few stools away from her at the counter. A man in a white button-up and a full head of hair. Normally, she would have clocked the man immediately as a civilian, someone whose self-conception wouldn't include participation in certain arrangements. Those men weren't a good use of her energy. But maybe that had been an error, her focus on more immediate gratifications—because where had that gotten her? She'd been overlooking the protection a civilian could offer. Something more permanent. Adrenaline coursed through her: this was a man who could turn things around.

Who started the conversation, him or her? At any rate, at the man's invitation, Alex moved to the stool next to his. His watch glinted as he made a point of dropping his phone in his pocket: she had his full attention.

"I'm Simon," the man said.

He smiled at her. She smiled back.

Here was the answer, the emergency exit she had always suspected might present itself.

Alex was hitting all the correct beats, like she had been training for this exact moment, and maybe she had. She allowed Simon to order her a real drink. When she laughed, she covered her mouth with her hand, as if she were especially shy. She watched him take this gesture in, like he took in her two modest glasses of white wine, her napkin spread primly on her lap. The conversation came easy. Alex must have looked, to Simon, like a normal girl. A normal, young girl, enjoying her life in the city. But not enjoying it too much: she turned down a third glass of wine but accepted an after-dinner coffee.

Everything had gone right. Simon asked her on a date. An actual date. And then another. Alex stopped seeing the other men. Avoided certain triggers, parts of the city. Alex never invited Simon to her apartment. She stopped answering late night calls. Resisted the urge to take anything of Simon's: the pearly cufflinks, the cash he wadded carelessly on his nightstand.

When did things get dire—a few weeks later?

August was right around the corner, Alex still stalling

Dom, trying to figure out who she could crash with if—
when?—her roommates kicked her out. Her apartment
keys vanished from her purse—or had the roommates repossessed them? She spent a whole night waiting on the
stoop until the nicest roommate finally came home from
his late shift. His face, like everyone's seemed to lately, fell
at the sight of Alex. At least he let her upstairs to shower,
though he wouldn't let her linger.

Then Simon had swooped in to save the day.

His house out east. He'd love it if she came with him for
August. She could stay through the month. He had a fun
party every Labor Day—she'd have a good time.

Alex abandoned the shared apartment without paying
the outstanding back rent, though she left behind most of
her old clothes, all the cheap pressboard furniture, as a partial payment. Alex ignored calls and texts from her former
roommates, blocked Dom's number. Dom would get over
it, at some point. No one from what she was already thinking of as her old life knew about Simon, knew where Alex
had gone. None of the people she had, in whatever way,
vague or acute, wronged.

She had disappeared herself—it had been easy.

THE REST OF THE summer she would spend here, with
Simon, and then in September—Simon had his place in
the city. There was talk of Alex moving in. Whenever
Simon alluded to any possible future, Alex dropped her
eyes; otherwise, her desperation would be too obvious.
Simon still believed Alex had her apartment, and that was

important. Keep up the appearance of self-sufficiency, let him feel he was navigating all of this. At this point, restraint was best.

SIMON.

He was a kind person, mostly.

He had shown Alex photos on his phone of himself as a young man, handsome with an avid face. He was in his fifties now, but that full hair was still there, and he was in good shape. It was all the halibut that crowded the freezer, the white slabs he grilled with so much lemon that Alex felt her mouth vibrate. He had a trainer who hooked him up to electrodes that shocked his muscles to tightness, who suggested ice baths and organ meats, all the novelty add-ons of the professionally healthy. Simon maintained such psychotic discipline because he seemed to believe even the smallest lapse in vigilance would result in catastrophe. And probably he was right. Occasionally the control dropped: Simon took a jar of peanut butter to the couch, eating with fastidious care until it was empty, the spoon licked clean by his surprisingly pink tongue. He gazed sadly into the scraped jar, as if offended by the sight.

Simon had a daughter who didn't live with him, and an ex-wife on the other side of the country, but there was no rancor, not that Alex could sense. Simon always left the room to talk to his daughter on the phone. Caroline had the dark glossy hair of the wealthy, the groomed eyebrows and garments in dry-clean-only fabrics. One of those daughters of the rich who were pitiable because, in the end, they could buy everything but beauty. Alex had only seen photos of Caroline, a skinny girl always clutching her own elbows, a girl who appeared to be frowning even when she was smiling. She hoped desperately to become a singer. Alex saw sorrow in the daughter's future but that was probably just projection.

Simon's house out east was near enough to the ocean. The living room ceiling was twenty feet high, cut with beams. A polished concrete floor. Big paintings that, by pure dint of their square footage, implied high value. Simon's specialty was the secondary market, and Alex cultivated a thoughtful expression when Simon showed her a run of JPEGs or if they went to a dinner at a collector's house. Sometimes she tried to guess the price of things, or guess what Simon might say when they were alone. But Alex never guessed right—there were too many invisible contexts. Maybe there had been a poor showing for similar work at the evening sales. Maybe an artist had used certain materials that tended to degrade, making the piece too volatile to be covered by insurance. If the wrong person had owned something beforehand— a newly flush collector with a naïve eye, tech CEOs under federal investigation—that could taint it in some way. The value was based on a network of factors that were constantly in flux. Sometimes the work was a mere idea of the work, existing only as an image emailed back and forth, collectors reselling a piece they'd bought before they'd ever even seen it in person.

This game of convincing people how much things were worth—in that way, she and Simon were not so different.

———

THE LAST WEEKS HAD passed pleasantly. It had been easy to slot herself into Simon's life here: its textures and habits were so finely woven that Alex had only to submit. They went to his friends' houses for dinner, assistants emailing first to inquire about any dietary restrictions. None, Alex always chirped back. That was the point of Alex—to offer up no friction whatsoever. They went to garden parties in the buzzy, buggy afternoons and Alex stood there while Simon talked and drank white wine. His friends looked at Alex with unspecific smiles—maybe they assumed they had met some previous time, had confused Alex with one of Simon's other young women. Nice to see you, they always said, the safe phrase allowing the possibility to go in either direction. Having fun? someone might say, finally directing a question to Alex, and she would nod but their eyes would have already slipped back to Simon's. They were sometimes patronizing, Simon's friends, but she had long ago become inured to the disapproval of strangers. All those times she had sat in public across from men twice her age, men with sweating, exposed scalps. She felt the presentiment that she would be looked at and understood how to keep herself steeled against those stares.

But this was not that. This thing with Simon. She leaned into Simon and he kept talking but dropped a hand to her low back. On the ride home, he'd tell her about his friends. Their private lives, their hidden problems. And Alex would ask questions and egg him on and he'd flash her a smile, his pleasure suddenly so boyish.

This was real, her and Simon. Or it could be.

During the day, Alex watched television in the sunroom, read magazines in the bath until the water got cold. She went alone to the beach, or swam in Simon's pool. On Mondays, Wednesdays, and Fridays, a woman came to do laundry and clean. Alex spent hours being chased from room to room by silent, industrious Patricia, who took in Alex's presence with the same unmoving expression she took in any mess.

It wasn't hard. None of it was hard.

Every once in a while, Alex took one of Simon's painkillers to stitch the looser hours together, though she did not share this information with Simon. She was on best behavior. If she drank from a glass, she rinsed it immediately and put it in the dishwasher. She wiped away the leftover ring on the table. Didn't drop wet towels on the bed, or leave the toothpaste uncapped. Monitored the number of pills she cadged to avoid Simon's detection. Made a point of cooing over Simon's dog, Chivas, who Simon kissed on the mouth.

When Simon texted that he was almost done working, Alex splashed water on her face and brushed her teeth. She changed into an expensive T-shirt Simon had bought for her, then sat around, waiting, like the end of every day was a first date.

Had Simon ever had to wait for Alex, did Simon ever anticipate her arrival?

No. But who cared?

These were small concessions considering what they allowed.

———

OF COURSE SHE HAD not told Simon about Dom. She had not told Simon a lot of things. She'd learned early on that it was necessary to maintain some distance. Keep up a few untruths. It was easy, and then easier. And wasn't it better to give people what they wanted? A conversation performed as a smooth transaction—a silky back-and-forth without the interruption of reality. Most everyone preferred the story. Alex had learned how to provide it, how to draw people in with a vision of themselves, recognizable but turned up ten degrees, amplified into something better. How to allude to her own desires as if they were shared desires. Somewhere, deep in their brains, the synapses fired, chugging along in the direction she set out for them. People were relieved, grateful to click in to something bigger, easier.

And it was good to be someone else. To believe, even for a half moment, that the story was different. Alex had imagined what kind of person Simon would like, and that was the person Alex told him she was. All Alex's unsavory history excised until it started to seem, even to her, like none of it had ever happened.

Simon believed that Alex had graduated from college last year and had just moved to the city. He believed Alex's mother was an art teacher and her father coached high school football. He believed Alex had grown up in the middle of the country. He asked her, once, why she wasn't close to her family—she said her parents were angry with her for not going to church anymore. "Poor little sinner," Simon said, though he seemed genuinely moved by the idea of

Alex being alone in the world. Which wasn't untrue. Simon thought of Alex as a real person, or enough for his purposes. Alex spoke of the possibility of grad school and this seemed to soothe Simon, imply a modest life of self-improvement. Ambitious in the mildest version of the word.

THERE WAS STILL DEBRIS on the road back from the beach, leftovers from a summer storm, but most of the larger branches had been cleared away. The thin sunlight erased any memory, sugar bright on the cedar-shingled houses.

All the back roads looked the same. Trees meeting overhead, making a hollow cut by the occasional driveway. Roads lined by the same deep summer green, green packed so tight you couldn't see anything beyond. The houses were hidden behind hedges and gates, offering no navigable landmarks.

Alex's mind was elsewhere, so she didn't quite register the street she had turned onto. A sudden movement among the trees made her glance over. A deer, maybe. There were so many of them here, forever darting across the roads.

The sound of a car horn got her attention. Another car was driving toward her. The driver honked again, more aggressively. This was a one-way street, Alex realized. Too late. She tried to back into a driveway to turn around. She must have miscalculated the distance: the noise startled her, until she understood it was coming from her car. Or, rather, coming from Simon's car. The rear bumper made audible contact.

The other driver didn't even stop, didn't even slow.

Maybe if she hadn't been so flustered—the riptide, Dom, the painkiller shroud—this wouldn't have happened. Already Alex was practicing what she would say to Simon, calculating exactly how childish she'd have to act to escape his anger.

Alex left the car running while she got out to look at the damage. She had hit a stone retaining wall with the rear bumper, one of Simon's cherry-red taillights cracked open and missing a not-insignificant piece. She located it in the dirt, now just a scatter of red plastic. Maybe five hundred bucks to replace, not the worst. Though who could tell with these fancy cars, their particular mechanics, special parts? The imported paint. At least the bumper was only a little bit crumpled. She looked around, as though there might be help coming from some direction, someone who might arrive and take control of the situation.

Simon would be unhappy, his beloved car. This would be a mark against her.

The rest of the car looked okay, but as she scanned she kept her gaze a little blurry—better, for the confession, if Alex didn't know the full extent of the damage. Anyway, it seemed minor.

AS SHE STEPPED INSIDE Simon's house, the humidity dropped away instantly, the air-conditioning shocking the afternoon into a slight unreality. The day erased itself.

Simon's office was in a separate building on the property—Alex could see the ceiling fan going through the window, which meant Simon was inside, working. Good. She didn't want to see him yet. She was too rattled.

Don't think of the car, don't think of Dom, don't name this new feeling of dread.

A quick swim, she decided.

The screen door to the backyard had been manufactured in such a way that it was impossible to slam; it closed behind Alex in slow-motion silence.

Simon's assistant, Lori, sat at a table by the pool with two cellphones in front of her. She lived an hour away, in some cheaper town, woke up before the sun rose to drive to Simon's. She had a tattoo of a rose on her left forearm and a live-in girlfriend who sometimes dropped her off but never got out of the car. Among other duties, Lori was in charge of Chivas, Simon's dog. Lori was always trying to train Chivas to wear a tiny hiking backpack so he could carry a water bottle when she took him for walks. Whenever they returned, Lori spent an hour cross-legged on the floor, eyes squinted, checking Chivas's fur for ticks with unbroken attention that bordered on the erotic.

"It's the worst season on record," Lori had noted, multiple times. "Ticks are everywhere. The deer are crawling with them."

Now Chivas was barking steadily at the man in uniform who was crouching in the grass, servicing the gas grill before the Labor Day party. When the dog leapt half-up on the man's back, the repairman looked to Lori for help. Lori didn't say anything.

Alex could see a few holes in the lawn where Chivas had gone after the gophers. Simon would be annoyed, though he adored the dog—didn't mind its watery blue eyes, didn't mind the pale growths festooning its muzzle.

Alex draped the big beach towel over one of the metal chairs and pulled it into the sun to dry. She felt she was moving at a normal speed, doing normal things.

"How was the beach?" Lori said, barely looking up.

There had been others before her, Alex knew, other young women with weekend bags and hopeful, careful bodies, other women who drifted into the kitchen at ten in the morning to drink coffee someone else had made for them, tugging their cotton underpants out of their ass and looking around for Simon. Thin girls in camisoles who ate yogurt standing up. But Alex had outlasted them, had passed into another, more permanent realm. They were ghosts; she was real. Alex lived here; her clothes were in the closet. For the rest of the summer, anyway. She was no longer vulnerable to Lori's opinion.

"Really nice." Alex made herself smile, made herself catch Lori's eye. Hard to guess exactly how much Lori disliked her. "The water was perfect."

Before she got in the pool, she stretched, long enough that Alex could feel Lori was watching her. Could Lori sense something was wrong?

Alex dove into the water.

THE POOL WAS NARROW but long, perfect for laps, which Simon executed daily with manic focus. He told Alex he exercised so much because when he'd gone to business

school in Europe, he'd gotten fat from eating hamburgers—
that's all he knew how to order. Since then, he was obsessed
with never being fat again, up at six A.M. to work out on a
machine where he climbed the equivalent of eighty flights
of stairs, then to the pool where he swam feverish laps until
the sun rose.

Even with all those early morning laps, he was a poor
swimmer, with a habitual stroke too ingrained to ever improve.

"Maybe try this way," Alex said, the first day she was
here, showing Simon a stroke that would lessen the strain
on his tricky back. "It takes the pressure off."

Simon corrected his stroke for a few lengths, reining in
his wild effort, then reverted back to his old form.

"You're doing it again," Alex said, making her way to
Simon through the water. "Let me show you."

"It's fine," Simon said, his voice clipped, shaking off
Alex's hand.

She made herself laugh a little. She sat on the pool steps.
Simon went back to his laps, the water churning in his
wake. All this energy he expended. Simon said something
to her that she pretended not to hear. Alex made her hands
into a scoop and gathered the floating leaves, the torn blos-
soms on the water's surface. She made a wet pile on the
concrete that edged the pool and tidied it absently. So that
was more information to file away—don't correct Simon.
Alex plucked a bee from the pool by the filmy wing and
added it to the pile of other dead things.

Who would clean them up? Someone. Not her.

———

AFTER A FEW QUICK laps, Alex floated on her back. She could hear her heart in her ears. She inhaled for four counts, held it for four counts, exhaled for four counts. Straight above was the cloudless sky, a blue that seemed pulled tight. The airport was on the other side of the highway—a small plane arced across her vision, slowing for a landing.

Alex did ride in a helicopter once, with Simon, on their way out here. The noise had been deafening, a noise out of war movies, and it was odd, this heart-churning racket paired with the dreamlike sensation of rising straight into the air. It had been nighttime, the last hour before the airport's enforced curfew. The helicopter seemed to be flying extraordinarily low, enough that she saw, amidst the dark ruffles of trees, the illuminated swimming pools that dotted the landscape, pockets of blue and green hovering out there in the blackness. She kept bracing for a crash—as if such blatant excess deserved swift punishment.

A muffled sound, a bad feeling: Alex opened her eyes to a shadowed figure standing by the pool. It was Lori, her hands on her hips.

"Sorry?" Alex said.

"I said, do you need anything before I head out?"

SIMON'S BEDROOM WAS IN the back of the house, down a long hallway. It was quiet inside, the curtains drawn against the daylight and the heat. The bed was made so tightly. Such shocking cleanliness, edging on the perverse. She wanted to throw herself on those perfect uncreased sheets, but didn't. The perfect sheets, the chilly rooms: they were stupid things, taken one by one, but all together they were a convincing substitute for a life. One where suffering seemed to have no place, the idea of pain or misfortune starting to fuzz out and seem less likely. And who could argue with that, with wanting to be protected? No problem was unsolvable. Could she imagine the trajectory continuing upward? Good fortune accruing and accruing, the world suddenly opening in any direction, like one of those trick boxes, the sides falling down and revealing there were no more limits.

Even this thing with Dom could seem manageable. Like she could fix it.

How? She didn't know, exactly.

Alex calmed herself by making an inventory of the room, watching the trees move behind the curtains. She pretended not to notice the voicemail notifications on her home screen. She played a game on her phone that involved collecting diamonds before a black turtle could eat them. She kept playing until the turtle finally ate all the diamonds.

YOU LOSE, the screen said, the words vibrating, and she dropped the phone on the bed.

THIS PART WAS COMFORTING, the getting ready. Taking concrete action, executing the familiar set of steps. Alex had gotten good at it, over the years, this ceremony of preparation.

She took her time that evening, working up a trance. The bathroom went steamy, the rolls of toilet paper rippled in the humidity. With all her careful labor, the afternoon seemed farther and farther away. Alex stared at the mirror long enough that her face went abstract, too, now just light and shadow.

She used her fingers to dot foundation on her forehead, under her eyes, along her jaw. Brisk work with a damp sponge to spread it all out and disappear the flaws. Then she had to bring herself back to life: blush, a pearly highlighter at the brow bone. She darkened her eyebrows with short strokes—more realistic, the short strokes. She caught her own eye in the mirror as she silently pumped an eyelash curler.

Thirteen, fourteen, fifteen times.

Like a lot of the other girls, Alex had found out quickly that she was not beautiful enough to model. The lucky ones realized this sooner rather than later. But she was tall enough and skinny enough that people often assumed she was more beautiful than she was. A good trick.

Thin brown hair cut at her shoulders. Short fingers with filthy nails—how could a girl in this century get such dirty fingernails? Add it to the running list:

Keep fingernails clean.

Keep breath sweet.

Don't leave toothpaste in the sink basin.

She shaved her underarms, dragging the razor in the shape of a cross. Then went over the skin again, Alex wincing at the scraped feeling. The skin was smooth, when she finished, stinging a little in the bitten places. Her hair was on the edge of dirty, one more day before she had to wash it but okay for tonight, brushed back. Simon didn't like it falling in her eyes—she hit it with oil to keep it smooth, keep everything in place.

"THERE SHE IS," SIMON SAID, coming into the bedroom. The sight of him was like a tonic—here it was, Alex's life. Just as she had left it.

When Simon was done working for the day, he always seemed a little bewildered. He kept patting his shirt pocket absentmindedly for his phone.

"Wow." Simon looked her up and down like he always did, the gesture so amplified it was almost slapstick, a cartoon wolf in a suit.

"That's a great dress," he said. "You have great taste."

Simon had bought the dress for her.

Most of the clothes Alex owned, now, were gifts from Simon, the brand names like vocabulary words in a foreign language. Her old stuff she'd left in the apartment—it was crap, most of it. Not even worth the resale value—dresses stained with deodorant, the suede heels she'd had resoled multiple times. She suspected Simon was trying to make her appear older than twenty-two, these clothes he chose for her in dark colors. The linen shirts, the trousers, skirts with hemlines that hit her knee. The clothes were still fitted, of course, still marked her waist and breasts. It was just a more oblique way of achieving the same end, more palatable because it was less obvious.

The earrings she was wearing were another gift: Simon had presented the earrings to Alex inside a box inside a cloth bag inside another bag, and the act of opening the many layers extended the whole process to a grotesque length. Which maybe he had intended. She hadn't said thank you: the other girls had taught her that. You don't thank them—you smile and accept what they give you, as if it was something that already belonged to you.

"So pretty," Alex had said, holding up the earrings, "I love them," and the strange part was she really did, the drops of silver. Like earrings she might have chosen for herself. Occasionally she believed that she and Simon were actually in something like love.

"Aren't you going to keep the box?" Simon had said, and Alex nodded and immediately corrected herself, smoothing the bag into a clean fold and re-coiling the white ribbon.

SIMON SAT ON THE BED and Alex joined him, her hand going automatically to the back of his neck. She kneaded hard, then scratched his hair. Lightly. Very lightly.

"Don't stop," Simon said.

These moments were nice—Alex was giving him something tangible, playing her nails along his scalp. Simon lay with his head in her lap like a child, his eyes closed. Alex studied him from above. He was fairly handsome. He was trying to drink more water and had started dumping sachets of mushroom powder into his metal water bottle. Alex had tried a sip: it made the water taste swampy and expensive.

"You smell good." Simon's eyes were still closed.

"I took a shower," she said.

"You went to the beach?"

"Yeah."

Alex pressed her fingers harder on Simon's scalp, not letting herself dwell on anything that had happened after the beach. No fucking up of the car, the hundreds or possibly thousand dollars of trouble Alex had created. Make it so the tape started at the beach lot, the drive home uneventful, the reel ending with Alex parking the car. Alex could tell Simon about the rip current. The moment she believed she was in danger. She could tell him about Dom. But she didn't.

"Waves were a little big," Alex said. "But nice."

"Mm." Simon was quiet for a minute, letting Alex rub his neck. "Maybe you should wear the blue dress instead," he said. "Tonight. It gets chilly on the water."

"Sure," Alex said, her voice light.

Silence.

Normal, she told herself, everything was normal. She worried Simon could sense her unease. But of course he couldn't. His eyes were shut. Alex let her hand laze to his crotch, watching Simon as she did. His mouth automatically parted, his lids going heavy. He opened his eyes to look at Alex, then shut them. He widened his legs, pulling Alex to the floor by the wrist. How easily these things went.

Alex knelt beside the bed. Simon was lying back. Alex undid Simon's pants, keeping a mild expression on her face. It took Simon a while to get fully hard; her mind wandered, then returned. Her thoughts located themselves in different places around the room. The tree branches flashing out the window. The painting over the bed, a recent addition. What had happened to the old one? He got sick of things so quickly. She would have to fix her makeup, after—though she couldn't appear to care. Alex felt Simon surge in her hand. Alex caught his eye, looking, as they all seemed to prefer, right up at him. Her dress was probably ruined—fine. Simon wanted her to wear the blue.

TRAFFIC WAS BAD, EVEN on a Monday, the main highway packed in both directions. Simon sighed, flicking through the radio dial, then starting over again. Alex's knee was bouncing, her nerves jittery. She made herself stop.

Everything, Alex told herself, was fine.

Simon hadn't noticed the damage to his car's bumper. Or—this would be best—he noticed and just didn't mention it. Was this possible?

"It's Monday, where are all these people coming from," Simon muttered. "Jesus."

Stop-and-go traffic, the air smelling of exhaust. Simon kept trying to see around the cars in front of them, as if he could scout some alternate route invisible to everyone else. And it was possible he could—all these back roads out here, people zigzagging around, greedy for even a few extra minutes.

"You're quiet," Simon said, without looking at Alex.

Alex shrugged. "Just tired."

Alex tried to slow her thoughts down, match them to

the crawl of traffic. It was soothing, even, to try to submit to the larger forces at work, the mental static that traffic allowed—there was nothing Alex could do to improve this moment, no angle to consider, no moves to play through. She smoothed her dress on her thighs.

Her purse was in her lap, a soft leather the color of tobacco. Another gift from Simon, it had come with its own cloth storage bag and a special polishing wipe for the hardware. Bags, the other girls had taught her, were the one thing that actually had resale value. None of the other men had ever gotten her nice stuff: plasticky lingerie in too-bright colors, a pair of wan satin tap shorts, cheap stockings that stunk of chemicals. Like they got some punitive pleasure from withholding access to objects with real worth. Alex took very good care of the purse, monitoring any scuff. The first time she had seen a blemish, an inadvertent fingernail scratch, she felt actual sorrow.

Her phone was in her purse, and, if she shifted, she could check the screen without Simon seeing. But why did she want to check? It could only be Dom, texting again with exhortations to Answer. The. Fucking. Phone. And anyway, Simon didn't like Alex to be on her phone when they were together. He had never said as much, but Alex felt him watching, making his internal notes of disapproval. Best behavior, Alex told herself. She didn't touch the phone.

The party was at a woman named Helen's house. Her first husband drowned, Simon told Alex on the drive over. While scuba diving, or something like that, he couldn't remember. One of those freak accidents the rich suffer—too many people kept them in too good of shape for them to die from natural causes. Life had ceased to be dangerous, the oxygen tanks and hormone tests and syringes full of B vitamins warding off the old killers.

Traffic was at almost a full standstill.

Simon snapped the radio off. Music didn't seem to give him any pleasure—Alex liked that he didn't pretend otherwise. Younger men had to make everything mean something, had to turn every choice and preference into a referendum on their personality. They had made her uneasy, the men she'd seen who'd been closer to her own age. The possibility of exposure was too great. Much better to have the buffer of an entirely different generation: the older men had no context for Alex, couldn't even begin to inadvertently piece together any semblance of her real self.

Alex let her hand rest on Simon's knee. Out the window, the houses and storefronts passed, then a stretch of empty land. A new development going up, whoever wouldn't mind living right on the highway with all the noise. You could get used to anything, was the point.

"Oh shit," Simon said. "Well, here's the problem."

Traffic snaked around the scene of an accident. A white convertible was crumpled by the side of the road, a chunky SUV askew in the road behind. Two cop cars were parked on the shoulder with their lights going but no sirens.

There were no victims in sight, no injured parties, just a cop in an orange vest, waving traffic along.

Simon whistled, slowing down to look.

"It's that left turn," he said. "It's the worst."

"Maybe everyone was fine." Alex's voice sounded brittle: she tried to soften it.

"Doubtful." Simon was somber, shaking his head, though Alex detected a note of excitement. "No one's walking away from that alive."

Even though Alex understood that they were driving in Simon's car, and even though Alex understood she had only had a fender bender that afternoon, a minor fender bender, Alex had the sudden feeling, for whatever reason, that she had been inside the white car. That she had died, here on the highway. It was a dumb thought, but she couldn't shake it. Maybe she was going crazy. At the same time, she knew she would never go crazy—which was worse. She'd been almost jealous of the people she'd known in the city who'd totally cracked up, spiraled into some other realm. It was a relief to have the option to fully peace out of reality.

Simon crossed the main road, turning onto a smaller road, and then another. Houses were set farther back until most everything was hidden behind a wall or a hedgerow. Alex could smell the ocean getting nearer.

"You know," Simon said, gesturing out the window, "all this used to be potato fields. Hard to imagine, huh?"

It was not the first time he'd said this. It seemed to please Simon, imagining the process by which something worthless became something valuable. But it wasn't so hard to imagine—just take away these houses, the big fat boxes waving American flags over the front doors, and it was land, green and golden and not in its way so different from the place Alex had come from.

2

THEY STOPPED AT A metal gate flanked on both sides by a high wooden fence, a voice glitching over the intercom. Simon repeated his name twice before the gate swung open and they drove in on the pale gravel. Directly ahead, a semicircle of cars was parked in front of the main house. Alex could see a tennis court, a pool behind a smaller gate.

Alex kept her face blank and mild, though she felt a jolt at the obvious nearness of the sea. She poked her tongue along her top teeth, feeling for anything errant.

Simon cut the ignition. "Shall we?"

The door of the main house opened and a pug came trotting toward them. A man in a black polo and black pants followed, but the pug got there first, clamoring around Alex's ankles.

"Welcome," the man said. "This way."

There were candles flickering inside the house in big hurricane vases. Even so, the entryway was too dark, disorienting after the sunshine. Alex turned to make sure Simon was behind her.

"Onward and upward," Simon said, his voice echoing strangely, the pug's nails clicking along the marble.

THE BIG ROOM THAT led to the patio seemed partially filled with mist, a dampness from the fog that had breached the windows. Beyond the patio was the spread of the ocean. The sun would set soon, the light already faltering.

The patio door was open. There, framed in the doorway, was Helen.

She was all in black, a sleeveless dress with a kind of cape hanging down the back. Her blond hair was pulled tight in a bun at her neck. How old was she? Alex couldn't quite tell—her skin had been professionally blasted into the face of a bland thirty-year-old. Her dark eyes wobbled until they finally focused on Simon and Alex.

"Simon," Helen said, stepping toward him, opening her arms. "I wasn't sure if you were coming."

They kissed on both cheeks. Helen turned to Alex.

"And who," she said, "is this?"

Alex made herself cheerful, a Girl Scout cheer. Who would be threatened by a Girl Scout? Deferential, scrubbed clean, this was the pose she had learned to take with older women. Still, Helen looked Alex up and down, lingering on each area of note. Alex watched her take in the information of the dress, the purse from Simon. Probably someone like Helen knew exactly what each item had cost.

"Thank you so much for having me," Alex said. Better,

always, not to compliment the house, not to indicate unfamiliarity with these places.

"Oh, sure," Helen said, her attention falling away.

Helen had a touch of the daffy about her, but maybe it was just the effect of her cape streaming down her back, twisting in the breeze. Alex let Simon take her arm, let him lead her toward the tables set up on the terrace.

The guests were looking out on the ocean, or huddling under a fabric tent, full glasses held with both hands. Alex scanned the guests, always vigilant. But a quick glance around and no one looked familiar, no man staring at Alex with a worried question in his face.

Most of the women wore boxy shift dresses that showed off their slim legs. How many units of energy, how many hours of exercise did those legs require? Their wrists were weighted with gold bracelets, the same over-large scale as their earrings. The women had a funny, girlish air—their tiny steps and uncertain smiles, satin bows in their ponytails— though most of them were probably over sixty, raised in a time when childishness was a lifetime female affect.

On the terrace, two gray-haired men in rubber waders and overalls had set up a raw bar and were expertly dispatching rocky oysters with sharp knives. Alex had seen these men before: they'd been at more than one party she and Simon had gone to in the last few weeks, tending to their bed of crushed ice, passing out the oysters in their little cups of brine. The host never failed to point out their grizzled presence, to remark how they had caught everything *that day*. Alex felt some camaraderie with the men— here, like she was, to perform.

Helen was staring at Alex's dress. Helen asked if her dress was by a specific designer.

"No," Alex said. It was.

Something was off in Alex's tone, enough that Helen gave a little frown. Hopefully, Simon hadn't noticed. Rein herself in—Alex forced a smile.

ALEX THOUGHT THAT THE man who brought them each a glass of wine was the same man who had let them in, but it was just someone dressed in the same black polo.

"Nice view," Alex said—and it was. From where she and Simon were standing, the sand was invisible. There was only water, flat and silvered, appearing to stretch from the edge of the terrace to the hot-pink line of the horizon. What would it be like to live here, to occupy this unfettered beauty every day? Could you become used to the shock of water? The envy acted like adrenaline in Alex's body, a swift and enlivening rush to the head. It was better, sometimes, to never know certain things existed.

"Come look at the sunset," Helen said, clutching Simon's arm. Helen didn't quite include Alex in the invitation but Alex followed anyway.

THEY STOOD AT THE edge of the terrace, at the top of the wooden steps that led to the water. The sand was tinted purple in the last of the light. Farther down the beach, a dog ran silently in and out of the line of waves.

Helen surveyed her stretch of beach. Something made

her stiffen, let out an aggrieved exhale. "Well," she said, "look at that. I hope they're enjoying themselves."

Alex followed Helen's stare to a pair of beach chairs set up under a large umbrella. Alex could make out a couple sitting there, chatting. They were in jeans, one was in a plaid shirt—obviously not Helen's guests, no one Helen knew.

"I should bring them a glass of lemonade," Helen said. Her laugh startled Alex. "People must just feel so lucky, coming across these empty chairs. Just for them!"

Helen turned to search for help. When a staff member came over, she murmured instructions, her fingers waving in the direction of the beach chairs.

The three of them watched the uniformed man make his way across the sand. When he leaned down to talk to the couple, they burst out laughing, not at all chastened. The couple took their time getting to their feet. Exaggerating their exit. The uniformed man stood sentry, and when he was satisfied that the interlopers were continuing down the beach, the man began to dismantle the umbrella and efficiently fold the chairs.

THE SUN HAD SET, the staff scrambling to adjust for the new darkness. They turned on the outdoor lamps and lit the citronella candles. Alex's name had been scribbled on a place card, an obvious last-minute addition. Simon was sitting at another table. He waved at Alex with comic exaggeration. Alex blew him a kiss. An Austrian man was seated to Alex's left. His forehead was smooth as an egg. His family ran a department store that had many locations across

Austria, some department store that was a hundred years old. He came here every August.

"Nothing like it," he said. "Our friends all come, too."

"It's beautiful here," Alex said, dully.

"It is." The man sighed. "So beautiful."

Everyone said it was beautiful out here. How many times could this sentiment be repeated? It was the polite consensus to return to, the bookend to every conversation—a slogan that united everyone in their shared luck. And who could ever disagree? The place was so beautiful that people didn't need to do anything. And no one did, judging by the table conversation. Nobody seemed to busy themselves beyond the expected ways: working on their backhand, cooking outdoors, going on a walk before the day got too hot.

The only other reliable conversation, besides the weather or the temperature fluctuations of the ocean, was the discussion of exactly what time people were planning to leave this beautiful place, how exactly they were planning to avoid traffic. From the moment they'd arrived, Alex had heard people invoking their departures, considering in detail the precise logistics of their exits.

By the time the first course appeared, the Austrian was telling the table about some terrible crime in Munich, something that happened earlier in the summer. A woman had killed five babies.

"Her own?" Helen said. She was flitting from table to table, dropping into conversations. She seemed to consider herself the host of a grand salon.

"Yes, I think so. And the other daughter, you see, she found the babies in a freezer."

"Five?"

The Austrian nodded.

"The freezer must have been very big," Helen said. "What brand?"

The Austrian didn't know.

"Shocking," Helen said, her voice getting louder, "isn't it? We haven't seen anything like this in nature. A mother killing her own children. That woman last week in Los Angeles, leaving her infant to go shoot people. It's unprecedented. Science," she said, "is confounded."

Alex was barely listening—nature, science, morality. Sounded about right for these people on a Monday evening in August. She made a half-hearted attempt on the blended green soup in a shallow porcelain bowl in front of her.

Helen's second husband was at the next table over—Simon had pointed him out before dinner. He was much younger than Helen, thirty-five or so, the youngest person here besides Alex. How would he and Helen even have met? Alex imagined one of these pseudo-foundations, a pseudo-board of which the man might have been an advisory member. His hair was long—he was smart to keep it that length, a style that emphasized his youth. In combination with the suit and his white shirt, loose at the throat, he was an appealing presence. Alex watched him talk to the woman on his right, grabbing her hand for inspection then holding up his own to compare—some joke, the woman obviously flattered by the attention.

A member of the staff hovered at Alex's side to pour more water. When Alex leaned back to let the woman refill her glass, her face was suddenly near enough that they made accidental eye contact. Alex looked quickly at her plate, to be polite.

MIDWAY THROUGH THE BLACK COD, a boy came loping down the steps from the house in big, youthful bounds. His hair was wet and dark, his sweatshirt zipped up, and he veered straight to Helen, bending down to kiss her cheek. He grabbed a piece of fish off her plate with his fingers.

"Jesus," Helen said, swatting him, but beaming around the table. "My son," she announced. "Theo."

The boy smiled. His features were mushy and adolescent—Alex couldn't guess whether he would end up being handsome. But he had the gift of seeming very polite even as he chewed with his mouth open.

"And what are we up to?" Helen said, pulsing the boy's hand.

"Bonfire," the boy said. "Just a few people. We'll come back and say hi, don't worry."

OVER THE NEXT COURSE, Alex watched them trickle in, Theo's friends: boys in swim trunks and sweatshirts, a girl in cutoffs that yawned up her ass crack. Another kid, clean, angelically blond, his track pants low on his hips. The teenagers huddled on the patio, drinking beer. They left their empty bottles for the servers to silently clear away.

Later, when Alex looked over, she saw the girl taking photos of the boys on her phone, all of them fluent in the language of posing. There was only a second where the glint of braces was apparent on the angelic blond boy's bottom teeth—he'd learned how to hide them, Alex figured, smiling with his mouth closed.

When she turned back to the table, the Austrian was staring at her expectantly.

"Mm," Alex offered, a neutral enough stopgap, and this seemed perfectly acceptable. Amazing how little you had to give, really. People just wanted to hear their own voices, your response a comma punctuating their monologue.

Did Alex know, the Austrian said, that in certain island countries, women dressed in clothes that denoted their hierarchy, and every man could have multiple wives? Didn't Alex think that level of clarity was beautiful, that ability to meet desires without shame?

"This," the Austrian said, rapping his knuckles on the table, "is a very shame-based country."

Didn't she think so?

Alex nodded. She felt loopy, unable to exert her usual control. Alex made herself stop thinking. She searched out Simon at his table. When Simon waved at Alex, Alex kissed the air in his direction and smiled.

AS THE NIGHT WORE ON, Alex kept catching sight of Helen's young husband with different older women, always touching them in some innocuous way, the drift of his fingertips coming to rest on a woman's tanned, bony arm, or his hand lingering by the small of a woman's back. He was good at it—and it was fun to watch him, to see whether he could keep this up. Where was Simon? On the other side of the terrace, talking to a sunburned block of a man: a retired general, his arms crossed and a sweater tied around his neck.

Alex's unease was taking shape, a desire for the night to sharpen into action. The Austrian was regaling the table, now, with how wonderful Helen's breakfasts were. He had started to list the foods that were available at her famous breakfasts, the grains and the juices. Alex only realized she was smiling when her cheeks started to ache. Helen was going on about some app she had invested in. The app, if Helen was to be believed, was perfecting a technology that diagnosed illness from a breathalyzer you plugged into your phone. Helen said certain phrases with emphasis: *SDKs. Daily granularity.* Someone must have just taught her what these terms meant.

"Our art needs more technology and our technology needs more art," Helen bleated, looking into the middle distance.

Alex drained her wineglass, then her water glass. The ocean looked calm, a black darker than the sky. A ripple of anxiety made her palms go damp. It seemed suddenly very tenuous to believe that anything would stay hidden, that she could successfully pass from one world to another.

The sight of Simon across the patio should have been more comforting. Alex excused herself and got to her feet.

"I'll be right back," she said, though no one was listening to her.

THE STAFF WAS BUSY, in and out of the kitchen and the patio. The rest of the house was quiet. There were framed sketches all along the hallway, plans for something—probably the leftovers of someone important. People like Helen loved to display the artifacts of creativity as if that implicated her in the process.

Alex followed the hallway, opening a door on an empty room. Shelves lined the walls. A lamp cast a circle of light on a leather armchair. There was a white flower in a vase and a Duraflame in the immaculate fireplace. It was a non-room, dead and unused.

The things on the shelves were ugly—a poky brass paperweight, an ornate teak ball that smelled like amber. She paused to study a small piece of stone, carved to smoothness. It fit perfectly in Alex's fist. It was matte black, marked by a few air holes, some striations of green and blue, and the weight was nice, heavier than expected. Maybe it was supposed to be an animal, a few little knobs that could be legs. She closed her fingers around it.

"Can I get you anything?" a voice asked.

It was a man in a black polo. Just one of the staff.

"I'm looking for the restroom." Alex turned easily, dropping the stone into her bag. "If you could just point the way?"

THERE WAS NO CABINET to look through, no pills to skim—it was a guest bathroom. A tube of lipstick on a high ledge—obviously Helen's, stashed away for party touch-ups. Alex was about to take it, but the lipstick was a stubby burgundy. Not very flattering. A lit candle made jumping shadows on the baseboard. Alex's forehead was shiny. Sweating, she was sweating. She pressed toilet paper to blot the shine. Nothing in her teeth. Tense, this feeling of urgency rising with nothing to come up against.

Alex sat on the lid of the toilet, slipping off her shoes and pressing her bare feet onto the chilly marble floor. She played absently with the little stone animal. Maybe it was valuable. Or maybe it was worthless.

It was inevitable, a few glasses in—she took out her phone and opened her messages.

Dom. She would finally respond.

She was drunk, yes, but she blamed the house, too— certain places made you feel that all problems had solutions. Like she could defuse this Dom thing. And why couldn't she?

Alex would talk to Simon. Tonight. Lay out the situation in heavily redacted form. He'd be in a good mood, tipsy and generous. They'd have sex when they got home. But in her experience, men didn't get more magnanimous after sex—they retreated into themselves, became closed off. So better to talk to Simon on the drive back. Her hand on his knee. She'd say Dom was an ex. Eke out a few tears, and she'd be drunk so they'd come easily, and even just imagining this future conversation, Alex's eyes got watery— maybe she was more afraid of Dom than she'd realized.

How would she twist it into a palatable story?

She'd figure it out in the car. And Simon would know exactly what to do. Exactly how to fix the problem.

She typed out the text to Dom.

Srry i'll call you tomorrow. Promise.
Everythings gonna be fine

A blue bar appeared, her text slowly winging its way to Dom's phone, but it never loaded fully, a red alert popping up instead.

Not delivered.

No cell service.

No service in Helen's hallway, either. Or in the big living room. One of the staff saw Alex tilting her phone back and forth.

"There's better service on the beach."

ALEX WALKED DOWN TO the dark sand. Out of sight of the house, a bonfire was going on the shore, larger than she would have expected. A Jeep had been driven right onto the beach. Around the flicker of the bonfire, Alex saw the kids from earlier, Theo and the others. The group had tripled in size. Someone's phone was playing music, amplified in an empty metal bowl. Girls sat shivering on boys' laps, their bare shoulders cloaked by beach towels. The fire was going strong, the size almost frightening—but what could burn, here on the sand?

Alex kept walking, her phone held out in front of her. When a few bars jumped in and out of visibility, she squatted in the sand, trying to refresh her messages, but then the darkness nearby clicked into focus and there was a couple writhing on a towel. It took Alex a moment to recognize the boy from earlier, Theo's blond, pretty friend, whose hand was down a girl's unbuttoned cutoffs, working frantically. They didn't notice Alex.

"God," the girl said, her voice drunk and wet, "do whatever you want."

Alex made a face.

Her phone dinged—the text had sent.

Almost instantly, three dots appeared. Dom was typing.

> u say ur gonna call and u never do
> I heard ur out east

How had Dom possibly figured out where she was? Alex cycled through the possibilities. Did one of her roommates know? Had Alex told someone? It didn't make sense. She had the sick feeling that Dom would never let this drop. That she would never be able to get away from him, not really.

She typed out a message.

> *We can talk tomorrow.*

His response was immediate.

> Now. Call me.

She stared at the screen. Another message from Dom.

> Alex?

The phone started to ring, the screen flashing.

She turned it off.

BY THE TIME ALEX returned to the party, the dinner dishes had been cleared, the tables now cluttered with cheese plates and silver trays of dry-looking cookies.

Could everyone see how jittery Alex was?

But no one noticed her: they picked at the cheese, or stood bunched by the outdoor heaters. The party had gone a touch sloppy. Visible sweat stains, a few of the women's ponytails losing steam. Simon and the retired general had been joined by the general's wife, a sturdy woman with a dress that was too formal, the hemline grazing the floor. Simon caught Alex's eyes and widened his own. Alex knew that meant Simon wanted her to join him. Normally, Alex would go instantly to Simon's side, her obedience cheerful and frictionless. Tonight Alex smiled back at Simon but didn't go over.

Simon's expression flickered with displeasure.

Tense. Alex was tense. She didn't want to see Simon when she was riled up like this, off her game. Making bad choices. Dom knew she was out here. This whole thing would be tricky. She'd talk to Simon later. On the drive home. No more stalling: she'd tell Simon everything, or a version of everything. They'd figure it out together.

While Alex had been gone, someone had refilled her wine. Alex flagged down a server and got a vodka tonic instead. Helen was petting her pug with clawed fingers, seemingly unaware of her husband across the terrace with yet another woman.

Alex was now drunk enough to drift into the husband's orbit.

"Hi," Alex said, raising her drink.

The woman he'd been talking with looked annoyed at Alex's intrusion. "I'm going to get my sweater," she said, ignoring Alex. "I'll be right back."

"I'll be right here waiting," Helen's husband said. He had an accent but it seemed forced, something that required work. Alex still hadn't seen him and Helen interact.

"You're very patient," Alex said, when the woman had gone. "Doing your public service."

A look passed between them—and there it was, the barest shift of energy, of recognition. The husband's face recalibrated, dropping one layer of falseness.

"I'm Alex," she said. "You're Helen's husband, right?"

"Victor," he said. "Do you know Helen?"

"My boyfriend does. Simon." She took a sip of her drink. "Fun party."

"It is."

"Helen seems great," Alex said, keeping her voice bland.

"She's an interesting lady," Victor said. He was being careful. Alex could admire his dedication. What would it take to get Victor to crack, to break character?

"Have you guys been married long?"

"Five years."

Alex raised her eyebrows but didn't say anything. At least Simon was a real person. Easy to tell yourself he was pleasant, desirable. She couldn't imagine someone choosing Helen. And this wasn't temporary—Victor had fully committed, made a life out of this, or at the least, decided to call what he had a life.

"You're out here all summer?"

"Sure, another few days or so," Victor said. "Till Labor Day."

"Us too. Simon's having this party. This Labor Day party."

"Mm."

Alex made a gesture at the water.

"Do you just wake up every morning and jump in the ocean? That's what I'd do."

"Sometimes," Victor said. "Helen prefers the pool."

Victor seemed amused by Alex, but wary. Alex tried to hold his gaze, not let it drop. She was unsure herself of what exactly she was doing. What the game was here.

"Can I see it?"

"The pool?" Victor shrugged. "I guess."

Leaving the house, leaving the party behind—the air felt better, immediately, as if they'd been suddenly cut free. The path was lit by bulbs recessed into the ground that cast the foliage above into cutout shapes, like wallpaper. The gate to the pool stuck—Victor had to pull hard before it opened.

"After you."

The pool was a clean hollow of light, and it was bigger than Simon's, bounded by a brick patio. Alex could imagine how nice it would be to swim its length, a few easy pulls of water. Alex slipped off her shoes and grazed a foot in the pool. It was warmer than the air.

Victor stood behind her, hesitating, but when Alex sat down to put her legs in the water, Victor sat next to her.

"I almost drowned today," Alex found herself saying. "In the ocean."

"Oh, man." His concern appeared real.

"I don't know. I'm a pretty good swimmer. I think maybe it was a riptide."

"Those things are scary," he said. "No joke."

The silence between them wasn't uncomfortable.

Alex smoothed her dress. "Simon got this for me," she said. "This dress."

"It's nice."

Alex shrugged. "A little severe. Right? He likes everything a little severe."

She pulled her phone from her bag. It was still turned off.

"Service isn't great," Victor said. "It's the one thing about this place."

"Is that how she keeps you locked in here? Your calls for help don't go through?"

"Hey now," Victor said. He smiled, but Alex could tell talking this way made him nervous.

"Sorry." You couldn't press too hard, Alex knew, couldn't say certain things out loud.

"She's great," Victor said. "A great lady."

Alex was too drunk. She could feel that she was grinning insanely. She tightened her grip on the phone and moved her feet in the water. "Too bad I don't have a swimsuit," Alex said. "The water's perfect."

"Oh, just go in."

"I don't really think it's that kind of party." Alex took another drink. "Or do you all jump in together after dessert, am I misreading the vibe?"

"She really isn't so bad," Victor said. "Helen."

"I didn't say that."

It was dangerous, talking this way—the information out in the open, something they were naming.

"You go in first," Alex said. "It's your house, isn't it?"

"Oh, yes," Victor said. "All this. As far as the eye can see."

"Where did you live before?"

"London," he said. "Then Brussels. Now here." He held eye contact.

Alex had the idiot thought that somehow Victor would be able to help her. With this Dom thing. If she just explained the situation. Alex and Victor weren't so different. He seemed like he might understand how easily things got complicated.

She smiled at him. The thrill was familiar. The giddy anxiety of watching yourself and waiting to see what you would do next.

"I'll go in if you go in," Alex said. A bad idea had its own relentless logic, a momentum that was queasy but also correct.

"What if someone pushed you?" he said. "What then?"

"You wouldn't."

A beat, a question in the air waiting to be answered.

Alex wasn't sure he would do it until he actually did, Victor swooping toward her, wrapping Alex in a bear hug—they wobbled together for a brief second before he shifted his weight and they both hit the water. Alex came up laughing. Her drink had fallen in the pool, the lime wedge adrift, the glass sinking to the bottom in slow motion.

Her phone, she'd been holding her phone, and it was still in her hand, dripping wet.

"Fuck," Alex said, but Victor was laughing, too, plucking at his sodden shirt. He drifted toward Alex in the water, his features wavery in the pool lights. They weren't touching but they were close. Alex's dress was heavy and floaty at the same time. They made eye contact, and he seemed to be feeling what she was feeling: that this was correct, the correct situation, both of them here in this pool. Alex kicked her legs to stay in place. Nothing had happened, not yet, but it was there between them.

"Alex."

The voice came from beyond the gate.

There, in the strange light, was Simon, his hands in his pockets. He watched them, unsmiling.

Ha ha, Alex thought. That man is my boyfriend, she thought. His daughter is not a good singer. I can't go back to the city because I've done stupid things.

"Want to come on out of there, Alex?" Simon said.

Victor had stopped laughing, had stopped smiling, but Alex couldn't make herself stop. She knew she was making it worse, laughing like this, but still, she floated for a second too long, waited a second too long before she slogged toward the steps, before she pulled herself out.

3

IN THE MORNING ALEX FELT, more or less, ordinary.

The curtains were drawn but the sunlight was bright behind them. So it was already late. A headache winked in and out but didn't fully announce itself. She shifted to the cooler side of the bed. Empty—so Simon was working, or pedaling away in the gym in front of one of the movies he watched in thirty-minute increments on the treadmill. Even exercising wasn't enough: every moment had to be leveraged, squeezed tighter.

Alex's body held clues to the previous night. An unsavory smell, sweat in the creases behind her knees, in her armpits. The sheets felt stale. The memory rose up—she had gone swimming, or been in the pool, anyway.

Simon had been annoyed. Alex was remembering that part, had a flash of the drive home: the car heater trained full-blast on her soaked dress, Alex sitting on Simon's jacket so she didn't get his upholstery wet.

Had he actually been angry?

There were many ways to keep knowledge from yourself, to not think too hard about things you didn't want to confirm.

Alex sat up and groped for her phone. When she turned it on, the icons appeared, but then the screen flickered into gray. Fuck—the phone had gone in the water. Broken? When Alex turned it on again, everything seemed fine. Her hands shook. Just a little.

She didn't bother to check her messages, see if any fresh poison had arrived overnight. How exactly had Dom found out she was out east?

Unpleasant, unpleasant—she had to talk to Simon. It was time.

Alex brushed her teeth, then let the water run warm so she could splash her face. She started to feel better. Look more awake. She went through the routine, brightening her eyes, patting color into her cheeks. This labor felt virtuous. And if she didn't stop to consider it, the nausea seemed to go away. Alex was fine. It was all fine. She'd been stupid last night, reckless, but she hadn't actually done anything with Victor. Her phone wasn't actually broken. She'd talk to Simon. He'd know what to do about Dom.

She hadn't ruined anything. Misfortune hadn't touched Alex: it had only come close enough that she felt the cold air of a different outcome hurtling past.

THE HOUSE WAS QUIET. Lori must have been here— someone had left coffee in the French press and an empty mug on the counter. The coffee was still warm. The hemp milk from the fridge left clumps floating on the coffee's surface. Alex tried to poke them up with a finger. No one was in the yard, either. She opened the fridge again: There was the juice, the jams. A health bread that toasted up dense and nutty. It all looked and smelled too intense. She closed the door. Better to skip breakfast.

THE PATIO WAS EMPTY. The pool was empty. Simon was probably working.

After they talked, Alex could go to the beach, take one of the bicycles in the garage. Simon was always bothering her to use one of the bikes, like it was Alex's responsibility to enjoy things so he didn't have to. Or Alex could just swim here. The pool looked especially nice today, a rectangle of blue, the surface reflecting the sky.

Alex changed into a one-piece. A swimsuit that Simon liked. She inspected an ingrown hair in the crease of her thigh, a bump that got worse as she picked. She forced herself to stop digging with her fingernail, but the damage was already done.

THE DOOR TO SIMON'S office was closed. Alex knocked, then started to push it open.

"Hello?" she said.

Simon glanced up at Alex, then back to his computer.

"All okay?" Simon asked, eyes on his screen.

"Just saying hi."

Something in the tone of Simon's voice made Alex think she should have put on real clothes. Shoes, at least. She pretended to be interested in the books on the shelves. It occurred to her that there was still time to go back to the house, wait this out.

"Do you have something you want to tell me?" Simon said, finally looking up at her.

How could he possibly have found out about Dom? No, it didn't make sense. Could Dom have somehow figured out that Alex was staying here?

"I saw the car this morning," Simon went on.

Alex smiled, involuntarily, a smile of pure relief. Before she could correct herself, Simon noticed the smile. It seemed to visibly disgust him.

"The bumper," Simon said, "the taillight."

"What about it?"

Simon didn't respond; Alex pressed on.

"Someone hit your car last night?"

"Alex." Simon sighed. "Lori said it was there yesterday afternoon, she saw damage."

"I didn't notice," Alex said. "I'm sorry."

Simon smiled at the corner of the ceiling.

"Okay," he said. "You didn't notice."

Alex tracked Simon's glance, the way it didn't quite meet hers. That's when she started to worry. Time to make her exit.

"I just came in to say hi," Alex said. "Sorry to bother you."

She turned to go. She was almost safe, almost to the door.

"Big plans for today?" Simon said.

"Oh, nothing," Alex said, turning around. "Maybe the beach. Depending."

"I was thinking," Simon said. "You might go back to the city today. There's a train in an hour and a half. Or later, if you like."

"Sorry?" Alex laughed a little.

"I have work, Caroline might want to come for a bit." Simon made a gesture toward the desk, the invisible shape of his obligations.

"I can take care of myself," Alex said. "I don't need anything, really. If you and Caroline want to hang."

It almost felt like excitement, this urgency that took over, the vibrating sense that Alex had to fix what had gone wrong. Was *going* wrong. Simon wasn't looking at her. Her swimsuit had ridden up her ass but she forced herself not to pull it out.

Alex kept smiling hard.

"Or I could stay somewhere else for a few days," Alex said. "I'm sure there's room somewhere, give you guys some space?"

"I'm not sure that makes sense," Simon said.

"Or I can meet Caroline. I'd like to."

Simon pushed his chair back from his desk. "It's not a good time, Alex."

Alex could imagine what she must look like to Simon from where he sat at his desk. A skinny girl, barefoot, in an expensive swimsuit Simon had bought for her. Another problem to solve.

"Are you mad at me?"

It was a terrible question, she knew as soon as she said it, a question that always contained its own answer. Alex could see Simon was no longer engaged, that he no longer felt implicated in whatever drama Alex was creating. A switch had been flipped. That was the worst part—to watch how swiftly Simon absented himself, a professional affect taking over.

"Let's talk in a week or so, a few days," Simon said. He spoke like no one had ever been wearier than he was. He was trying to appease Alex, manage her like he managed his clients.

"But my phone is broken," Alex said. She heard how meager that sounded. It seemed unfair, criminally unfair, how cruel Simon was being.

"You went swimming with it."

"He pushed me in. You know he pushed me."

Simon pinched the bridge of his nose. Alex could feel how few minutes she had remaining, how suddenly all this was drawing to a close. She was light-headed. She thought of the bed she had left that morning—she had gotten used to the fact of the bed. Now it was disintegrating.

"I don't have anywhere to stay," Alex said.

"That can't be true. Don't you have your place?"

Alex stared at Simon, trying mentally to pedal for some traction, but there was nothing. The situation didn't allow for Alex's anger, or this sudden forlorn feeling that came over her.

"Please." Alex felt her face drop.

"You want money?" Simon said. "Are you asking me for money?"

"No," she said, cheeks hot. The calculations were too grim to perform; of course she would need money.

"This wasn't how I wanted this to go," Simon said. He glanced at his computer screen, trying to do so unnoticed. "Lori can take you to the station. She'll get you a ticket."

Simon picked up his phone, thumbs working hard, though Alex could tell he was looking at nothing. Could Alex just stand here until he changed his mind? Use the brute fact of her presence to wait this out? As long as she didn't leave the room, could all of this go another way?

Simon looked up at Alex, but his expression was quizzical, as if a stranger had wandered into his office. Then his eyes softened: just a degree, but enough that Alex noticed.

"I'll call you sometime," Simon offered. "Maybe when Caroline leaves."

ALEX GATHERED HER CLOTHES while the housekeeper hovered near the bedroom doorway, the nervous sentinel. Had Lori posted the housekeeper there? What was the woman supposed to stop Alex from doing? Stealing? Alex packed her black weekend bag, an oversized tote, with the clothes Simon had given her. The dresses in their drab colors, the trousers with the whiff of the office. Alex thought about leaving behind everything Simon had bought for her—dumping all the clothes in a pile on the bed—but even as she imagined the gesture, she knew she would never do it. She could sell some of this stuff, if she had to. It had been dumb to take the tags off. To assume any of this was permanent.

Alex folded everything carefully before putting it in the weekend bag. She saw stains she hadn't noticed on a silk shirt, an aura of sweat in the armpits. All these lovely things she had ruined.

In the bathroom, she packed her bottles, her ointments. There were pills in the cabinet: Simon's sleeping pills, his painkillers. She skimmed off a few of the sleeping pills and added them to his remaining painkillers. No reason, now, not to take the whole stash. Before she packed away the bottle, she took one of the painkillers with a handful of water from the faucet. She deserved it.

It felt, for a second, like Alex loved Simon, felt like the abyss Alex was facing was the prospect of a life ahead of her without this person, this person that Alex loved. Simon's world would seal over, the rooms of his house would forget Alex's presence. She had been fine here. She'd been protected. But even as she felt her eyes get wet, there was a catch, a self-consciousness, an asterisk on any sincere feeling. She would have to find a place to stay. She would need to hold off Dom. The horrors of these everyday tasks started to loom. Life flattened so quickly to these dull logistics— how stupid Alex had been to think that she could relax.

Alex found a fifty in the pocket of Simon's pants, a pair he'd left in the hamper, then picked up and put down one of his watches twice before she finally dropped it in the purse. The purse Simon had bought for her.

———

THE DAY WAS BRIGHT and the sky was clean. Lori had her sunglasses on, cheap gas-station sunglasses whose lenses were blue mirrors. She was waiting by her car.

"Ready to go?"

Simon's car was already gone.

"Where is he?" Alex said.

"Not sure," Lori said.

Instead of going to Lori's car, Alex listed off in the direction of the office.

"Don't," Lori called after her. But what could Lori do? She wasn't going to physically restrain Alex.

When Alex opened the door, the office was empty.

"Told you," Lori said, from behind her. Alex didn't know what she'd expected—some last chance, some opportunity for appeal. She had always managed something.

Lori didn't wait for Alex to follow her back to the car, but of course Alex did.

BEYOND THE WHITE CLAPBOARD station and the broad concrete platform, a line of trees shivered in the breeze, a ripple of green. A green deeper than green. It all seemed too vivid. It would only take a few hours, a single transfer, and Alex would be back in the city. And now a membrane would close over this summer, sealing it off. It would become something that had happened, something that was over. A life she had gotten right up to the edge of. Alex had known exactly how lucky she was: that hadn't been the problem.

LORI WAS CHATTY ON the car ride to the station, almost manic, her tone gossipy and cheerful. The situation must have been familiar to Lori—perhaps this happened regularly, some young woman, some girl, needing to be spirited away while Simon kept himself conspicuously hidden, deputizing Lori to clean up his mess.

You were the exception, until you weren't.

Lori's car was cluttered: coffee souring in paper cups, a metallic sun shade folded in the backseat on top of a sleeping bag. The interior smelled like Simon's dog. Alex's hangover had crystallized, hijacking her nervous system.

"It might be nice," Lori was saying. "Being in the city."

Alex didn't respond, watching out the window as Lori drove, passing through the many shaded lanes until they got close to the station, close to town. There were restaurants she had gone to with Simon, roads that led to the houses of his friends. None of it was available to her anymore.

"You know," Lori went on. "The city empties out. In August. It can be great."

When Alex didn't say anything, Lori looked over.

"He's a complicated guy," she said. "It's not you."

Alex didn't know why Lori was suddenly being nice—apologetic even.

"I'm *fine*," Alex said.

"He's kind of a child, to be honest," Lori said. "Totally incapable of being in the real world. Useless. If I wasn't around, he would probably starve to death."

Alex studied Lori's face. Lori hated Simon, had always hated him—that was obvious now. Strange Alex had not noticed it before.

ALEX LET LORI BUY the train ticket. Lori kept the receipt—for Simon, Alex supposed, tallying her expenses. Or maybe she was supposed to present it as proof Alex was gone.

"Is that all?" Lori said, as Alex stood there with her single bag. It wasn't a question.

4

ALEX SAT ON THE PLATFORM. On a nearby bench, two guys in faded chino shorts and baseball hats chattered away, their knees spread wide. They cradled giant plastic water bottles and only stopped speaking to take dramatic gulps. They were talking, now, about an eclipse that summer, a partial eclipse. Discussing how the moon was going to start to wobble. Not this second, apparently, but soon. The moon wobbling up there in the sky, and we'll all be fucked then. The prospect appeared to excite them. When they noticed Alex, it only made them talk louder.

The louder they talked, the more Alex felt her headache pulse, piercing the painkiller fuzz. You could occasionally be overcome by dislike for strangers: if these boys got zapped into nothingness, would the world really miss them?

But who would really miss Alex either?

Alex flipped through a free magazine from a stack on

the platform. Interviews with local restaurant owners and culty exercise instructors with amphetamine grins, a summer gift guide for hostesses that featured a lot of blown glass. A limited-edition rosé produced by a supermodel, now in her fifties. The magazine was mostly ads. Looking closer at the interviews, she saw that those were ads, too. One whole page was taken up by the headshot of a beefy realtor, in a suit and no tie, smiling in a queasy way.

Alex's breath was stale, sweat gathering along her hairline. There was an apple in her bag, a green apple, and a package of flavored almonds. A squished protein bar. The air seemed extraordinarily heavy. Another punishment. Things toggled swiftly between real and unreal.

Alex looked through her phone. The names scrolled past—some people she had met once, men whose last names Alex had never known.

> *Chris Party*
> *Don't Answer*
> *Ben's friend gramercy*
> *86th Street*

A list of people she had either forgotten or alienated in some way.

How many months of back rent did Alex owe her old housemates? Anyway, Dom seemed to know she'd lived at that apartment. She was not welcome at the Mercer, not welcome at the Mark. Alex could think of no one to call, no one to plead her case to.

She started a text to Simon.

Can't we talk?

She watched the cursor blink—then erased the text.

The train was coming in thirty minutes.

ALEX CALLED WILL. He was still in the city. Or she thought he probably was: they hadn't spoken in a year. Maybe more. But they'd been friends, hadn't they? She'd apologized to him, she was pretty sure.

"Hello," Will said, after the second ring.

Alex stood on the shady part of the train platform. "It's Alex."

He exhaled and let out a sharp laugh. Not even a pause before he launched right in.

"Don't call me again," Will said, "seriously." She heard him mutter something to whoever he was with, continuing some conversation, and then, without ceremony, he hung up.

Alex tried Jon.

"Hey"—the line sputtered a bit. Alex paced in the sun. "It's me," she said.

"What's up?" Jon's voice was flat. Jon was one of the last people Alex had been seeing before she met Simon, a semi-regular.

"Nothing." Alex laughed. "You at home?"

"It's Tuesday. I'm at work."

"Oh." There was a long silence. "It's Alex," she said.

"Yeah, I know."

Not promising.

"So," Alex said, "I'm thinking of coming back to the city."

Jon had dropped the phone or something, a rush of noise through the speaker.

"Hello?" Alex said.

"I didn't know you weren't here," Jon said.

His voice was flat, faint—not angry, just uninterested, deeply uninterested.

"Yeah. Well," Alex said, her pacing constrained to tighter and tighter spans, "I wasn't, but now, you know, I will be."

"Great."

Alex could picture the face Jon was making, up there in the recirculated air of his office. Alex had run up a hefty hotel bill on his card, she vaguely remembered—staying on an extra night, letting the staff call her Mrs. Anderson, or whatever his last name was. He had not been pleased. She kept the details out of focus.

"I was thinking," Alex said, "maybe I could stay with you for a bit."

She'd only been to his apartment once: a landlord-white studio in Tribeca. He had pee pads in the corner for his dog and a pull-up bar in his bedroom door.

"Um." The line was quiet. "I don't know if that's a good idea."

"Just for a week. A few days." Silence. "We have fun," Alex said, pitching her voice into a softer register, "don't we?"

Jon made a noise of pretend regret. "Alex. It's just," he said, "not a good idea."

Alex's phone died before she could respond. She turned

it back on. When it came to life, a bar of static was wavering across the screen. She shut the phone down.

Not a good idea.

That was the second time someone had said that to her
today.

She looked at her phone, out of habit, though she knew
it was off. Her watery reflection stared back from the screen.
Who else was there to call?

The station clock said it was almost noon. Alex could
feel the tops of her arms getting hot, the first prickle of
sunburn. She moved into the shade.

Had Simon already been informed of her departure?
Simon.

He was annoyed with her, yes. Right at this moment.
But she knew Simon. The parts of him that were lonely and
greedy and afraid of not having the things he wanted—he'd
start to miss her. Soon enough.

And hadn't he said he would call her? Hadn't he made a
point of not closing the door completely? He was too smart
to say things he didn't mean.

She replayed their last conversation with a mental
squint. And replayed it again.

It was becoming clearer, now. The situation. How to
play this through. He'd been sending her a message, Simon.
Asking her to wait, give him a few days.

How had she not understood? A pause—that's all this
was.

Simple. Alex would stay out here until Labor Day. Just
until Simon's Labor Day party.

Simon would be a little drunk, at the party. He'd be expecting Alex, maybe even worried she might not show up. Worried she had somehow missed his signal, failed to understand his invitation.

Then Alex would walk in. She would make her way straight to Simon. She'd apologize, she'd appease him. And then what? Then Simon would take her back, because that was the whole game he'd set up, both of them hitting their marks, and all would be well.

It was obvious, now that she thought about it. Less obvious: how to burn the next six days.

THERE WAS SOMETHING LIKE four hundred bucks in Alex's account. Maybe a little more. She hadn't checked since she'd been out here, because she hadn't needed to: Simon had taken care of everything.

It wasn't enough—whatever way she circled the number. She could get a hotel room out here for one night. Maybe. But there weren't even hotels here, just the old Victorian inns filled with people's most disliked relatives or the milky Europeans. More than ever, this place seemed like a collection of houses, everywhere she looked, or more like a collection of gates. A good trick, when you thought about it. How everything was private, everything was hidden. The better to keep you out if you didn't belong. It was unthinkable, enraging, how many of these houses were empty.

THE TRAIN ARRIVING FROM the city pulled into the platform and the doors shuddered open. A rush of people exited—a woman with a baby strapped to her chest, a couple armed with tennis rackets, moody teenagers who looked around, preemptively impatient, for the housekeepers who had been sent to pick them up. People aimed at someone or something, some end point awaiting their arrival.

The last passengers poured from the train, laughing and shrieking as they surged onto the platform. There were ten or twelve in a group, all in their early twenties, dressed for a certain type of leisure. Everyone was talking too loudly, performing the fact that they were on vacation, liquor bottles poking from tote bags. This year, women were supposed to buy tiny basket purses, as if they were Jane Birkin. Alex studied a girl carrying a basket purse. The unfortunate effect was to make you realize that the person holding the purse was not Jane Birkin. The girl wore a long floral dress that looked brand new, probably purchased expressly for this trip.

They were house-share people, Alex figured, fifteen or twenty people crowding into a flimsy new spec house, bottles of tequila bought cheaply in the city and transported wrapped in beach towels. They would leave here Monday night, imagining they had gotten close to something, had some rarefied experience. The truth was that the world they were imagining would never include them.

THE TWO GUYS WHO'D been waiting on the platform stood to join the group. They were shaking hands all around, introducing themselves—so, Alex understood, no one knew each other that well. A boy clapped another boy on the back while they compared something on their screens.

When one of the girls looked at Alex, Alex perked slightly, out of habit.

"Hi," the girl said, her voice rising in a question.

"Hey," Alex said, waving. "Hi."

The girl smiled reflexively; girls were so polite, so ready to make others comfortable.

Alex stood up when the girl came over.

"How was the ride?" Alex asked.

"Oh," the girl said, "okay. Kind of third-world, though—everyone, like, pushing and shoving." She wore tiny pearl earrings, a light Patagonia sweater. A tropical-print skirt that showed her pale legs. "So hot today, huh? But the train is so air-conditioned it's, like, freezing."

Alex laughed, but she was watching the girl and watching the people behind her at the same time. Alex angled her body toward the girl.

"I'm Alex. I think we've met, maybe? Right?"

"Yeah, totally," the girl said, blinking rapidly. "Hey. Lynn."

"Right, Lynn," Alex said. "I remember." Things were just happening, taking on momentum. "What's the plan now?"

"Um, I think Brian called a car?" Lynn shrugged. "Or we might have to take a few trips, depending."

One of the guys who'd been waiting on the platform came over.

"We're just gonna take a taxi," he said. "It's fucking expensive but I'm burning vacation time sitting here."

"Should I come now? With you?" the girl asked. "Shouldn't someone text Brian?"

"We should just go now," Alex said. "Let's text him from the taxi."

The guy looked at Alex and there was just a stutter of confusion, a slight double take.

"Yeah," he said, "yeah. Good."

And like that, Alex was piling into the backseat of a minivan taxi. The driver seemed already weary of the group as they loaded in, and so was Alex. Their voices were too loud, the jokes predigested, leached from some sitcom or movie. But Alex smiled. Important to smile. Everything would be fine. There wasn't enough room in the minivan: Alex had to sit on one of the boys' laps.

"Comfy?" the boy said. Was he pressing his crotch into her ass? Alex kept smiling.

ALEX WAS TRYING TO find a clean glass, but there were none in any of the kitchen cabinets. Just a sleeve of red plastic cups and a few used coffee mugs in the sink. When she opened the dishwasher, it was grim and humid, smelling of beer. No glasses there either. Music pulsed from the backyard and scrambled any attempt to think clearly. Hard to imagine the people staying here could stand it, much less the neighbors.

A girl came in the front door, rolling a big suitcase behind her. "Where should I put my stuff?" she asked.

Alex couldn't hear whatever the girl said next over the music.

Alex gestured at the staircase. "Try the first room upstairs."

The house was new, with fake plaster columns, a double-height living room with blocky wood furniture and cushion covers that could be put in the washing machine. It smelled like air freshener and potato chips bought in bulk. The counter was covered with liquor bottles in giant industrial sizes, the marble beneath glazed with spills. She'd already checked out the pool outside. It looked a little gray. Every so often, the mechanical pool cleaner jerked along the bottom, a half-inflated raft drifting on the water's surface. Beer bottles dotted the surrounding tables and spilled out of a black garbage bag on the grass.

Alex changed into a bikini in the bathroom. A bikini was the correct choice for this place, for these people. The bathroom was disgusting—a hairdryer left plugged in, a towel streaked with self-tanner wadded on the floor. Stains marbled the toilet bowl. She flushed the toilet with her sandaled foot.

Alex hid her bag in the closet. She found a room with four bare twin mattresses and a futon and put a sweater on the futon to claim it.

She filled a plastic cup from the sink faucet, drank it down, then tipped in some vodka. She brushed her hair out with her fingers, ran her tongue along her top teeth. She made a second drink, this one with much more alcohol and some room-temperature cranberry juice, and took both cups with her to the backyard.

She surveyed the scene: a group playing beer pong, beer sloshing onto the patchy lawn. An audience of girls hung back in bikini tops and wedge heels, clutching anxiously at their elbows, expressions frozen in pretend interest. The setup looked taken from a low-rent porno, no one quite good-looking but intent on action.

"Here," Alex said, handing the stronger drink to the guy lying back on a lounge chair who seemed like he might be the one in charge. Was this Brian?

He was surprised, Alex could tell; trying to make out Alex's face from behind her sunglasses. "Thanks," he said. He was not very handsome, forcing a shape to his features with aggressive facial hair.

Alex tipped her glass against his in a hollow meeting of cheap plastic.

"Cheers."

Alex drank it down, and he followed her lead.

"This was a good idea," Alex said. "Getting out of the city."

"Right?" the man said, taking in the fact of Alex's easy smile, her swimsuit. Alex felt him relax, shift from slight confusion to stunned pleasantness, a willingness to go along with the idea that they might know each other from somewhere. It always happened this way, Alex pushing in close enough that people paid attention, that they felt edgy. Easy to turn that edginess into adrenaline, interest, indulgence.

ALEX WAS DRUNK ENOUGH by late afternoon to be having something like fun. It wasn't fun, exactly—it was just that the moments were slurring into one another and she didn't mind losing the thread.

Who cared about Lori, whatever she would report back to Simon? Simon's grim dog studded with ticks. Alex's life with Simon seemed a million miles away, part of a story that did not involve her now, not right this minute, and when she tried to call up Simon's face, there were only the details that came unbidden: The magenta vein that seamed along the length of his dick. How he liked an index finger in his asshole. His orgasms that had always sounded mournful, alarmingly so.

Alex did not know what time it was. The music was loud, endless. Could you live like this forever, in some alternate universe ruled by immediacy? Already the group seemed to have cycled through many incidents, many dramas. On the way to get more ice, Alex counseled a crying girl in the bathroom; even the crying had an air of forced cheer, though the girl was slumped by the sink, a position that exacerbated a slight double chin. She wore a tiny silver *E* on a chain around her neck, and she kept touching the letter as she cried.

From what Alex could discern, the girl had an on-again, off-again thing with one of the guys here, and he'd snapped at her when she'd tried to kiss him in front of his friends. Alex sometimes felt lucky to be exempt from this ordinary mess. Her arrangements, at least, made some attempt to meet both people's needs, offered a shortcut that bypassed all this swampy trouble. Who would want to be this girl in the bathroom, weeping over a ruddy-faced guy who wouldn't acknowledge her in public?

The girl's right breast kept falling out of her swimsuit top.

Alex tugged the swimsuit back in place.

Alex brought the girl a glass of water. The girl stared at the glass.

"Come on," Alex said, "drink. Drink the whole thing."

The girl spilled half of the glass's contents on her chest. She studied herself with mild surprise.

"Shit." She wiped with a half-hearted fist.

Alex tucked the girl's hair behind her ears.

"You're okay," Alex said, "you're just fine."

When the girl calmed down, Alex asked to borrow her phone.

The girl nodded, woeful, and pushed the phone along the floor toward Alex.

Alex checked her email—no word from Simon. Why would there be? Well, the watch. She had taken Simon's watch. Bad, she thought to herself, very bad, but at this moment it didn't feel bad. Only funny, in a far-off sort of way. Would he be mad about it? She'd bring the watch back at the party. He probably hadn't even noticed.

Alex opened a new email message but she could feel the girl nearby and she didn't know what to write or to whom. Alex signed out of her email, then cleared the history. As Alex rubbed the girl's heaving back, it occurred to her that she could take the phone. Use it until she could figure out how to get hers fixed. The girl hiccupped; Alex patted her more gently. She left the girl's phone by her side. Best to hold off until she'd gotten through a night here.

ALEX MUST HAVE GONE SWIMMING—hard to imagine she'd gone in the dirty pool, the water probably half beer at this point—but how else had her hair gotten wet? She could smell the chlorine. Her swimsuit felt damp. She should change into dry underwear, avoid infection, but that

seemed like a lot of effort. The guy sitting next to Alex—
was this Brian?—was trying to show her a photo he'd taken
of a deer he'd seen in the garden.

"They're always, like, just chilling in the yard," he said.
"They don't even seem afraid."

It's true, Alex thought idly, there were so many deer out
here. Sometimes she caught sight of a few deer bounding
across Simon's backyard, the dog losing his mind loping
after them. Who knew how the deer got in, considering the
wall around the place. But they did.

What was Simon doing at that moment? Finishing
work, making dinner plans. Finalizing logistics for the
party. Calling his ex-wife, or calling some new girl—he
was the type who always kept someone in reserve, who
wouldn't tolerate a gap, an instant when he might be alone
with himself. And maybe he'd go out with another girl,
waste an evening, but it would only remind him of Alex.
Make him miss her even more. He'd be glad to see her at
the party. Simon wouldn't need to know how she'd spent
her days out here. He'd be embarrassed for her: Alex with
this guy, his sunburned nose, his knee-length swim trunks.
The soft push of his belly, like he was practicing for middle age.

"I actually freaked for a second," the guy said, moving
through his photos, "when I saw this fucking wild creature
just standing there."

Alex was barely paying attention to the passing photos,
the guy swiping through multiple images of a roan-colored
deer until he swiped too far and suddenly a dick, like a big
blurry finger, filled half the frame.

"Fuck," he said, "sorry."

He glanced at Alex, apologetic, fumbling the phone back in his pocket. She blinked dully. She lay back on the lounger. The sun felt good. The guy kept talking but Alex wasn't listening—he probably couldn't tell, behind Alex's sunglasses, if her eyes were opened or closed.

WHEN ALEX WOKE UP, the sky was dark, the yard lit by floodlights. She was freezing, still in her bikini, a towel draped over her legs. A few people were clustered around the ping-pong table, bags of ice ripped open and melting at their feet. The music was playing but at a lower volume. Alex heard but could not see someone vomiting along the fence. Her phone still wasn't working. She kept it with her anyway, clutched in her hand.

The digital clock on the stove read one A.M. The futon upstairs that Alex had claimed had been taken by two girls, sprawled under an unzipped sleeping bag. All the other beds were occupied.

She opened another door down the hallway. The overhead light was still on, a guy asleep facedown on the fold-out couch. His shoes were kicked off and a sheet was only half pulled over the mattress. He was snoring.

Better than nothing.

Alex flicked the light off. She lay on the side of the mattress with the most room. The man stirred and reached out a hand in her direction. She let him make contact with her shoulder before patting his hand and shifting out of his reach.

She slept well enough, though she woke up in the middle of the night when someone opened the door and turned on the light.

"Oh shit, dude, sorry," then laughter, the light turning off, the door closing. More laughter. The laughter was unkind. Alex didn't care. She wouldn't see these people again.

IN THE MORNING, WHEN the man woke up and clocked Alex, then his wallet open in front of her, his eyes widened, hardened, so that she saw there was really only one thing to do.

"What the fuck?" The man grabbed his wallet. "Who are you?"

"Oh god." Alex made herself laugh, fluttered a hand at her throat. "I'm so embarrassed. I was just, like, double-checking your name."

He was sitting up, still staring at her, though his eyes snapped down to her breasts in her swimsuit. She laughed again and reached out to touch his knee.

"Last night," she said, "sorry, we were both pretty drunk."

The guy scratched his fingers through his hair, blinked at Alex. Alex sensed his unease but moved closer.

"It was fun, though," Alex said, smiling, and looked at him with lowered eyes.

"Yeah?" A smirk was forming as he downloaded this new information, pleased with this vision of his past self.

"Really fun," she said, breathy, and sometimes it was this easy, her face tipping up until they were kissing, his hand moving roughly to her breast. Her response clicked in easily—her arms going around his neck, her head tilting accommodatingly to the side. It was automatic, the murmur of pleasure that she had made many times before, would make many times again.

"Fuck," he said, his cock surging. Entranced by the sight of his hand on her. He had a smeary face, peppery blackheads. Easy to make the noises, to position the body.

When he took her nipple into his mouth, it dropped her abruptly into the moment—suddenly her body was involved, her brain forced to recognize what was happening. A flush radiated through her—then what? Then nothing.

You could perform a constant filtering of whatever you were feeling, taking in the facts and shifting them to the side. There was a static that moved you from one moment to another, and then another after that, until the moments had passed, turned into something else.

And really, it was nice, having a strange hand on her. She had never minded that part.

LATER, WHEN ALEX MADE her way to the kitchen, she saw the ravaged pizza boxes, a gallon of milk sweating on the counter. She was suddenly very thirsty.

A blonde in a floral cover-up was polling the girls on the couch on the correct way to make White Russians.

"Morning," Alex said, making herself smile, but no one—the blonde or the girls on the couch—smiled back. One of them actually frowned.

The coffeepot was empty, scaly with calcium. After Alex located a bag of Costco-brand coffee, she started to run the water, bunch up a paper towel to scrub the sides of the pot. The energy in the room seemed off. Some static in the air. When Alex glanced over, the girls on the couch were whispering.

"Not very cool," one of the girls muttered, looking over at Alex.

"Sorry?"

"Nothing," the girl sang out, smiling harshly, but the other girl's face trembled and Alex saw it was the girl from the bathroom.

"You hooked up with Matt." This was recited in a monotone by the blonde now sloshing milk into a plastic cup and stirring it with a finger.

The guy on the foldout couch, Alex surmised.

"That's my boyfriend," the trembling girl said.

"I didn't know," Alex said, trying for the appropriate solemnity.

The girl looked near tears, her friend rubbing her back in firm circles that seemed to churn up her outrage.

"What's your name again?" the friend said.

"Alex." She kept cleaning the coffeepot, the paper towel disintegrating, as if this effort would help, would forestall what was coming next.

"And who did you say you knew? 'Cause none of us"—the girl gestured around the room—"remember you."

"Brian," Alex said. "He invited me."

"Brian?" The girl on the couch shook her head. "Fine, okay, *Brian*. What's Brian's last name?"

———

ALEX WALKED FOR A while in the sun. For some stretches, where the trees met overhead, the road was shaded. Even so, the humidity meant she was sweating. Her forehead was wet, her neck, too. She lifted the hem of her shirt and tried to summon a breeze. Her sandals chafed. Every so often, she had to stop, had to bend down to wedge a finger between her skin and the sandal straps. Her weekend bag was small enough that it looked like a beach bag, not a bag containing everything she owned, and that was important. Important not to look desperate, out of the ordinary. She was a girl walking along the side of the road, and as long as she kept to these quiet streets, it wasn't so unusual.

She knew which direction the ocean was, knew she was getting close when she crossed the highway, darting quickly before a delivery truck. Traffic was bad, people heading back to the city. But was today Wednesday or Thursday? Wednesday. It would be easy enough to get a ride to the city—squint into the sun until her eyes were bleary and wet, then flag down a car. Explain she had gotten in a fight with a boyfriend, that he'd left her by the side of the road.

But what was the point? Simon's party was in less than a week. And there was nothing in the city. Jon was back with his wife, or that's what she figured from his tone. She was not welcome at her old place. The city was a series of people who had known Alex for too long. And Dom was in the city—Alex started to play that scenario through, and the end point wasn't anyplace she wanted to find herself.

———

HOW LONG HAD ALEX stayed with Dom? In that strange apartment? At least two days. Maybe more.

It now seemed stupid. And obvious what would happen next, obvious how Dom would react. But at the time, it hadn't been obvious.

Alex woke up in the afternoon on the last day. Her throat was burning. The apartment was empty. No sign of Dom. He was gone, attending to whatever shadowy errands made up his life.

She had a vague memory from the night before of Dom pulling the sheet back, her hand ineffectually trying to cover herself. But it had the patchy quality of a dream—maybe that's all it was.

She studied her stye in the bathroom mirror: mostly gone. The merest tint of pink.

There was a nest of bloody tissues in the wood trash can. The sight was alarming, at first glance, but they were just leftovers from one of Dom's frequent nosebleeds. She took a brief, scalding shower. The robust water pressure reminded her that the water in a shower was supposed to have actual force.

She had to search for her underwear: the twisted cotton briefs had somehow ended up under the bed. There would be a fresh pair in her purse, if she could find her purse.

Nothing in the fridge but a murky jar of gherkins, a stony cheese embalmed in many layers of plastic wrap. A box of hormone suppositories that was unopened and also expired. Vegetarian frozen burritos in the freezer. She wasn't hungry anyway. Food seemed just a concept.

Alex finally located her purse, the suede drawstring dumpling with its gold hardware. A fairly good fake, though the gold was too shiny. She got a glass of tap water and started to idly wander the rooms.

It was Dom's fault for leaving Alex alone. In that apartment. He'd gotten lax, that way. Careless.

And some things had not changed—Dom still used the same hiding spots. Didn't he owe her?

Alex took it all. The cash, too.

And now everything was gone. The money had been dispensed to cover various debts, buy her a little more time. Though less time than she expected, considering the shocking amount of cash, an amount that had seemed life-changing. It had made only the slightest dent, in the end.

The drugs were gone, too. That had been almost immediate.

Alex had assumed her theft would go unnoticed, or rather, that Dom would notice but that in some distorted way he wouldn't mind. That he would think of it as an expected loss, the cost of doing business.

Or maybe Alex had known, in some part of herself, that she was ruining everything, known how bad things could get, and maybe she had done it anyway.

NOTHING FROM ALEX'S PHONE. It was a dead rectangle, useless, but somehow still comforting to palm, slim as a prayer book.

Alex kept walking along the highway.

She didn't know how far away Simon's house was, but she had a sense of the general direction. She imagined showing up suddenly, opening the door onto the walled estate. But it was still too soon. Lori would deal with the situation. She would call someone else, if necessary, if Alex really proved herself too difficult to manage. It was pleasurable to imagine causing Lori trouble, to imagine forcing her to make her disgust perfectly clear. Simon would never get involved: people like Simon hated having to actually say things out loud, preferring subtler poisons.

Of course Alex wouldn't actually do it. Of course she would keep herself in check. And Simon wasn't actually angry with Alex, just annoyed, and that annoyance would dissipate soon. The party was the correct goal, the correct context to reappear in Simon's orbit—Alex just had to busy herself till then. Wait this out.

Five more days.

BY THE TIME ALEX made it to a beach, one she didn't recognize, the sun was too harsh to stay out for very long. She changed into her swimsuit in the cramped beach bathroom. The concrete floors were sandy, standing water collecting in the corners.

For a while, she sat on the bench in the shade. Cars left, other cars pulled in. She watched a father making the trek to the sand loaded down by folding chairs, umbrellas, a sack of beach toys, all the unwieldy props of family fun. Teenagers screeched up in a white Jeep, their dog leaping up their legs as they hustled a cooler to the beach. Three times Alex ambled to the cars people had just vacated and checked if they had left them unlocked. One car was open, but there was nothing inside—receipts, a stick of sunscreen, a pair of swim shorts drying on the dash. Six crumpled dollars in the center console that she folded into her hand. Pathetic.

After a while, the sun wasn't directly overhead and Alex could sit on the sand by her bag and try to appear content with her own company, soothed by the sound of the waves and the air vibrating with charged ions, and she even swam, knowing her bag would be fine.

A violent yelp, a splash—Alex glanced over at the source, a group of boys roughhousing in the waves. One of the boys lit up with a sudden smile. He was smiling at her, his hair a blond cap of curls. Alex smiled back—was this an avenue, a useful possibility? Some college boy? She floated for a while, pretending to be lost in her thoughts. At the same time, she was keeping track of the blond boy out of the corner of her eye, alert for any opening, but when he finally emerged onto the sand, it was to join a faction of adults with heads bent over their chubby paperbacks.

Alex sat with her bag and let the sun dry her body. She wished she had a towel. The lenses of her sunglasses were dirty but she could still study the scene: women in leggings power-walking along the waterline. Kids with their slim hips and rash guards running into the waves, shrieking in delight when they got knocked over. The group of adults carrying on a slow-motion conversation. The blond boy's eyes were closed, like he was absorbing the sun. When the air got softer, the adults made rumblings to leave. They started to pack up their chairs and shake out their towels, finished the last of their water bottles and tied back their wet hair.

ALEX FELL ASLEEP—BRIEFLY, but by the time she woke up it seemed like a different day—the sun low, the beach emptying. The adults were gone but the teenagers had stayed behind. They pulled on hooded sweatshirts. They threw a neon football back and forth with shocking vigor. Soon more teenagers joined them, all boys. There was a paper bag of beers that were promptly unloaded into a cooler, the boys setting up some paddle game that required a miniature net.

How much longer could Alex lie here without seeming out of place?

One of the boys had noticed her, a certain intensity aimed in her direction that she pretended not to acknowledge. It wasn't the blond one—some other kid with a concave chest.

She started to sit up, to fuss with her bag, when she saw the kid was approaching. He stopped at an anxious distance.

"Do you want a beer?" he said.

Alex decided to keep her sunglasses on. To take her time responding. Slowness worked just as well. "Excuse me?"

The boy had a little rat face, pinched. "I said, do you want a beer," he said, "because we, like, have some."

He was more confident than he should have been with a face like that.

Alex considered the boy.

Sometimes it was best to just say yes, to see how far something could go. It would either be a good choice or a bad choice, no way to know yet.

"Sure," Alex said. "Okay."

"Cool," the boy said, betraying only the slightest surprise. "Very cool."

THE RAT-FACED BOY OPENED a beer for Alex with overly exaggerated effort, as if it required great strength.

"Salud," he said, handing the bottle over. Still fairly cold.

A few of the boys gathered around a tiny grill. A guy ripped open a plastic pack of hot dogs with his teeth, then stabbed at the package with a penknife. He squeezed out the hot dogs, and the wet tubes plopped one by one onto the grate. Alex sat on an empty towel. The boy on the towel next to hers made himself small, and seemed to avoid looking at Alex out of politeness. It was the boy who had been playing in the waves, his blond hair now mostly dry.

"You look familiar," Alex said, a stupid thing to say, though the thing was he did seem familiar, from somewhere else entirely: his clean face, curly hair like a Valentine cherub. The track pants he had pushed up his calves.

"Oh yeah?" His jaw was a little soft, puffy, and his eyes were at half-mast. Stoned? Tired from the sun?

"I don't know," Alex said. "I think so."

The boy smiled at Alex, a shy smile that exposed the braces on his bottom teeth, and then it clicked.

"Oh," Alex said, "right. That party."

"Huh?"

"Helen," Alex said, "I don't know her last name. That big house on the beach."

"Mrs. R?" The boy furrowed his brow in a slow, amiable way. "You know Theo?"

Alex waved her hand. "Nothing," she said, "never mind, I just feel like I saw you."

Was the boy blushing? He took a drink from his beer, then pulled absently at the strings of his sweatshirt hood. His mouth was so pink, babyish, which made it somehow sexual.

"You're not old enough to drink," Alex said, "are you?"

His blush deepened. "I'm nineteen."

Alex would have guessed younger. She took a sip. "How old do you think I am?"

"I dunno." The boy laughed. "Twenty-four? Twenty-five?"

For a moment, Alex considered lying. But his face was so mild.

"Twenty-two," she said. With one hand, Alex was digging a hole in the sand, burying her fingers in the coolness underneath. "So old, right?"

"Nah," the boy said, as if she'd been seriously asking. "That's not old."

"Hey." The rat-faced boy clapped him on the back. "Can we have your keys? We left the vape in your car."

The boy tossed his friend a key.

"Thanks, man." The friend wagged his eyebrows like Alex wouldn't be able to see.

Together Alex and the boy watched him veer to the parking lot and unlock a boxy Range Rover.

"That's your car?"

"It's my dad's." The boy looked only a little embarrassed. He bit down on his bottom lip. His lips were chapped and rosy. When Alex leaned back on the towel, he glanced down at her body, then stared furiously ahead. Why did she find this sort of sweet?

"I'm Alex," she said. "By the way."

"Jack."

"Jack, huh?" They were both smiling.

"Where're you staying?"

"Just across the highway."

He nodded. "Cool."

She dumped the last dregs of her beer in the sand. "You want another one?"

There were three burnt hot dogs on a paper plate and a roll of paper towels beside them. She took a bite of hot dog: it tasted like charcoal, the center still cold.

Alex returned to the boy with a can of cheap beer. "It's the last one. We can share."

She settled herself a little closer to Jack than she had been before. He instantly sat up straighter.

"There are still some hot dogs left," she said.

"I'm a vegetarian," he said. "Mostly."

"Yeah?"

"I'm trying it out. I read this book?" He checked to see if she was listening. She nodded. "Um, *Siddhartha*. Have you read it?"

She shrugged in a way that could mean yes, could mean no.

"It's, like, basically about Buddha. He wasn't a vegetarian, 'cause you were supposed to just take whatever food you were offered. 'Cause they were begging?"

He checked her attention again.

"But it made me think, like, how to cause less harm." The boy seemed suddenly ashamed. "It's stupid, I dunno."

"Sounds good."

"Yeah. It's really good. Actually."

"Where's your place?" Alex said. "Out here."

"It's my dad's." He took a tea-party sip of the beer. "I mean, my dad has a place here."

"So you're staying with your dad?" Alex had been hoping for a house empty of parents.

"Yeah," Jack said. "My dad and stepmom. See? The house is, like, right over there. On the pond. It's really scummy this year."

She followed his pointing finger to a line of trees and the faint tops of houses.

"That one that looks like a barn?" he said.

A gray gable in the distance stood out taller than the others. So it was obvious that he had everything he needed.

Jack's phone dinged. He was instantly on the case. There was a stack of text messages on the home screen that he flipped through expertly.

"Fuck," he said. "I gotta go."

"You're leaving?" She was surprised, studying her own disappointment.

"Yeah, fuck, sorry, my sister just got in. It's, like, the one night I gotta see everyone."

"Too bad."

He looked unhappy to be leaving, too, his teeth trapping his bottom lip.

Alex held out the can. "You wanna finish this?"

"You keep it."

"Are you here for a while?" she said. "Maybe I could give you my number. And you can text, you know, if something fun is happening."

He blinked, taking this in. "Yeah," he said, "yeah, I can do that.

"Here, put in your number," he said, handing over his phone. "I'll call you, then you'll have my number, too."

His phone background was a pixelated mandala. Alex typed in her number, the number to the phone that barely worked.

Jack pressed send. She could hear the call go straight to voicemail, the voicemail that she had never bothered to change, so it said, *You have reached the voice mailbox of*—and then silence, a unit of dead air. Then: *Please leave a message after the tone.*

"Hi," the boy said into his phone. "It's me, Jack. I'm sitting with you right now. And now," he said, glancing at her face, "now you have my number."

WHEN IT STARTED GETTING DARK, Alex knew to walk away from the parking lot, to keep walking. Along the dunes, there were houses with their lights on, but they were far from one another and far from the water. The sand was still warm with the last gasp of stored heat. She kept walking until the beach was empty. To her left: the water. On her right, the dunes, the waving grasses, the wooden walkways leading to houses. One of the houses was probably Jack's, the family sitting down to some dinner of pesto salad and salmon and corn from one of the farm stands. The dad and the stepmom and the two children. Alex imagined Jack's sister was older, Alex's age.

Well, she thought, okay. Okay.

She did a round of box breathing, what that one guy had taught her—he was a corporate coach, took harried business calls while Alex zoned out in the sheets, watching CNN on mute and trying to ignore whatever gruesome leftovers were on the room service tray. He had narcolepsy, was prescribed a medication that he said was used by fighter pilots and ISIS bombers. He believed in breathwork. He listened to summaries of famous self-help books while he exercised with giant ropes. His son had died after a high school football injury—"my boy," he called him, smiling as he showed Alex pictures. Alex had cried—at that moment, she'd felt real affection for the man. He'd pressed a fist into her solar plexus, told her to inhale deeply.

"In for four, hold for four, out for four. And hold it."

Where was that man now?

She did another round of breathing, and then did it again. Better? Maybe.

———

BY THE TIME IT was fully dark, Alex had gotten far enough away from the parking lot that there was no one out, no one in any direction. Alex passed the white skeleton of a lifeguard tower. A metallic candy wrapper snapped along the ground.

How odd the ocean was at night—strangely placid, the waves unfurling in polite afterthoughts on the sand. The houses looked strange, too, looming on the dunes with the blank eyes of their windows, the size too unbelievable, like this was a soundstage. The mist in the air, the unnatural warmth, the moonlight on the pale sand; it would make sense if none of this were real.

What seemed so peaceful, the black stretch of ocean, was frightening when she got up close. It would be easy to lose yourself. One step into the water. Another. Simple, all the questions answered.

Was she spooking herself? Just a little. She sat on a piece of driftwood at the base of a dune. Fine. Not so bad, not so terrible. Maybe even boring, sitting out here, passing the hours, and boring meant manageable, though underneath that thought was another thought, an understanding that whatever this was, whatever she was doing, it was temporary. She could not do this forever. Just until—when?

Five days until the Labor Day party. Or four? No, five days.

Far off on the horizon, she saw a flash. A police boat, a lighthouse? Fireworks? But no, there it was, again: light-

ning appearing in bright silence. A storm out in the middle
of the ocean. A storm that was, at least, not here.

EVEN THOUGH IT WAS OVERCAST, Alex didn't think
she'd be able to sleep. Part of it was hunger. She'd eaten a
handful of tortilla chips from the boys, plus the hot dog.
Alex leaned back against the dune with her hands in her
armpits, a comforting childhood habit, feeling the ruff of
stubble. She took a sweater out of her bag. Groped around
until she found a pair of jeans. The sand was unavoidable
when she put them on: gritting against her thighs, the
backs of her knees.

She couldn't fall asleep. Her phone wouldn't even stay
on long enough for her to see what time it was. It was probably only midnight, if not earlier. Maybe it was good her
phone wasn't working. Better not to know exactly how
many hours she had to get through.

Maybe staying out here was dumb. Could things really
be much worse in the city? The city: she had an immediate
vision of the unhappiness that would be there, waiting for
her. Dom banging on the door, refusing to leave. (What
door? Where exactly was she planning to stay?) That was
too dramatic, Dom didn't do things like that—well, actually, he did, he had. His hands on her throat. That time he'd
stolen her phone from her purse, made her crawl on the
floor to get it back.

And what would he do now, now that he was really
angry? She wondered this but knew she didn't really have
to wonder.

The party was only a few days away. This was just a waiting period for Simon to cool off, a pause. Then everything would go back to the way it was.

Alex found the pill bottle in her zip purse and shook a few out into her palm. If she brought them close, she could identify which were painkillers, which were sleeping pills. She swallowed a sleeping pill dry.

She and Simon had taken Ambien and stayed awake a few weeks ago. It had been his idea, Simon learning about the possibilities of recreational use and sexual enhancement from the news coverage of a golfer's cheating scandal. Simon had promptly fallen asleep, but only after tearing up—a rare, frightening sight, Simon's hand pawing at his wet eyes, Simon saying, his voice slurred, how proud he was of his daughter.

"She's a great kid," he said. "Really. Caroline's had a tough go."

He had been concerned Alex was somehow recording him.

"Don't film this," Simon blubbered, "don't film this."

That had been the last thing he'd said before his eyes had closed, his head falling back on the pillow. His features had shifted as Alex looked at him, his face going fragmented.

So many of the men had been scared she was recording them, setting them up in some way. It had never occurred to her—it already felt enough like a setup. And why would she have wanted evidence, why would she have wanted to see herself, watch her body move, hear her voice gone to some unnatural, faraway pitch?

———

ALEX CURLED AROUND HER bag, waiting to feel tired. The lightning, wherever it was, had stopped. The ocean looked still, softened by mist. It was pretty at night, she decided, and probably too few people saw it like this, the indifferent beach empty of humans. It was just itself: a stark edge.

When the headlights appeared, they were distant enough that, at first, it seemed like a pair of flashlights. She sat up. Was this a sleeping-pill phantom, an optic jitter? But no, the lights got closer, and then there was the boxy shape of a car, the headlights making two columns in the mist. A car, headed slowly along the sand, headed in her direction. The pill was working, definitely. Her brain was lagging, each thought accompanied by its own woozy aura—the car, she understood, was coming for her. Coming to collect her. It was completely clear: he had located her, Dom. It seemed very obvious and very correct. Of course it had to happen like this.

For too long, she sat, frozen, watching the lights approach. And then she told herself, very calmly, to get to her feet.

The unsteady sand was a surprise, and she shouldered her bag and stumbled through the scratchy patch of tall grass and up and over the dune. She lay down, flat on her back, and who knew if she was hidden at all, and she stayed there, breathing hard, one hand on her bag, her other hand on her heart. The lights washed over the dune, over her body, brilliant as daylight—and then the lights were gone.

———

SHE DIDN'T WANT TO stay on the beach after that. Walking felt more difficult than it had earlier, her shoes sinking in the sand. When the houses started getting farther away from the water, separated, now, by small scrubby forests, it was easier to know what to do. She found an opening in the dunes and followed a path for a while, a series of boards laid on the ground like railroad tracks. There was sand everywhere, sand in her shoes, sand trapped in the legs of her jeans. When there were enough trees, she left the path and found a clearing. Her bag was fine as a pillow, one of her dresses laid out on the ground, packing down the dune grass. She tried to tamp the grass down more. Wasn't that where all the ticks were supposed to be hiding, in the grass? Better not to imagine what dark specks might find her in the night, tap into her bloodstream and funnel bacteria straight to her brain.

A girl Alex had met that first year in the city—back when Alex actually had a job, actually worked at a restaurant—told Alex that whenever she was scared, she just made herself believe that it was just a movie, whatever was happening to her. And who cared about a movie? It was all fun, wasn't it?

The girl had stopped coming around the usual places, the parties, seemingly disappeared, though people said she had just gone back to her hometown. She had been so tall, had worn those funny round sunglasses that made her look old-fashioned, her forearms dim with dark silky hair. She told a story about when some guy she was dating had gotten pissed at her, and how she sat there at some fancy dinner while the guy yelled at her, just taking it, just letting him rip into her, and how finally she picked up her full glass of wine and dumped it on the floor of the restaurant.

Now Alex couldn't remember the girl's name.

Alex blinked up at the sky, mostly obscured by trees, though the clouds had blown off. She made herself close her eyes. She realized she was still straining to hear a sound, waiting for some disturbance. But everything was quiet, even the ocean too far to register.

5

JUDGING BY THE SUN, it was close to noon.

Alex had been up early: a tremendous noise had startled her awake, panic flooding her system. Alex's hand went up frantically to cover her face, the other one reaching out to protect—who?

It took another second to understand the noise was just a deer, the sudden animal apparition crashing through the trees. The deer didn't seem to notice Alex at all, didn't care about a girl sitting alone on the ground.

Now Alex was walking along the shoulder of the highway, just until she saw a street she knew, though she could feel a few drivers craning to look at her, the whole thing too exposing, too unusual. No one else was walking anywhere—not on the highway, anyway. Only the occasional bicyclist passed her: men sheathed in toy-colored spandex who pedaled recumbent cycles with grim focus.

Alex kept walking, the temperature pleasant enough, at

least for now, and then she heard it. Someone calling her name.

"Alex?"

The voice was coming from somewhere behind her. Her pulse was racing—Dom? Simon? She forced herself not to turn around, to keep moving forward.

"Alex, hey!"

A white car slowed in the lane alongside where she was walking, then pulled onto the shoulder ahead of her, its hazard lights blinking.

And now a man was getting out of the car, waving at Alex. She didn't recognize the car, but as he got closer, she recognized the man—she'd forgotten his name but she knew his face. George's house manager. George was one of Simon's collector friends. She and Simon had gone to dinner at George's house the first week they'd been out here, an endless dinner where seemingly no one had fun, up until the very last minute, when everyone fell over themselves exclaiming how much fun the evening had been, so fun that they had to do it again very soon.

"I was driving the other way," the man was saying to Alex, "and I thought that was you, so I turned around. Is everything okay?"

He was young, in his thirties, and handsome in a boring, professional way, dressed in his button-down and khakis.

"Nicholas," the man said, touching his chest. "I work for George."

"Oh, sure," Alex said, "sure." She waved her hand in the air. "I just"—she paused, considering the scene. "I bicycled to the beach and then—" Alex laughed a little. "I guess someone took my bike." She hiked her bag higher on her shoulder. "And my phone's dead."

"Oh, man," Nicholas said, "really?" He pushed his hands through his hair, his distress genuine. "No way."

She gave a shrug.

Nicholas was so kind. It was his job, she guessed. When she and Simon had gone to George's for dinner, Nicholas had been the one who asked her if she had any dietary restrictions. When Alex went looking for the bathroom, Nicholas led her straight there. And Nicholas was the person who stood, stoically, as George and Simon discussed the difficulty of finding a chef, segueing seamlessly into the recent rape accusation against a basketball player that didn't quite add up, and what had the girl thought would happen, George said, asking a man into her dressing room? Alex had eyed Nicholas: he didn't react. Like Alex, he had made himself into vapor, the better to allow things to pass through him.

After dinner, Nicholas had brought a plate of warm cookies to the table.

"I shouldn't eat these," George said, finishing his third cookie.

It had been one of the rare nights when Simon had decided to drink, to really drink. Without Alex realizing it, Simon had gotten almost blackout: at the end of the night, Nicholas had driven them both home in Simon's car, Simon's eyes heavy as he slumped against her in the backseat. She hadn't considered what Nicholas had done after he had dropped them off and parked the car in the driveway, hadn't wondered how Nicholas had gotten home.

"Where's Simon?" Nicholas asked.

"Back in the city for a few days," she said. "Just for meetings. So I'm at the house alone."

Her voice sounded airy enough, sounded casual, and Nicholas didn't seem to think any of this was so strange.

"Let me give you a ride home," Nicholas said. "Or you want to drive around and look for your bike? Maybe someone ditched it."

"Maybe." Alex shaded her eyes with her hand. Beside them, traffic was whizzing past—fancy car, fancy car, fancy car, landscape truck. Fancy car.

"You know," she said, "I think I just got a little too much sun. I just feel a little dizzy."

"Why don't you come by the house for a minute? I just have to drop some stuff off. We can charge your phone, feed you."

She glanced at the highway, glanced at her bag.

"Where's George?"

"He's coming back out on Saturday," Nicholas said. "I'm getting everything in order, you know. Fill the refrigerators, pump up the bike tires."

He smiled at her, Nicholas, his job to take care of things.

IT WAS GOOD TO be in a car, to move at that speed. The windows were down. Alex could see an extra white shirt hanging from the hook in the backseat, a case of water. A freshly strung tennis racket. Nicholas was listening to an oldies station, cheery Motown.

"Can I have one of these waters?"

"Of course," he said. "Take two."

The bottle was warm from being in the car—she drank the whole thing.

"Hot out there?" he said.

"Oh," she said, "not too bad yet."

"Good thing I found you. You want to call Simon from my phone?"

"That's okay," Alex said. "Maybe in a little bit."

"Sure, sure."

It was Nicholas's job, of course, to be this agreeable. It was even part of his job to look like one of them and not like an employee, to dress like someone's nice son-in-law who just happened to anticipate your every need and tend to it discreetly. Maybe the lack of uniform made people more comfortable with the idea of another person being so deeply embedded in their life, as if Nicholas hung around just because he liked it, just because he enjoyed their company.

When she and Simon had gone for dinner, it had been dark, and now, in the day, she saw George's house was much bigger than Simon's, the property larger by many orders of magnitude. There was a pond she hadn't noticed before, obviously man-made, with a wooden dock and lily pads rimming the edge. The lawn was seamless, the green flat and unchanging.

"Let me just unload the groceries," Nicholas said, parking on the cobblestone apron of a smaller garage.

"Can I help carry anything?"

"Absolutely not," Nicholas said, his arms filled with bags. If any of it was a strain, he didn't let on.

She followed him to the front hall, dropping her bag by the door, then on through the living room. Art on every wall, vibrating with dense color. A Persian cat stalked past, pausing for a haughty moment before leaping onto a glass coffee table. The couch was an undulating wave of upholstery, oranges and yellows, some sixties Italian thing that looked vaguely like a sea of breasts. The distance between the furniture in the room was unnaturally large. Through the windows, everything outside was varying shades of green.

"I'll just go to the restroom," Alex said, shouldering her purse.

"Down the hall," Nicholas said, "you remember where?"

IN THE BATHROOM, ALEX splashed her face with water, rinsed out her mouth. A cluster of pimples had formed along her hairline: she resisted the urge to fuck with them. Her eyebrows looked too faint, her cheeks just slightly sunburnt, lips peeling and dry. She tried to fix everything as quickly as possible—filling in her brows, patting concealer under her eyes, around her nostrils. She wet toilet paper with hand soap and rubbed under each arm. Not so bad, and even her hair looked better after she braided it, her scalp faintly gritty with sand. She swept a scatter of sand off the sink and onto the floor. She blotted off her lipstick with more toilet paper, then flushed away the whole mess. An inspection of her fingernails. She scratched them against the bar of hand soap, then ran them under water as hot as she could stand.

There. Immaculate.

———

ALEX HADN'T BEEN INSIDE the kitchen before: unlike the rest of the house, it looked like it hadn't been updated. It still had the plain wooden cabinets from the fifties, painted light yellow. Floral wallpaper with tiny pink rosebuds marching tightly on a diagonal. At a desk, there was a landline and a monitor setup, screens showing a grid of black-and-white security footage. A small plastic buzzer with a button—a garage door opener, Alex thought, but then she read the label. PANIC.

Nicholas opened the refrigerator and started pulling out six-packs of Pellegrino from white grocery bags, then bottle after plastic bottle of orange juice and grapefruit juice. He lined up everything on the shelves at right angles.

"This'll take just a minute," he said. "Can I get you a drink or make you a snack?"

She took a stool by the counter. "I mean, I'd love a little something, if it's not a problem?"

"Of course not." He closed the refrigerator and folded the empty bags into precise thirds. "The chef won't be out until Friday, late, but what do you feel like?"

"I don't want to put you to any trouble."

"Please," Nicholas said, "it's my pleasure. I actually like cooking, it relaxes me. And I hardly ever get to do it."

Amazing how he almost made you believe everything he said—she could learn from him.

He opened the refrigerator again, peered inside. "I can pan-fry a piece of salmon with some vegetables?" He looked at her. "You like fish, right? Or a quick salad?"

"I mean, that all sounds great. Whatever's easiest."

"Go, sit outside, I'll bring it to you."

"No, god no," Alex said. "Can't I help?"

"I've got it. Enjoy the sunshine."

"Seriously," she said, "I'd rather sit in here with you."

"As you wish."

Nicholas pulled out a pan and unwrapped a piece of bright pink fish from butcher paper. He appeared graceful, relaxed, though probably he wished she would leave him alone to work. It was likely easier for everyone when the lines were drawn more clearly, but surely other people had performed this way for Nicholas, tried to demonstrate how unlike the others they were, how comfortable they were fraternizing with employees. She had experienced her own version of it: the men who asked her endless questions about herself, faces composed in self-conscious empathy. Waiting with badly suppressed titillation for her to offer up some buried trauma. Men who insisted on her coming first, as if this was proof of their fundamental goodness. It wasn't bad, it was just annoying. Because actually it required more energy from her, required more fake emotion scrounged up to match theirs.

Alex drained the glass of water Nicholas poured for her, the welcome shock of ice making her realize how thirsty she still was.

The dinner with George had been unpleasant, here in his dining room with black marble floors and black lacquered chairs. He'd been trying out a new chef. George's voice—warbling, reedy—was unsettling, plus how quickly he got bored, obviously bored. It made everyone anxious, conscious of needing to herd his attention.

His wife was extremely thin, a model who had decided, later, to become a painter. Based on the dinner conversation, being a painter seemed mostly to consist of thinking about real estate, the wife on a constant search for a more picturesque studio. She wore a maroon sweater with lime green cuffs over a stiff white button-down, red lipstick, and kept her purse on the chair next to her, its teeth zipped in a sharp smile. While everyone else had been served a bowl of sorbet, the wife had, without comment, been served a bowl of blueberries: she ate them one at a time. All through dinner, she had barely spoken to Alex, her frail, nervous energy aimed at her husband. George hadn't spoken much to Alex, either. Alex was a sort of inert piece of social furniture—only her presence was required, the general size and shape of a young woman. Anything beyond the fact of her sitting in her chair and nodding along was a distraction. Occasionally, Simon put his hand on the back of Alex's neck, or patted her shoulder.

Over the course of the dinner, Alex lulled herself into a trance state, the boredom almost like a drug, something you could lean into, gorge yourself on. Simon told her that George's wife demanded that George never be alone with another woman. As if any woman would throw themselves at George's tiny frame, overcome by passion. But better to believe your life was valuable, under attack, than the alternative.

"ARE YOU SURE YOU'RE not hungry?" Alex said. "This is so fucking good."

"I already had lunch," Nicholas said.

Who knew if it was true? Maybe Nicholas was meant to appear free of needs, any human hungers.

She would have felt more inhibited, usually, eating in front of him like this, but she was too hungry to care. And the salmon was good, the salad, too, soggy with oil and lemon juice. Whenever she drank from her water glass, he refilled it from a carafe, almost without her noticing. Her phone was charging on the counter where Nicholas had plugged it into the outlet.

"So," Alex said, "how did you meet George?"

Nicholas had been an actor, he told her, or had tried to be one. He'd been in a few things, even had a fairly good run on a soap opera, which was actually not a bad job. Really. You learned a lot. They taught you how to be professional. Show up on time, keep yourself in shape. Learn your lines. None of it, the success, had stuck in the way he'd imagined. He met George at a party where Nicholas was working for a caterer; George had hired him away. Nicholas said he had a daughter on the West Coast.

"Or West, anyway. Reno. Not really the coast."

"Really?" Alex held the linen napkin to her mouth as she finished chewing. "You don't seem old enough to have a kid."

"She's five. Bella."

"Can I see a picture?"

Nicholas pressed his phone and flashed the home screen at Alex: she saw a photo of a blond girl with a butterfly painted on her cheek. The girl looked frazzled and anxious, her smile pinched. Who took care of the girl, what was her life like?

"She's beautiful," Alex said.

"Thanks," Nicholas said, glancing at the screen before pocketing the phone. "Yeah, it's hard not seeing her all the time, but this is a really great job. And I get back to visit when I can."

"And you sleep here, in the house?" It was certainly big enough.

"When we're here and not in the city, yes. There's a staff apartment," he said. "It's on the other side of the garage."

"It must be pretty weird. This job."

Nicholas shrugged. "Oh sure, I mean, every job is a little weird."

There it was, the famous discretion.

"Yeah, but this is pretty nuts, right?" She raised her eyebrows at the kitchen, the lawn outside, a green so deep it appeared to echo.

"It's certainly not how I grew up," he said.

"Me either."

There was a pause—neither of them elaborated. She scraped the last of the food from the plate, used a finger to wipe up the remaining oil before bringing it to her mouth.

"So good," Alex said. "Thank you." She stood to take the plate to the sink.

"I've got that," Nicholas said, smoothly, as though carrying her dishes would give him the greatest pleasure, and only after he insisted twice more did she hand the plate over.

"How's your phone doing?" he said. "Let me know when you want a ride back, I'm happy to run you over. I can call a car, too, if you'd rather."

She tried to turn on her phone. It was no longer producing even a sputter. The screen was black and inert, a void of pure indifference. Her pulse spiked, though she kept her expression cheery.

"Sorry, I think my phone is just totally dead," Alex said. "I don't know what happened."

"I can take a look at it."

"I mean, sure, if you wanna try. Go for it."

Nicholas used a different charger, then tried a different outlet. He disappeared for a while. While he was gone, Alex petted the cat, its fur the same ginger color as George's hair. The cat looked mildly irritated by her attention.

Nicholas came back, waving the phone apologetically. "I thought it might work if I plugged it into a computer."

"Nothing?"

"It turned on for a second, it seemed like. Then nothing. There's a place in town that might be able to fix it," he said. "I can take you there on the way to Simon's. You about ready to head back?"

Alex smiled at him, then down at her hands.

"George isn't back for a few days," Alex said, "right?"

"Saturday," Nicholas said. "First thing."

"Do you mind," Alex said, "I mean would it be just totally horrible if I just hung out here for a while longer? I'm such a baby," she said. "I hate that house when it's empty. I get so scared, it's kind of pathetic."

Nicholas was obviously taken aback, but was good at not appearing surprised. Surely he had dealt with worse.

"I mean, yeah." He rubbed the back of his neck. "I've got a few more things to do."

"But I wouldn't be in your way, right?" Alex said. "If I just hang here and read or something? And you can kick me out whenever you need to, really."

She made herself look down, counting out a few seconds before she looked back at him. She held his eye.

"I'm really sorry to ask," she said, "I'm so embarrassed."

There it was, the flicker of responsiveness, the barely perceptible glance at her breasts.

"Of course. Let me just text Mr. H and let him know, but I'm sure it will be absolutely fine."

Alex touched his arm.

"Nicholas," she said, "listen, do you mind just not telling George I'm here? I don't want Simon to know." She let her mouth tremble slightly, then bit her bottom lip. "To be honest, we're kind of fighting," she said, "and I know he'd be furious I was at his friend's house. Bothering you. He can get really mean."

She said this in an almost whisper, a reluctant confession, and Nicholas's brow furrowed as he took in this information. She rubbed her bare arms and smiled at him, a brave smile.

"I'm really sorry," she said. "I hope that doesn't put you in a weird position."

"No," he said, "no." He exhaled. "I mean, I'm sure it's fine if you want to hang for a while. Right? No harm in that."

"Thank you," she said, going up on her toes to hug him. She could smell the faint tang of her underarms, but hopefully he couldn't. He kept a businesslike distance as he patted her shoulder.

"Of course," he said. "Happy to help."

ALEX SAT IN THE shade with her legs in the hot tub. The sunlight warped the surface of the pool. She was reading a memoir she'd found on the living room shelf, an old hardback whose butter-yellow pages were brittle enough that she could pierce them easily with a fingernail.

Somewhere on the property, she heard someone operating a leaf blower, then the sound of a lawnmower. Occasionally a man in long sleeves and a baseball hat walked past the pool carrying a garbage can filled with weeds. When she nodded and waved, he just looked at the ground. So much effort and noise required to cultivate this landscape, a landscape meant to invoke peace and quiet. The appearance of calm demanded an endless campaign of violent intervention.

"Do you want a towel?" Nicholas said, passing by on his way to the garage. "Sunscreen?"

"Please don't worry about me," she said, "I don't want to put you out at all."

He showed her how to use a key hidden by the gate to open a small bar area: pool toys hanging on the wall, a small sink and refrigerator. She should feel free, Nicholas said, to take anything she needed.

All this abundance was its own intoxicant. She changed into her pink two-piece that still smelled of chlorine. She drank a Corona and three mini bottles of water from the refrigerator, then spent ten zoned-out minutes covering her body with sunscreen from an amber tube, sunscreen that smelled woodsy and expensive. She felt vaguely turned on, her skin sliding around under her hands, newly aware of her swimsuit pressing her crotch. She put the sunscreen in her bag. A party favor, useful for later. Like her new sunglasses: she'd found a pair in a bowl on the living room table when she'd gone inside to pee, big tortoiseshells whose green lenses sharpened the world into shockingly precise detail.

Four days until Labor Day. It seemed like a long time. Enough that she didn't worry too much about what exactly might happen between now and then.

Her skin glistened in the sun, her hands were slick from the sunscreen, and when she dipped her legs in the hot tub, she saw a veil of oil start to spread, a rainbow radiating from her skin—she was dirtying the water, sand sparkling on the steps, but so what? Someone would just clean everything again.

"Sit with me," Alex called, the next time Nicholas passed. "Please?"

She was a little drunk, even off one beer. She swallowed a burp. She pushed the sunglasses up on her forehead.

"How is it?" Nicholas said. "Want me to turn on the jets?"

Hard to gauge whether he was annoyed or not, having to deal with the needs of this person who did not employ him.

"Come sit with me," Alex said, "please." She patted the warm stone beside her. "I'm lonely."

"I've still got to do a few things." Nicholas cocked his head.

ALEX HAD FALLEN ASLEEP. For a second, waking up, she was disoriented. Then it clicked back into focus. The line of lounge chairs along the pool, the yellow swoop of a sculpture in the lawn nearby. Though the air smelled like cut grass, the landscape truck was gone, and the day, another day, was almost over.

She inspected her cleavage, pressing on the skin to see if it turned white. But no, she had somehow avoided getting sunburnt. That was lucky. Wasn't she a lucky girl? Just the ghost of the fish in her mouth, the grainy aftertaste of the beer, another bottle half empty on the table beside her. When she picked it up, the beer was warm.

The book was splayed open on the ground—she had read almost twenty pages, but couldn't quite recall what the book was about. A memoir by a woman whose mother had loved her too much. Whose brothers had loved her even more. A problem of emotional excess, psychological gout.

When she got to her feet, all the blood rushed to her head. She walked into the pool with one hand lifting her hair above her shoulders to keep it dry. The pool was heated to an amniotic degree, the water silky and smelling of minerals. She let her hair fall. She held her breath, ducked under. An easy lap. She surfaced at the far end. There, back at the other end, where she had just been, was Nicholas, his white button-up glowy in the dusk. His hand was up in a wave. She swam back toward him and stepped out of the pool, squeezing the water from her hair.

"Feels nice?" Nicholas said.

"Perfect."

She grinned at him, grabbing a towel from the lounge chair. She wrapped it around herself, holding it just under her bikini top so it pushed up her breasts. She wiped her nose with her forearm.

"Saltwater pool," she said, "right?"

"Yep."

"Do you go in ever?"

"In this pool?" He made a face. "No."

"Even when they're not here?"

He shrugged. "Maybe once or twice."

Admitting even this small transgression seemed like a step forward, though Alex suspected it was a lie. She rubbed each leg briskly with the towel, then started to braid her wet hair over one shoulder. "Can I see your place?"

"It's not that big," he said.

Was he embarrassed? Or just impatient. No, she decided, he was curious.

"But, yeah," Nicholas said, "you can see it if you really want."

"I do," Alex said, "I really want."

———

THE STAFF APARTMENT WAS a box with gray tile floors, though at least the air-conditioning was strong, the rooms almost too cold to be comfortable. Most of the furniture was white and plastic. There was an older television mounted to the wall, a black leather couch. A few *Surfer* magazines on the coffee table. Everything was very neat.

"You live here all year?" Alex said.

"Just when Mr. H is out here. Otherwise, we're in the city."

We, he said, as if he and his employers were a unit.

She sat on the couch—she'd changed into cutoffs, though she was still in her bikini top and an oxford shirt she left unbuttoned. When you were quiet long enough, let the silence really settle, people usually felt too uncomfortable to gather their thoughts. To form those thoughts into a question, like, for example, why was Alex still here?

"Do you want a drink or something?" Nicholas said.

She brightened. "What do you have?"

"I can make literally anything you want. I went to bartending school."

"Really?"

"Oh yeah," he said. "I'm a scholar. Bartending school and three semesters at the Actors Studio. So what's your drink?"

"Dealer's choice."

He decided to make a tequila drink that needed fresh herbs: he took her out to show her the garden. It was under the purview of a master gardener, he said. There were tomatoes among the humid prickly vines, a patch of basil that made the air smell thick and grassy. She saw squash, in the shade of their big leaves, and Nicholas bent down as if to pick one, though he did not, his hand only resting on its ridged skin.

There was a beehive in the back. "There's chickens, too," he said, "do you wanna see?"

This offer, she assumed, appealed to people from cities.

NICHOLAS WANTED TO MAKE a different drink, next, something that had a float of dark rum on top and required him to psychotically jackhammer a cocktail shaker over his head. He poured the drink into the glasses from a dramatic height. Soon enough they had each had two.

How did the coke appear?

From somewhere in the immaculate staff apartment, coke Nicholas parceled out in bumps, silty white piles that they snorted off the key to the garage. It wasn't very good, an immediate speedy drip in Alex's throat, but, more importantly, there seemed to be a tremendous quantity. Some spilled down her front when she brought the key toward her nose, but she didn't care—not at that moment. They could get more, if they wanted it. Wasn't that true? Even though her heart was racing, she was calm, imagining a pearled line of possibility stretching on without end. She could always get what she needed. Wasn't she taking care of herself? Hadn't she managed to avoid going back to the city, hadn't she kept things moving forward out here?

It was probably late. The sky was totally black. She'd

taken a quick shower in Nicholas's bathroom. Her hair was still wet, but at least it was clean, slippery. The air conditioner made a constant industrial whoosh that eventually became white noise. She plugged her phone into the wall, and that alone felt like an improvement, a deposit on the future promise of connection. When the screen turned on, she did not click on Dom's name (twenty unread texts), but saw two texts from a number she didn't recognize: a dolphin emoji, a text that said *what are u up to tonite?* It took a moment to realize it must be the boy from the beach. Jack. The boy with braces. Her phone died before she could write back. She didn't know if she even wanted to: it was hard to conjure up more than his blond curls, the boy pointing to the big, far-off house. What book had he been reading? *Siddhartha.* Right.

Nicholas tried to play music from his phone before finally giving up.

"The Wi-Fi in here is really bad," he said. "Basically nonexistent."

He knelt on the rug, floating a CD on delicate fingertips into a chunky old stereo.

"A CD player," Alex said. "Why the fuck do you have a CD player?"

"A classic," he said. "Do you know this song?"

Nicholas didn't seem to mind when Alex didn't respond.

He crawled over and arranged a few lines on the cover of *Surfer* magazine. They knelt on either side of the coffee table, not quite looking at each other, in the way people doing drugs often did not quite look at each other.

"You first?" he said.

A little bit dizzy afterwards, she leaned her head back against the couch. Even after showering, she still smelled like that expensive sunscreen.

How late had it gotten? She was fuzzy on the details of their conversation, how exactly they had landed on this latest topic: Nicholas had, apparently, many years ago, almost been cast in a big studio movie. It was not the lead—but, he said, even so. He made it sound as if he had been promised the role. A life-changing role.

"It's just," Nicholas was saying, "I would have been good. For real."

"I'm sure," Alex said. "I'm sure you would have been great."

"It was so fucking close," Nicholas said. "It was down to me and, like, two other guys. Two other guys!"

"You would have been amazing," Alex said. Was her voice too loud? "So fucking great," she said. "One hundred percent." As she said it, it seemed true. She felt genuine affection for Nicholas. He deserved good things.

They had finished their drinks, their glasses empty except for a few twisted leaves of mint—she should try to have some water. They both should have water; Nicholas's cheeks gone a bit red. She had the thought, again—that she should get up and drink water. She didn't move. Now Nicholas was talking about George. She supposed she had asked.

"He's been good to me," Nicholas said. "He's a good guy."

Alex must have made a face, Nicholas's voice gone suddenly strident. "I'm serious!" he said. "He's great."

She stared up at the ceiling, her heart pounding hard enough that she could feel it. It wasn't unpleasant. She put her hand on her chest. "If you say so."

"A lot of people aren't. But he's tidy, clean, and he's got a good heart, so you know, that's pretty good. Considering. He's not mean."

"How'd he get all his money? How much does he have, anyway?"

Nicholas neatened the lines on the table, bent to do another quick one. He snorted hard, then sat up. "I really," he said, "don't know."

"Fifty? A hundred? More?"

He shrugged.

"Fuck." Alex slumped lower on the couch.

"Family money. Now he has a foundation."

"I don't get it."

"I dunno. He likes art. What have you got in there anyway?" He toed her bag with his shoe.

"Nothing," Alex said, "just clothes." She pulled her bag in front of her.

It was funny to her, suddenly, this bag she'd been dragging around, this bag full of all her possessions. She lifted out a pink sweater. "Feel this, it's so soft."

"Clothes? Why do you have a bag of clothes? Weird," he murmured, peacefully, "so weird."

Nicholas lay his head on his folded arms.

They both were a little giggly, a little sweaty.

"What about this?" Alex held out the small onyx rock from Helen's house. It was cold in her palm. "Do you like it?"

Nicholas opened one eye to study the rock, then sat up to hold it.

"So heavy," he said. "I like how heavy it is."

She took it back, wrapped it in the sweater. She shoved the bundle further down her bag.

"What is it?" Nicholas said. "Is it fancy?"

She didn't answer, but that didn't seem to bother him. Nothing seemed like it could bother either of them, a calm lull settling over the room.

"How'd you meet Simon?" Nicholas said, after another stretch of silence.

"At a party. We knew the same people."

Did he believe her? Nicholas seemed about to say something.

"What?" Alex said.

"I don't know," he said. "You like him? He's so much older. You're what, twenty-five?"

"Twenty-two."

"Yeah. A baby! Don't you want to be with someone your own age?"

Alex shrugged. "I love him," she said, watching Nicholas's face.

ALEX WANTED DESSERT, which is how they had ended up in the main house, Alex following behind Nicholas as he disarmed the security system. She couldn't stop laughing.

"Shh," he said, but he was laughing, too—this was like a parody of a heist movie, his finger to his lips, his exaggerated, cartoonish insistence on quiet. Who would ever be able to hear them? They could yell if they wanted to, Alex screaming at the top of her lungs, and nothing would happen.

Even in the half-light, Nicholas's features were legibly handsome. He would have been a good actor, she decided. The living room lights were off—she held on to Nicholas's shirt as he led the way through the darkness toward the kitchen. She was barefoot. She didn't remember when or where she had taken off her shoes.

"Fuck," she said, recoiling—something warm and alive brushed against her leg.

"It's the cat," Nicholas said. "Chill, Maria," he cooed, "just fucking chill. I should actually feed her." He flicked on the kitchen lights.

"There's gelato in there," he said, nodding at the freezer. He squatted down to the cat, its eyes almost wholly obscured by fur. "You hungry, Maria? You starving?"

Alex opened the freezer door—there was a bottle of vodka, four pints of pale green gelato, and ten boxes of unopened perfume.

"What's all this?" She studied the back of one of the cellophane-wrapped boxes.

"It's Greta's," Nicholas said. "The wife." He was filling a tiny silver bowl with water while the cat wound itself around his ankles. "She's worried they would discontinue it."

"Right." Alex took out a pint of gelato. "Don't you hate them? I mean, you can tell me. I don't care. I don't even know them."

"I told you. I like them."

"I can't believe someone fucks George. Who would want to fuck George?" She couldn't stop laughing. "I mean, really."

"He does okay," Nicholas said.

"Shut up."

"I'm not joking." Nicholas said the name of a well-known actress: famously pretty, famously tiny.

"No," Alex said. "Really?"

"Oh yeah," Nicholas said. They stood at the kitchen counter, taking turns scooping at the gelato with a spoon. "She has Lyme disease."

"Isn't that fake?"

The gelato tasted like basil. She let it melt on her tongue, then passed him the spoon.

"She had to move out of the city," Nicholas said, "to a place with no insulation and no nearby cell towers. It's in her brain, you know, that's where it goes." He sucked the spoon clean.

THE FIRST SWITCH ALEX hit in the living room controlled the spotlights: only the art was visible, hovering in squares of golden light in the black room.

"Let's go back to my place," Nicholas said. He was lying on his back on the living room floor, petting the cat who was walking back and forth along his stomach, kneading his shirt with her paws.

"I just wanna see all this first," Alex said. The pint of gelato, half eaten, was in her hand—she couldn't find the lid.

Some of the art she didn't recognize. A photo of old actors, flecked with paint. Some still from a vampire movie? A scratchy line drawing on a neon yellow clay panel. But some of it she did. There was a modern piece, brutal and primary colored, basically a museum poster except, bizarrely, that it was real.

"Is this serious?" Alex said, stopping in front of the painting.

"What do you mean?" Nicholas was still on the floor, his fingers working the cat's ears.

"I don't know." She got up close to the painting. "Why isn't it covered by glass or something?"

"There's all this temperature control in here," Nicholas said. "Like, humidity control. The windows are tinted. UV protection. There's a generator in case the power goes out."

"Do you ever just come in here and think about all this stuff, how long ago it was made, whatever?" Alex put down the pint on a side table, licking her fingers clean where some gelato had dripped. "You can see the brushstrokes. Doesn't that freak you out?"

Nicholas got to his feet. He turned on another light.

"I don't really spend all that much time in here," he said. He came up beside her. "And they're not that old. They keep the really old stuff in the city."

"This one's insane," Alex said. "What the fuck! How is this here and not in a museum, right?"

She squinted, then pulled him by the hand so they were standing close to the painting.

"What do we think? Good or bad?"

"I mean, good, right?" Nicholas seemed to be getting slightly nervous. She could feel that his hand was clammy. He dropped her hand and wiped his palm on his pants.

"It's like I'm getting high off this," she said. "Like, just purely off the estimated value, a contact high."

Up close the painting was just colors. Blue, like the sky, like the lines painted on the bottom of the pool.

"Can I touch it?" Alex said.

She didn't look at Nicholas, but she could hear him breathing.

"What?" He laughed on a slight delay. "Touch it?"

"Like, just for a second," she said. "Not even a second."

He didn't stop her, Alex pressing the pad of her index finger to a line of blue, then pulling away as if she'd been burnt.

"Okay. Well. I did it."

Nicholas laughed, but he was bending down to pick up the cat, not really watching her.

And why did she do it again, why did she follow the impulse to reach out her hand again, let her fingertips linger?

"Hey," Nicholas said, his voice suddenly sharp, and maybe this harshness had startled her, made her jerk away. It hadn't been conscious, surely. A little stutter, a little slip of her fingernail—but there it was, a scratch. A scribble in the paint. She stared at it. She stared at her hand.

She had done a thing that could not be undone. And even though there was mostly just shock, regret, was there also something else jolting along underneath, something like a thrill? Like the time when one of the men had slapped her and she smiled, afterwards, not knowing what else to do. He slapped her and she had smiled like an idiot. It seemed to surprise them both.

She resolutely did not look at Nicholas, who walked over, the cat held tightly in his arms.

His eyes went straight to the scratch.

She wanted him to be more angry than he was. Instead, Nicholas seemed like he was about to cry. He looked, strangely, like a little boy, like a scared little boy, and that was worse than anger. He studied the painting for a while. The second he put the cat down, the animal bolted, disappearing in the darkness beyond the doorway.

"It's okay," Alex said. She wanted to reach for his hand but found she could not. "It's okay, right?"

Nicholas's eyes were closed. He didn't acknowledge her. "You can't see it," she said. "Not really. Can we fix it?"

A stupid suggestion; there was no possible way for them to fix this.

She sat down beside him. They were silent. Nicholas finally opened his eyes. He got abruptly to his feet, stalking toward the kitchen. He only stopped to grab the open pint of gelato from where she had abandoned it on the side table. Even from the couch, it was obvious the container had left a ring of condensation on the wood.

"Let me clean that," Alex said, jumping up. "Please."

"Just get out, okay?" Nicholas said. He spoke without ever looking directly at her. "Let me deal with this. Just go wait at my place."

WHEN NICHOLAS RETURNED TO the apartment, Alex was sitting, primly, at his kitchen table. As if good posture could somehow improve the situation.

"I'm sorry," she said.

He didn't answer. He poured himself a glass of water and drank the whole thing at once. He seemed deadly, deadly sober.

"Let me call you a car," he said. "You have everything, right?"

"Can I just stay here tonight," she said, "please? Please?"

His face hardened. He looked like he was about to say something, but stopped himself.

Alex stood up, grabbed his arm. "Please? Simon's not home. I don't want to sleep alone."

"It's easier," Nicholas said, "to just get you a car."

NICHOLAS LET ALEX WEAR one of his T-shirts and a pair of boxers. They were printed with surfboards, strangely juvenile. She lay in the bed beside him. He slept in a white T-shirt and long gray pajama pants, his back turned from her. She studied his shape for a while in the dark. She could tell he was still awake. He was not a bad person. He had a daughter he loved. She had caused him trouble. He had only been kind to her.

Alex scooted so her body was curled against his, her breath on his neck. He didn't move. She pressed her breasts against him, her hand going toward his crotch.

"Hey," she whispered, "listen—"

He recoiled. "Jesus."

Alex had started to pull her shirt up over her head. He grabbed her wrist with what felt like excessive force. She could see the whites of his eyes in the dark.

"See," Nicholas said, "see, your whole shit doesn't work on me."

"What?" she said.

"Do you think it's not obvious? What your deal is? You think I can't tell?"

She felt her face fall.

"Why are you like this?" he said. And he was really asking. Expecting some explanation, some logical equation—x had happened to her, some terrible thing, and so now y was her life, and of course that made sense. But how could Alex explain—there wasn't any reason, there had never been any terrible thing. It had all been ordinary.

When she was quiet, Nicholas shook his head. Disgust. "I'm going to sleep on the couch."

"I'm sorry," she said. "I'll leave you alone. Okay? I'm sorry."

He moved as far away from her as he could while still remaining on the mattress.

Was this shame, this coil of dread, her head pounding? Every thought was too exposed, the room lacking any softness. Things were too much like themselves. They had done too much coke—her heart was weak and fragile, her eyes ached in their sockets. She wished she had a painkiller. She wanted to get up and find one in her bag but didn't want to make any noise and remind Nicholas of her presence. She could smell herself, could smell her sweat.

Her hand reached out to Nicholas, hovering by his shoulder. She didn't touch him.

"Please don't tell," she whispered in the dark.

He was already asleep, or pretending to be.

———

IN THE MORNING, NICHOLAS had only spoken to her to announce that a car was arriving in—he checked his phone—eight minutes to drive her back to Simon's. Alex made coffee in the machine in the empty staff apartment. Then she waited in one of the dew-covered Adirondack chairs by the pond, her ass getting damp as she watched algae drift toward the lily pads. Her phone was still dead— she'd been too out of it, last night, to bother to even keep it plugged in. Stupid.

The algae clumped on the water's surface, broke apart. Someone's job, surely, was to skim off the algae, no matter that the pond served no actual purpose. When the driver finally arrived, the black SUV idling in the driveway, Alex looked back at the front door. Maybe Nicholas would come out to say goodbye. Offer a last-minute absolution.

He did not.

The driver zoomed in on the map on his phone. "We're heading to Daniels Hole Road?"

She let herself imagine the driver taking her all the way to Simon's. Alex getting dropped off with her bag, Alex opening the gate and walking inside. Of course, she would not do it. Of course she wouldn't deviate from the plan. But even so, nice to feel that she could still enter Simon's life. At any moment. He wasn't so far away.

"You can just head that way. But I'll jump out before then."

"Do you have an address I can put in?"

What was her plan exactly? She'd know it when she saw

it. What the next move was. She made a loose gesture. "I'll just let you know when to stop."

"Whatever you want."

She plugged her phone into the backseat charger.

Three more days. That's all she had to get through.

Alex watched the roads pass through her sunglasses. Were these George's wife's sunglasses? Everything looked much more tolerable in their green tint. More like a video game or something. A world adjacent to the actual world. Out the window, a small plane was descending, disappearing. The car drove by the starkness of a golf course with a few pairs of golfers trundling along, a lone cart cresting the barest hill. Golf was one of the only things Simon deigned to watch on television: golf and tennis.

Alex had never watched with him. Had never even feigned interest. In retrospect, she could have been more accommodating. Been more vigilant. She had started to believe that it hadn't been an exchange.

ONLY TEN MINUTES OF driving before they hit the main road, nearing the center of town. Alex leaned forward.

"Sorry," she said. "Could you just drop me off here?"

"Here?" the driver was saying. "Just here?"

"Yes," she said, "it's fine, just this curb is good. Thanks."

6

THERE WASN'T MUCH TO the town: a few clothing stores, the fancy grocery store and the not-fancy one, a dinky movie theater. A church refashioned into a real estate office, the single intersection piling up with cars. The women she passed on the sidewalks looked like mothers and daughters. Most of them dressed alike: white cropped pants, expensive sandals, pearl earrings. Their skin was always good, even if they weren't attractive. They were dressed to invoke the wives they either already were or would one day become, future domestic totems.

At the round tables in front of a coffee shop, men in baseball caps and polo shirts sat with younger versions of themselves, all of them looking at their phones, their legs splayed in their shorts. No one was speaking but even so, they were united by some primitive affect, obviously family.

She considered a restaurant patio. The awning was cranked open, most of the tables unoccupied. It was still early, the lull before lunch really began. Without really knowing what the plan was, she smiled at an older man sitting alone at an outdoor table, a ruff of skin pooling at the base of his neck. He looked at Alex, then looked away. He didn't glance over again. Maybe even he thought she was too desperate.

ALEX WALKED DOWN ONE BLOCK, then crossed the street and went back up another block. She went down a side alley: nothing there except a few trash cans, leading to a parking lot that abutted the main road. There was the less fancy grocery store, and behind that was the green of a small scrubby park with a gazebo, a few benches in the shade of the poplars.

The grocery store was busy, with only one register open. The aisles were filled with locals, people she had not encountered elsewhere. These, she assumed, were the year-round residents, people who looked the ages that they were. Citizens of the real world.

Alex got protein bars, a plastic bag of nectarines. Saltines and a jar of peanut butter. A plastic tray of chicken tenders. A box of blister patches, makeup remover wipes. A tiny chub of travel deodorant. The smaller items she dropped in her bag, keeping her face calm as she did so. So much of getting away with things was the outward insistence of normalcy. The rest of the larger stuff she would actually purchase—another useful method, to buy at least a few items. Legitimize the endeavor.

Alex swiped her debit card at the checkout. Was it taking an extra long time to process? She had enough money, surely. Even so, it seemed possible the transaction might not go through. Like Dom might have somehow wormed his way into her account, drained it all.

The cashier had said something, something she'd missed, and he was staring at her, waiting for Alex to respond, his fingers poised over the machine. For a second, she assumed the card had been flagged, that she was in trouble. Or that the cashier had somehow been alerted that there were items in Alex's bag that she was not planning to pay for.

"Are you a rewards member?" the cashier said. "I just need the phone number."

"Oh, no. No phone number."

"If anyone in your family is a rewards member," he said, "you can just use their phone number."

When she shook her head, the man smiled at her, conspiratorial. "Tell you what. You can use mine," he said, scanning a laminated card. "And we just won't tell, will we?"

His warmth took her aback—maybe he thought they knew each other. But she was a stranger, and Alex had the urge to make sure he understood this, to make clear that she didn't deserve his kindness.

ALEX FOUND THE BENCH in the small park with the most shade. The chicken tenders were warm and salty. The aftertaste was unpleasant. She considered making herself throw up, perform a swift and nasty maneuver in the nearest trash can. She couldn't muster the energy. The nectarines were unripe. A waste.

So many more hours to get through.

Alex gathered her things and exited the park. She passed a cemetery, crowded with headstones and plinths, knocked into one another like bad teeth. The sight made her jittery, the abrupt presence of death surrounded by a white picket fence, a child's idea of a fence. The sun had gone behind the clouds. Overhead, a small plane was pulling an advertising banner. The plane turned around, chugging in the direction it had come, so now the banner was snapping along backwards, the message indecipherable. Whatever it was that they were trying to sell.

"On your left," someone called out, a bell dinging, so Alex had to back onto the grass. A man and a woman— probably not so much older than Alex—pedaled past on mint-colored beach cruisers, beach towels rolled in the wicker baskets. What sort of day lay ahead of them? Some easy waste of the afternoon. What possible worries would they have?

Alex must have appeared this way to others, those afternoons she burned through at the beach. Eating a bag of cherries that Lori had packed with ice. Combing her wet hair with her fingers, taking one last swim before eventually making her way back to Simon's. She missed that version of herself.

Alex knew she should stay in town, should figure out a place to fix her phone. Text that boy from the beach. Jack.

Instead she found herself heading in the direction the couple had bicycled, found herself watching the pair of them pedal along, watching them coast before they passed out of sight.

A few more blocks with her bag bouncing against her side, her sandal strap tindering a new blister, and she regretted not parking herself in town. But then the houses got more hidden, and that meant she was close.

THE PUBLIC BEACH WAS BUSY, even on a cloudy day. Everyone's faces were made similar by sunglasses, a kind of Easter Island stare. The big hats and button-downs. Only the children moved at any pace other than unhurried languor.

The parking lot was full, a line of cars edging slowly forward, waiting for a space to open up. People waiting for their turn at fun. Alex cut across a car's path. The driver must not have noticed her—the car lurched ahead and almost hit her. She glared at the windshield—it was tinted, no place for her anger to land.

Alex had the sick sense that she was a ghost. Wandering the land of the living. But that was dumb, a dumb thought. It was just when the day was hot like this, hot and gray, anxiety moved closer to the surface.

She was wearing her swimsuit bottoms under her clothes and changed into her top in the bathroom stall. When she emerged, there was a mother at the sink struggling to pull a soaking wet swim diaper down a baby's chubby legs. The mother grimaced at Alex.

"Sorry," the woman said, and scooted away from the sink.

"No worries." Alex smiled at the woman. Smiled at the baby.

She was trying to be good, she realized. As if it would

matter whether or not she smiled at a harried mother. Like it would somehow help things along with Simon, a cosmic reparation. Would Nicholas say something to George? Or Simon? But how would Nicholas explain allowing Alex to stay, letting Alex loose in his employer's house: maybe he wouldn't say anything.

Alex needed to sit in one place and try to think of what to do. She found a patch of unclaimed sand and lay with her head resting against her bag. She still had the book from George's house and held it overhead to block the glare.

She read the same paragraph three times. She slapped at a gnat on her stomach, turned the page. The daughter had just tried to commit suicide the night before her mother's second marriage. The daughter had gotten too much love, was the gist of the memoir, so much love that it had crippled her and now she had to correct it by getting even more. It made Alex uncomfortable, someone demanding love so overtly, showing all her cards. As if it were that easy, as if love were something you deserved and didn't have to scramble to earn.

Useful, anyway, to have something to read, some obvious, visible task that legitimized her, meant her presence somewhere wasn't so strange. She abandoned the book when her phone turned on, for a brief moment, then sparked to life long enough that she caught a glimpse of the home screen before it shut off. Better than nothing. She had assumed there might be an outlet by the bathroom. There wasn't.

A place to plug in her phone: that was a task, an aim,

eminently reasonable, and it was okay, she decided, to not think beyond that, not yet.

TO THE LEFT OF the main beach, more beach, more crowds. To the right, an open expanse. Alex went right. A ways down, there was a brick building with a brick terrace edging onto the sand and bright blue umbrellas set up in tidy lines. As she got closer, she saw a private lifeguard, dressed differently from the public one, who surveyed a square of ocean marked off with buoys. Odd to see brick at the beach, this squat brick building with its wide terrace. It didn't look right, too cultivated and old-fashioned for this landscape.

This must be the club. A place she had never been, only heard about. The beach club was for the worst people, Simon said, a place where all their noxious allegiances to race and class could be laundered by nostalgia. They turned away most applicants. It occurred to her, remembering Simon's disdain, that probably he had applied and been rejected.

Alex hung off to the side. After a while, she could tell which people walking past would veer up the steps and into the club and which people would not.

The club looked sparse, almost military, but no matter. It didn't make a difference what was behind a rope, really, it just mattered that there *was* a rope. The people on the terrace needed the people walking past, just as the people walking past needed the people on the terrace.

The only drama came when an outsider stopped to rest

in the shade of an umbrella and sat down on one of the beach chairs. The woman glanced around, face open as a dinner plate, trying to understand where exactly she had found herself. Not a minute passed before a man in a polo shirt came over and bent down to say something to the woman—Alex watched this happen, watched the error being corrected. Like the couple at Helen's party, ejected from the sphere where they didn't belong, only this woman was apologetic, eager to participate in her own removal. The man, Alex figured, was some more subtle version of a bouncer, sifting through the social information on offer and deciding who was an interloper and who was not.

The crowd on the terrace sat around tables with drinks in their fists, cast in shadow from the blue umbrellas. Lots of older men, skin burnt to the same rust color as their overly baggy swim trunks. The women in collared blouses, untucked, with neat chino shorts. The social groups were separated by gender. Except for the polarized sunglasses, it could have been a scene from sixty years ago, the men gathered in primal council, nursing their brown alcohol, the women and children at separate tables, eating chicken tenders with saltwater hands.

Alex could just go up to one of the men. Approach a table with only a few men hunched over their watery cocktails, a manageable audience. Easy enough. You waved your fingers, you spoke in a voice just a tick too quiet—they got flustered, trying to follow what was happening. Any glitch in the usual order of things, the expected social script, made people anxious, off balance. Even a glancing touch at their elbow, the barest squeeze of an arm, could short-circuit any wariness. Suddenly they were newly suggestible, eager to find steady footing in whatever story you offered.

And men did not, it turned out, mind being approached by a young woman—not usually, anyway. They did not immediately assume that her motives might be murky, their vanity allowing for the possibility that she had been drawn over by the sheer force of their personhood. But not really sensible to try that here. The air was too domestic, dripping with the proximity of family and other blunt moral concepts. It had a chilling effect: the wives nearby, the children.

Alex just needed to be seen with anyone who had already been approved, and that would be indication enough that she belonged.

The nannies might be the right move: women in rash guards and cheap sunglasses, kneeling in the sand with toy shovels to help children dig holes. Their bodies were practical, bodies that didn't bear the evidence of an excess of time and money. The children wore classic boater stripes and salmon-colored trunks. The nannies wore blindingly bright shirts from some restaurant in St. Martin or Mustique, carried plastic sacks from Citarella that held bags of soggy baby carrots they'd mete out to their charges.

The children were in their own realm, tripping along the shoreline, only circling back to the nannies to submit to another application of sunscreen. Children were too much like Alex. Tolerated but not needed, not powerful.

A YOUNG GIRL WAS toting sand in a bucket, her face grim, occupied with her task. She walked by close enough for

Alex to touch: Alex reached out for a brief graze of the girl's shoulder.

Before Alex could say anything, the girl's eyes widened in alarm. She hurried back to a towel where a woman was lying. A mother, Alex saw, not a nanny, and that wouldn't work. Alex waited for the girl to say something to her mother, to point out Alex, but the girl just dumped the contents of her bucket and busied herself patting the sand smooth.

Another kid broke away from a group, a group obviously under the purview of a nanny: a woman in long pants and a wide cloth hat, shaking sand off a flotilla of towels. The boy flung himself into the shallow waves. Then ran in dizzy circles on the sand before passing out dramatically on his back. How old was he, six? Hard to gauge children's ages.

He seemed to sense Alex was watching him. The boy sat up and glanced in her direction. She smiled and gestured for him to come over. She waved again, more urgently, and he crab-walked most of the way toward her before getting to his feet. When he arrived, he didn't speak. Just panted, his bare chest heaving.

"Hi," Alex said, "hi. Are you having fun?"

She smiled, gently, as if they were sharing a joke.

"I don't know you," he said.

"Sure you do. I'm Alex."

He squinted. Looked over his shoulder.

Alex followed his glance—back to the nanny in the hat, two little girls shrieking and plucking at her pants, and Alex waved at the nanny, so the boy could see her doing it, even though the nanny didn't.

"So guess what," Alex said.

The boy crossed his arms.

"You want to do something fun?" she said.

He appeared willing to let her try to impress him.

"Should we go up there and get something? I bet there's dessert up there, huh?"

"Sugar doesn't grow your bones."

"Nope," Alex said. "It doesn't."

The boy was visibly bored.

"Well, okay. I'm Alex. Where are your parents?"

He pointed generally in a far-off direction.

"Home?" Alex said.

He nodded. So that was good.

"I bet there's a pool up there?"

Another nod.

"Okay," she said, "you can show me the pool."

The nanny was actually looking over at them, now, from down the beach, and Alex watched her eyes alight on the boy and then on Alex, and Alex waved again, more confidently, mouthing nonsense, but appearing, she hoped, that she was conveying some message. She pointed to the boy, and then to the club. Ruffled the boy's hair—he softened automatically, and somehow the gesture, as she was doing it, felt genuine.

The nanny was coming over. Not ideal but okay. Okay.

"You're in trouble," the nanny said. But she was talking to the boy. "No more swimming without sunscreen," the nanny said. "Come here."

The boy tilted his face up, eyes closed. The nanny applied a layer of sunscreen from a tube, wiping the excess between her palms. She was brisk but calm, the exchange lacking any drama.

"You having fun, Calvin? You being good?" The nanny turned to Alex. "I'm sorry," she said, "I should have been watching him."

Did she think Alex thought she had somehow shirked her duties? Alex smiled hard.

"Oh, not at all, we're fine."

"Want to come play?" the nanny said to the boy. "Let your friend relax?"

The boy shrugged. "We're going to the pool."

The nanny looked to Alex again.

"If that's okay with you," Alex said. "Obviously. I'm Alex, I'm a friend of the family."

The nanny considered the boy.

"I haven't seen Calvin in a while," Alex went on. She smiled. "He's gotten so big. Haven't you?"

Alex held her hand out to the boy. She waited: this could go either way. But the boy grabbed her hand. A squeeze. Once, twice.

This seemed to soothe the nanny, though she still hesitated. Alex kept smiling. The nanny glanced back at her other charges, whose play fighting looked on the brink of turning into an actual fight, one kid letting out a piercing screech that made her wince. She turned to Alex. "All right," she said, after a second. "I'll be up in a bit. You behave yourself, Calvin."

"We will," Alex answered for both of them, a pleasant singsong.

———

THEY WALKED PAST THE man guarding the perimeter, Alex not even glancing in his direction, and up they went, up the wide steps and under the many umbrellas and onto the open terrace of the club. She had not even needed the boy.

He gazed off into the distance. "I can have ice cream, I'm allowed."

Alex had planned on cutting the boy loose, but he seemed pliant, happy enough, interested in what might happen next. It allowed for a different quality of day to present itself. At least she could get him ice cream.

A MAN HOVERED IN the open window of the snack bar, heat emanating in visible waves from the grill behind him. He was sweating, a fly circling near his forehead. Even the fly was moving slowly.

"Ice cream," the boy announced. "Vanilla."

"Good choice," Alex said. "Vanilla ice cream."

The man nodded. He was uninterested in the specifics of Alex and the boy, though his expression was arranged in a smile.

Behind Alex was the pool, smaller than she'd imagined, lane dividers floating on its surface. A woman in a navy one-piece waded back and forth with a small boy, her thin hair pushed into a baseball hat. A teenager sat with his feet in the water, a hamburger half-eaten on a plate. He didn't look up when a girl in uniform, probably his age, bent to pick it up and place it on her tray.

"How much?" Alex said, starting to open her bag.

"We don't take cash," the man said, like this was obvious. "Number?"

"Sorry? I'm visiting," she said, "I don't know the rules."

"The last name?" he said. "For the chit."

She looked at the boy, lost in his ice cream, a significant amount already down his chin.

"Last name, Calvin?" Alex nudged him.

"Spencer," the boy finally said.

"Spencer." Alex smiled sweetly.

The man did not care. He flipped through papers on a clipboard. He made a note. "Okay. One ice cream. Number 223."

"Do I need to sign anything?"

"Nope."

"Actually," Alex said, "I'll have an ice cream, too. And a cheeseburger. And a beer."

THE MAN HAD POINTED out the dining room where Alex could find a power outlet. The room was mostly empty at this hour, the buffet closed. Lunch was over, the tables waiting for cleanup: soiled plates on trays, stained napkins in polyester weave. Her cheeseburger was fine. The ice cream wasn't good. It tasted like the waxy container it had been scooped from. Still, Alex finished hers while the boy swirled his tongue around his own ice cream with unbroken focus.

Alex took a swig of beer from the plastic cup. Only the occasional staff passed in and out of the dining room. Women in their fifties with sun spots, a white-haired man in belted khakis, a teenager with a lush beard of acne.

She turned her phone on. There might be a brief stretch of usefulness, enough that she could read her text messages. Maybe Simon had texted. But she knew Simon—he wouldn't make the first move. It was on Alex to shift things forward.

If there was more from Dom—and of course there would be more—she'd just keep ignoring him. She'd deal with Dom after she fixed things with Simon. At the party. The party that was still days away. If she considered how many days, the panic started to rise up. Better to just try and figure out what this afternoon would look like. What Alex would do tonight. Keep the sphere limited.

The boy was still working on his ice cream. When he saw Alex watching him, he paused.

"Are you a good grown-up?" he said. Was she? He didn't seem too concerned either way.

"I'm not even a grown-up." She put her phone down. "How's the ice cream?"

He shrugged. Some had melted down his hand and dried so his skin looked strange and artificial.

"I have to pee," he announced.

A ding from her phone. Alex had new texts, she could tell, but they weren't loading fast enough to read before the phone shut itself off.

"You go to the bathroom," she said, "and I'll be right here."

Though, it occurred to her, this was a good place for them to part ways. The boy could head back to his nanny. She could apply herself to the phone problem. To the wasting-of-another-day problem.

"Come with me?" The boy was rubbing his crotch with one hand, the other hand holding aloft the last of the ice cream. "Please?"

THE WOMEN'S BATHROOM WAS well stocked: a bottle of mouthwash on the counter, tampons, a jar of Q-tips. Alex knocked back a paper cup of mouthwash and spit into the sink. Her tongue buzzed with menthol. The stalls were empty but someone had left a tote bag under the sink. Alex toed open the bag. She glimpsed a striped sweatshirt, three tubes of the same colorless chapstick.

The boy was already finished. He paused expectantly by the sink. "Shouldn't I wash my hands?"

"Sure." Alex was nudging the tote bag. Trying to sense whether there was a wallet inside. Something heavy, any-way. She squatted to feel around the bottom of the bag. A money clip: an ID, a credit card, a Christmas-themed gift card to Saks, a selection of folded fifties and twenties that looked almost ironed. A chunky silver barrette.

The credit card would be good, Alex thought, as long as she didn't need a PIN or a zip code, but how long before the owner noticed the charges? Alex wanted to take the whole money clip, but restraint was a good thing. Always. Hadn't the other girls taught her that? To never take enough

that you couldn't call the guy again, never fleece him so
badly that he cut off the relationship entirely. People, it
turned out, were mostly fine with being victimized in small
doses. In fact, they seemed to expect a certain amount of
deception, allowed for a tolerable margin of manipulation
in their relationships.

"I wanna swim," the boy said. "I could race you."

She had already taken two fifties and the silver barrette,
dropped them in her own pocket, but before she could decide whether or not to grab the credit card, the door started
to open. Alex straightened. Kicked the bag back where
she'd found it. By the time the woman entered, Alex was
washing her hands in the sink, drying them with a paper
towel with assiduous care.

The woman: blond, blue-eyed, her teeth white but not
exactly straight. A rugby shirt worn with blousy cotton ca-
pris.

Her eyes went directly to the tote bag. "Thank god."

As she bent to pick it up, Alex hustled the boy along.
But there was no need to rush—it didn't even seem to occur
to the woman to check that the contents of her bag were
intact. The bubble of safety was utterly assumed. The
woman smiled at Alex in the mirror. Alex smiled back.

Alex had not taken the credit card, had not taken the
money clip, and who would notice the fifties were gone, or
the measly silver barrette, amongst all that abundance? The
universe had protected Alex. Or the boy had, somehow.
There was no reason to feel anxious—the fear had been
transmuted, the way it often was, into excitement, the

memory always dissolving until it was only the idea of fear, and when had the idea of fear ever been a convincing deterrent?

THE WATER WAS BRACING, chlorinated: no saltwater pool here. Alex dunked her head and came up dripping. She wiped her nose, wiped her mouth. The boy held on to the side and kicked his feet in a frenzy.

"Watch me," he said. "Are you watching me?"

Another beer, ordered from the bartender, arrived in a plastic cup. Alex leaned on her elbows on the rim of the pool. By the deep end, a pair of fratty bros scanned the crowd with lizard eyes.

The sun came out from behind the clouds. It was not a bad day, here in the water, the funny weight of the boy clinging to her neck as she propelled him from one side of the pool to the other.

"I'm the baby," Calvin said. "You're the mom. You're taking me away."

"A trip. Sounds nice," she said. "Where are we going?"

"You know. I don't know. You're the mom."

"Should we go underwater?"

The boy looked equally afraid and excited.

"If you hold on tight, I can swim you under, okay? And then we'll come right back up."

He held his breath, a hand plugging his nose. The drag of his body weight was nice, the boy's hair waving in the water, bubbles trailing from his lips. Fun, she thought, they were having fun, but his arms tightened around her. She swam up to the surface. The boy swallowed a gulp of air.

"Were you scared?" she said. "I had you, you were okay."

He smiled but he was blinking too rapidly.

"Okay," Alex announced. "Time for a break." She lifted the boy up onto the side of the pool. "There," she said, and squeezed a wet knee. "You sit up here and you can see everything. You're the lookout."

He took to this task eagerly, then quickly got bored— what danger was there to look out for? Soon, the boy was back in the pool, forgetting to be afraid. Too busy splashing around to notice when his nanny stopped by to check on him. Alex did, though, waving at the woman, trying to answer the question in the woman's face with a reassuring smile. All was well, was the gist Alex was trying to convey, and the woman relaxed and continued back toward the beach, pulled along by her other charges.

ALEX TWISTED WATER FROM her hair. Drained the plastic cup, legs stirring idly in the pool as she tracked the boy's happy paddling. Her phone was charging out of sight. Her bag was safe, nothing to worry about in this exact moment. When her phone started working, she would text Jack, the boy from the beach. That made the most sense. But waiting until it got later was better, especially if she was angling for a place to sleep. Burn as many hours as possible here.

Another beer, she thought, why not, the day sponsored

by the kindness of 223, the Spencer family subsidizing this pleasant buzz, the tribal wholesomeness of this place its own comfort.

The boy grabbed at a pool noodle that floated past.

"That's mine," another little boy called out, and splashed toward them in water wings and goggles, the girl in the navy one-piece trailing behind. His mother, Alex had assumed, but then Alex saw her face—she was Alex's age, but her expression was sober and pinched.

"You can share," the girl said.

Alex nudged Calvin. "Give him back his noodle."

Calvin only narrowed his eyes.

The other boy splashed angrily. "It's mine."

Alex gentled the toy from Calvin back to the other boy.

"Sorry," Alex said.

"It's fine," the girl said, "he's supposed to share. Luca, be nice."

The boys regarded each other warily.

"They're friends from school," the girl said. "Luca," she said, nodding at the other boy. "My brother."

"Hi, Luca," Alex said. Luca was inscrutable behind his goggles.

"Luca has to wear wings 'cause he's still little," Calvin said. "But I could go in the deep end," he said, "I touched the bottom."

"Maybe you can share your noodle with Calvin?" the girl said.

This suggestion appeared to displease Luca.

"Sorry," the girl said. "I'm Margaret."

"Caroline," Alex said. Reflexively. Simon's daughter's

name—she was surprised she remembered it, surprised she had bothered to lie.

"Where's Rose?" Margaret said.

Not the boy's mother—the nanny, Alex decided quickly, the name sounding like an American replacement for a foreign one.

"Oh, on the beach," Alex said, smiling. "I'm just visiting."

"Cool," Margaret said. "I know the Spencers. I used to babysit Calvin, actually. Didn't I?"

"Sugar eats your bones," Calvin said, cheerily.

THE BOYS PLAYED TOGETHER in the shallow end. Margaret sat on the pool's edge and tapped at her phone. Alex considered asking to borrow it—Alex could check her voicemails, check her email—but the girl was wound so tight.

Margaret had tucked her hair behind her ears and it made her look poky and exposed. Alex had to restrain herself from reaching out to untuck her hair. "I like your swimsuit," Alex said.

"Thanks," Margaret said, and squirmed. She glanced at Alex's beer.

"You want one?" Alex said.

"Oh, no," Margaret said. "I'm fine."

"I'll get you one. My treat."

Easy to feel magnanimous, another round on 223.

"Back for more?" The man winked as he filled another plastic cup, but it was like vaudeville, a hollow flirtation that lacked any real feeling. Alex had worked enough restaurant jobs to be familiar with this flavor of exchange.

"Hot out there," he said. "The clouds should burn off before too long." How many times had he already said that today? He handed over the cup.

"Two twenty-three," he said, before she could speak.

"Right." She went to leave a tip—but it was impossible. Unseemly, maybe, to acknowledge that being served wasn't just the natural order of things.

Alex walked back to the pool. "Cheers," she said, handing Margaret the beer.

"Thanks," Margaret said. They watched the kids splash. "How do you know the Spencers?"

"My parents are friends."

"Mm," Margaret said. A faint rash had appeared on the girl's collarbone, her pale skin flushing. She floated her fingers over the rash, fluttering her fingernails but straining, Alex saw, not to make actual contact.

"Where's your place?" Margaret said.

"I mostly stay with the Spencers," Alex said, and pretended to be absorbed in finishing the last of her drink. She made a gesture—she had no idea in what direction.

Both kids were lying on their backs on the sun-warmed tiles, chatting to each other with adult affect. Alex's sunglasses, or George's wife's sunglasses, gave the scene a nice, benevolent cohesion. The frat bros were in the pool, now, fussing so you couldn't ignore them, one boy flailing on another's shoulders. Even this didn't bother her. It was nice: the buzz of guests, the heat. Margaret's shyness was endearing, in its way, how Margaret blinked as she waited for

Alex to steer the conversation. Margaret was saying something about college, the internship she was starting in a week, and Alex nodded along, but thinking about the future meant thinking about the whole days that would have to pass before Simon's party.

"I'm going to the bathroom," Alex said. "Can you watch Calvin?"

A QUICK DETOUR TO her bag for a painkiller—like a reward, a cherry on top of the pleasant afternoon. Alex didn't let herself think about how few pills there were left. On the way back, she ran into the bartender coming out of a side door.

"Hey, 223," he said, pointing at her. "You need a refill?"

She considered him more closely. He was around forty, his ears sunburned, his eyes crinkling in a friendly way— a lifer, she guessed, a career bartender. What did he do in the off-season?

"Maybe," Alex said. "But aren't you on break?"

He checked his watch.

"For eleven more minutes."

"Very exciting."

He laughed. "Oh yes."

Always interesting, this moment of possibility. She smiled at him without looking away—that was often all it took.

"You smoke?" He produced a black vape pen he twiddled between his fingers.

"I'll have a little," Alex said.

Alex followed him through a set of double doors. They pushed open into a back alley. Dumpsters, stacks of cardboard neatly tied with twine. The smell of fresh garbage that lingered, uncut by ocean air.

He glanced around. "Let's actually go to my car. If you don't mind."

THE CAR WAS A small hatchback with old fuzzy upholstery, a tape deck that drooled out a USB adapter. An inside-out wetsuit was folded thickly in the backseat.

"Sorry," the man said, sweeping the passenger seat clean. He made swift work of a passel of empty water bottles, tossing them in the back.

A prism on the rearview twitched and twisted on a piece of fishing wire.

He passed her the pen. When she inhaled, the end lit up green.

"Thanks."

"No problem," he said, taking another hit. He offered it to her again before tucking it away in his shirt pocket.

"You live here?" Alex said.

"Not here. Like, forty minutes west. Thirty minutes without traffic."

"Yeah," she said. "I'm not from here either."

Neither of them would say more about where they came from: that seemed correct.

"So you're a guest of the Spencers," he said, filling the silence. "Nice people."

"I don't actually know them," Alex said. She hadn't planned to say this.

He gave Alex a curious look. "You don't, huh?"

Was he attractive? Attractive enough. She shifted her weight. She licked her lips. None of this was lost on him. He took her in with a bemused air. Like someone watching a movie they'd already seen.

Alex started to move closer to him, leaning across the bulk of the center console. What was she doing? She hadn't wanted to kiss him, which she only realized when he tried to kiss her: she buried her face in his neck to avoid this. The finger he had pushed inside her felt good, startling and good, her swimsuit pulled to the side.

"You're all wet," he said. She moved against his hand. His mouth didn't smell bad but it was too near and emanating something, some overwhelming human element. There was a bubbly mole on his left collarbone, his eyes rheumy. Up close, she saw that he was older than she'd thought. Simon's age.

What if you spent decades like this? Serving these people? Too distressing to consider.

Alex stopped. The moment, whatever it was, was over. Alex pulled his hand away, gently. She readjusted her swimsuit.

She should get back to the boy. And anyway, she knew how this would go. And the man seemed to know, too. So it almost didn't matter whether it happened or not.

"You okay?" he said.

Alex shrugged. When she crossed her legs, her knees hit the dash and the glove compartment knocked open.

"Fuck," he said peaceably. He reached over to shut it, hard. "This car's falling apart."

"It's a nice car."

He laughed. "It's not. It's most definitely not." He tilted his head. "Wait. Are you feeling sorry for me?"

"No. Why would I feel sorry for you?"

"Your face right now." He smiled. It wasn't exactly a kind smile. "I like my life, you know."

"I didn't say you didn't like your life." But probably she had thought it, some fleeting expression of pity.

"I guess your friends are waiting for you," he said. He was nice enough to offer her an excuse.

She must have made a face.

"They're not your friends?" he said.

"I don't," she said, "know any of these people."

He seemed to think this was funny, laughing as he coughed.

"Yeah," he said. "I don't fucking know any of these people either."

MARGARET AND HER BROTHER were right where Alex had left them, but the boy was nowhere in sight.

Alex's first thought was doom, the boy at the bottom of the pool. Her chest seized up. A frantic scan of the water, the crisis already fated. Of course it would end badly, of course there would be a punishment.

But only a few seconds passed before Alex caught sight

of the boy, her eyes locking on Calvin. The relief made her feel almost insane. There he was, the boy was fine.

Calvin was being shuffled along by his nanny. He squirmed in the nanny's grasp, trying to wrench away, but the nanny corralled her charge steadily forward.

It had worked out fine, hadn't it? Nothing bad had happened to the boy. He had been repossessed by his proper caregiver, returned to his proper place, and what had Alex done that was so wrong? Fed him ice cream, dove to the bottom of the pool with his arms tight around her neck, the afternoon a small hiccup in the days of seamless pleasure that awaited him.

ALEX GATHERED HER PHONE and charger from the still-empty dining room. Her heartbeat was a little erratic, as if the worst had actually happened. The bartender was rolling down a metal grate over the grill's window. From this angle, in the harsh sunlight, she didn't find him handsome at all.

She wanted to leave. But where, exactly, would she go?

Through the window, she saw Margaret walking past, her outline swimmy through the weather-eaten glass.

7

AS SOON AS THEY pulled into the driveway of Margaret's house, a woman, dressed in a very clean T-shirt, khakis, and white Keds, hurried out to meet them. She tried to take Alex's bag from her hands.

"Oh," Alex said, "I'm good, thank you."

"Karen," Margaret said, with a touch of irritation. "We're fine."

Karen was, Alex assumed, the helper, or the house manager, or whatever they called her as long as it wasn't maid.

"Luca's with Mrs. E?" Karen said, and Margaret nodded, was saying something about not feeling well, leaving early.

"Your sister's in the movie room," Karen said.

They followed the woman to the side entrance of the low clapboard house, black shutters framing each window and a pool dropped neatly into the grass.

"We have the same donor," Margaret said, breezily, "so she's my actual sister. They're twins, her and Luca."

The little girl was watching *Finding Nemo* in a wood-paneled room, all the shades drawn. She was in a swimsuit with her hands folded solemnly on her chest.

"Say hi to your sister," Karen said, lingering in the doorway.

The girl didn't respond. In front of her, on a tray, was a bowl of macaroni and cheese and a plate of avocado slices, quickly browning.

For a moment, Margaret and Karen stood there, eyes on the screen. Alex was watching the girl on the couch—she was picking her nose in a daze. The girl withdrew her finger, scrutinizing her findings, then, after a quick glance at Karen, wiped it along the back of the couch, out of sight.

MARGARET'S BEDROOM WAS CARPETED in lilac, the curtains lilac, too, matching the upholstered bed frame. The bedside lamps were two sizes too big, but that looked to be the prevailing taste in lamps in this house: giant lamps, on every flat surface, alongside notepads and boxes of golf pencils, tissues in rattan tissue-box covers.

"This is your room?" Alex said.

She tried to picture Margaret as a young person. Though probably Margaret was one of those kids who had never seemed young. There was a die-cut shape of a butterfly on the wall and a few books on a shelf: a series of reproductions of first editions, still in plastic.

Alex turned over a copy of *To Kill a Mockingbird*.

"It's like a subscription," Margaret said. "A Christmas gift."

Alex sat on the bed, her phone charging on the nightstand, and Margaret sat at the desk, the desk's surface covered by makeup organized in Lucite cases. A tentative knock on the door frame: Karen stuck her head in, the sister huddled by her legs.

"Girls? Do you want to come with?" Karen said. "We're going to the tennis club."

A silver cross necklace was visible around Karen's throat.

"Nah." Margaret barely acknowledged Karen.

"It's the tournament," Karen said. Her hands rested on the little girl's shoulders. Sunscreen outlined the girl's nostrils. The girl had the same downcast features as Margaret, as Luca—the mention of tennis made her scowl.

"We're gonna win, hm?" Karen squeezed the girl's shoulders.

"Have you seen my blue shirt?" Margaret said, finally looking up. "With the buttons?"

"It's hanging in the laundry room," Karen said. "I can iron it tonight."

Margaret rolled her eyes.

"It wasn't even dirty," Margaret said, under her breath.

Karen kept smiling, as if she hadn't heard.

"We're headed out," Karen said. "Wish your sister good luck."

"Bye." Margaret was scanning her phone.

"Good luck," Alex said to the girl. The girl didn't react. And why should she? Alex was a stranger.

———

"so," MARGARET SAID, AFTER they heard the sound of the car on the gravel outside. "What do you want to do now?"

A beat, a space opening up for Alex to consider her outstanding debts. Keep it going, keep the day blurry. She shrugged.

"I don't know," Alex said. "Do you wanna drink a little wine?"

MARGARET OPENED THE FRIDGE. It was stocked with half-size cans of Coke, Jiffy peanut butter and bottles of white wine. Alex wandered into the pantry. There were unopened plastic containers of candy, some gift basket remnant. One of them: a see-through cube of sugar roses. Like lemon drops, only pink, petaled, pale with sugar. She dumped one into her palm, then took the candy in her mouth, sucked, moved it from cheek to cheek. Why were they so appealing? They were so dainty and girlish, but kind of grotesque, too, like little malignant growths.

Alex rattled the box. "Can I take these upstairs?"

"Yeah," Margaret said, two stemless glasses in her hand, an already-open bottle of white wine sloshing in the crook of her arm.

As they made their way to the staircase, they passed a small room with a twin bed, a single dresser.

"What's in there?"

"Karen's room," Margaret said.

The only visible possessions were a hairbrush and a toiletry bag lined up neatly on the dresser.

"Come on," Margaret said, "it's boring in there."

THE WINE HAD A sailing ship on the label. Margaret poured each glass almost full. It was so cold that it tasted like nothing.

"So," Alex said. "What's the deal with Karen?"

"Karen? I dunno. She's, like, our babysitter," Margaret said. "For, like, forever."

"And she lives with you guys?" Alex said.

"Yeah. My mom, like, helped her get a green card and stuff."

Margaret already sounded defensive. Best to drop it. Alex drank more wine.

"Sorry," Margaret said, "you think I'm, like, a total brat. 'Cause of the shirt. I know, it sounded really bratty, but I, like, told her, unless it's in the hamper, please don't wash it. And sometimes she, like, shrinks things, like my favorite things."

Alex shrugged.

"We love Karen," Margaret said, diplomatically. And, after she seemed drunker, she repeated herself. "We really do love Karen."

"Of course," Alex said. Of course we love Karen, she said in her head, but did not say out loud.

IT TOOK TURNING ON Alex's phone three more times before it stayed on long enough to write the boy's number down on a piece of paper. Jack's number. Nothing from Simon, of course, and nothing from Dom either, which was more surprising.

"Can I borrow your phone?" Alex said. "Just to text this guy," she said, "mine keeps dying."

The background of Margaret's phone was a tropical scene, palm trees bent against the sherbet sunset.

Alex composed a text.

> *Hey it's Alex from the beach. Phone dead srry, using my friends.*
> *What you up to today?*

"Is he cute?" Margaret said from the bed. She'd put on a lilac sweater. "The boy?"

Sometimes Margaret sounded like she was reading from a script, her lines ringing hollow.

"Yeah," Alex said. "Pretty cute."

"Tell me about him."

"I met him on the beach," Alex said. "I don't know. He's blond."

"Blond!" Margaret almost clapped her hands. "Cute! I love it."

Margaret's phone dinged. A text from Jack.

> Not much u wanna hang tonight?

Margaret was watching her, her head tilted. Margaret's expression, now fuzzed out with wine, made Alex suddenly uneasy. Margaret reminded her of the girls from that first restaurant job—something skittish and unsettled in her face, an obvious discomfort that painfully called up adolescence.

Alex typed a response.

Yeah or maybe earlier?

It would be better if Alex had something to do with her hands. Anything so she and Margaret weren't just sitting here.

"Let me do your eye makeup," Alex said.

"Now?" Margaret blushed.

"Yeah, why not?"

All the makeup on Margaret's vanity was expensive. It looked untouched.

"Here, sit here." Alex moved the chair near the window, into the light.

Both of their breaths smelled of wine, though Alex was sucking on one of the rose-flavored candies. Margaret tried one, too, audibly rolling the candy against her teeth.

"Yuck." Margaret spit it into her hand. She opened her fingers over the trash can, letting the candy drop in, then wiped her palm on her dress. "It tastes like perfume."

"Let's do neutrals, okay?" Alex said. "Like, grays, and this is a nice color, right, this sort of pewter one? Close your eyes."

Under the thin skin of Margaret's closed lids, Alex saw the tiny snakes of blue veins, the faint animal twitch of the girl's eyeballs.

First Alex put foundation on Margaret's eyelids. Then a pat of a shimmery pale color. The trick was to put it under the bottom lash, too, so it emphasized the whole eye. How many videos had Alex watched online, learning how to do this, how many hours had she spent studying the other girls: those girls who had lived with her in that bad apartment, girls who made pancakes late at night and cried for faraway mothers, girls who paused doing their makeup to take a delicate inhale off a joint waiting in the ashtray. They sat by the windows to get better phone service. They wore hoodies over tight dresses and didn't own suitcases. Alex was aware that some of the girls hanging around were very young. But she was also young. It was a matter of a few years sometimes. No way to be exactly sure. Alex didn't ask questions; she made enough coffee for them, she kept her door closed. When she heard one of them weeping on the phone, Alex did the girl a kindness, or so she saw it at the time—she left her alone.

Alex used a different brush to push an asphalt color along Margaret's lash line.

Margaret looked especially vulnerable like this. Her eyes closed, her face tipped upward. As if she would let Alex do whatever she wanted to her.

A framed photo stared out at Alex from the desk: Margaret and the twins and their mother perched on a piece of driftwood. They were all barefoot, a whiff of corporate cheer in their smiles.

"What about you?" Alex said. "Do you have a boyfriend?"

"No," Margaret said. "I've had them before, but, like, not this very second."

Alex found the biggest brush and fluffed it against her palm.

"Can you make, like, a kissy face?"

Margaret was eager to follow any instruction: she pursed her lips, her cheeks hollowing. Even though Alex had finished her eye makeup, Margaret kept her eyes closed.

Margaret was not, Alex could see, a happy girl.

"Perfect," Alex said, and worked the bronzer along the cheekbones, into Margaret's hairline.

"Can I see," Margaret said, her eyes flitting open.

"I just started," Alex said.

"Just let me look, for a second," Margaret said. "I wanna see."

Ignoring the mirror on the vanity, Margaret looked at herself through her phone camera. Her face wobbled on the screen.

"Cool," Margaret said, turning from side to side. "It's good. Wait, watch."

Margaret pressed a button and all at once her skin looked better, as if lit from within, an unnatural glow emanating from the whites of her eyes, now suddenly so white.

"Get in with me," Margaret said, "take a picture."

Alex hesitated.

"Come on," Margaret said.

"I hate photos," Alex said.

"Seriously, you have to. Just one."

Alex didn't want to feel sorry for Margaret or make an accounting of the need in her face. Alex bent down and pressed her cheek to Margaret's. On the screen, they both looked eerie, strange, their faces smeared into softness and their eyes extra bright. Alex considered the unfamiliar version of herself. It was weirdly compelling, this new avatar.

She looked reset, as if the last stretch of her life had not happened, as if you could erase things and start over just like that. Had she ever actually looked that clean and fresh and blameless?

But when the filter clicked off, it was worse. There was her actual face. In too much detail. A faint divot forming between her brows that she had not noticed before. A wrinkle? Alex backed out of range of the phone camera.

Margaret studied the photo, zooming in unhappily.

"You look good." Margaret stuck out her tongue. "I look like shit."

"That's not true. You look great. I like that sweater."

Margaret looked down. "You can have it if you want."

Alex smiled.

"I'm serious." Margaret shrugged her arms out of the sweater. "Take it," she said, "I don't even like it."

"I'm not taking your sweater."

"Seriously, I don't want it. Take it." Margaret tossed the sweater at Alex—it was warm.

"Well," Alex said, resting the sweater on top of her bag. "Thanks, I guess."

"Want me to text the picture to you?" Margaret said.

"I'm okay."

Margaret looked hurt.

"I mean you can. But my phone," Alex offered, "is basically dead." This explanation seemed sufficient. As Alex tested different lipsticks on the back of her hand, she watched Margaret post the photo.

Margaret refreshed the page, waiting for a like that did not come. She refreshed again.

Too sad, suddenly, Margaret and her phone, the powder on Margaret's cheeks settling into the light down that covered her face. Down was a side effect of starvation, as Alex knew from living with those professionally anorexic Eastern Europeans, their diet of popcorn and miniature bell peppers.

Margaret was zooming in on the photo again.

"You're, like, really pretty," Margaret said, her eyes slippery, aiming a crooked smile in Alex's direction. Was she flirting, in her clumsy way? If so, she wasn't aware of it on any conscious level. Probably the possibility was too foreign for her to recognize. What would she do if Alex sat next to her on the bed?

Alex had the thought, and then she was doing it, settling on the bed, scooting toward Margaret. Alex studied her from this new proximity. Margaret kept smiling. Uncomfortable to imagine how far she would let Alex go.

What was she doing? Alex stopped herself. She stood up.

"Do you have an eyelash curler?"

ANOTHER GLASS OF WINE and Margaret was napping, her expression peaceful, her dress hiked up her legs, her eyes dark with makeup and her lipstick already diffusing beyond her mouth. Her makeup might get on her pillowcase. Should Alex try to prevent this? But there were probably twenty pillowcases in the linen closet, what did it matter?

Alex sat in the desk chair. She flipped through a yearbook from the shelf: out fell a grid of school photos, Margaret as a twelve- or thirteen-year-old, in uniform, her hair pushed back by a velvet headband, gaze fixed on some point to the side of the lens. The photo depressed Alex, all the questions visible in the girl's face, the last moment before she found out how cruel the world might be. But really, why should Alex pity her? Margaret, in her home, with her family, her clothes cleaned by someone else. She would trundle forth into her future.

The bottom drawer of the desk had an unopened candle in a box, a velvet pouch stuffed behind. Inside the pouch was a jumble of earrings. All studs. Most of them were diamonds, though they were small. Like the earrings Margaret wore, twin pinpricks of light. Fake? No way to tell right now. She considered taking a pair, but decided against it.

Margaret let out an abbreviated sigh and nestled into her pillow, asleep.

At the last minute, Alex palmed a lone ruby stud that did not have a mate. In a way, she was being helpful, getting rid of it. What was more annoying than one of something, a reminder that the world was unreliable, that even valuable things went missing?

It was cold enough, in the air-conditioning, that Alex pulled the blanket over Margaret, covering her skinny legs, her immaculately painted toenails. Out the window, there was a play structure in the yard, a wooden turret and slide, and, farther away, the pool, half hidden by a tree.

"Hey," she whispered to Margaret.

Nothing.

"You awake?"

Margaret wheezed lightly, then turned on her side.

Alex's swimsuit was in her bag, still damp from the club, and no one was home, anyway, so who cared about a swimsuit?

THE POOL WATER WAS cool but not cold. If the sun were out, swimming would be nicer. But it was still overcast, the air heavy and gray. Alex sat on the step, hunched over her bare breasts. She held her left breast in her hand, studying the nipple, then ran her finger along the line of her thigh. Her pubic hair was growing back in. The ingrown hair hadn't really healed: a dime-sized aura of pink. Don't touch it, she thought, even as she dug in with a fingernail. She stopped only after the bleeding started.

Alex floated for a while. She was sucking on a candy rose, moving it from one cheek to another. She didn't feel like doing laps. Nice to just lie on her back, to feel half of her exposed to the air, the other half in the water. The water was cold enough that it made her aware of every part of her body.

Three days until Simon's party.

She floated in silence. Nothing but trees all around her.

A strange afternoon, here with this poor unhappy girl, now alone in this pool that, Alex felt sure, no one ever used. These were the type of people who assumed that there were rules, who believed that if they followed them they would one day be rewarded. And here was Alex, naked in their pool.

The pool was surrounded by trees: any slight breeze and they rained almost translucent white petals into the water. The petals were veiny and bisected. Like insect wings. Alex dove down to the bottom of the deep end, exhaling as she sank. It was colder down there, actually cold. Pressure on her temples. When she opened her eyes, it was just dim, the echoing sound of nothing, of a void. It was nice to be alone. When she looked up, there were pinpricks dimpling the water: was it raining?

Alex surfaced to drizzle on her face. Finally the clouds had broken. It wasn't bad, at first, light drops hitting the water all around her, almost as fine as mist, but then, in a big, visible curtain, she watched real rain move in: fat drops that splashed the water and were cold on her shoulders. She pulled herself up onto the side of the pool. Alex groped for her towel, still sucking on the candy rose, when she caught movement by the house: she was so surprised she bit the candy cleanly in two.

There was Karen in her blindingly white Keds, the little girl holding her hand, and they were both looking at Alex, who was naked, shivering. Karen did not seem shocked, or mad. She just seemed embarrassed.

How did the look Karen gave Alex seem to contain everything? Knowledge of exactly what kind of person Alex was.

Karen turned away and pulled the girl into the house. Before she disappeared behind the door, the girl glanced back, gaping openly as Alex covered herself with the damp towel.

———

MARGARET WAS SITTING UP in bed, her makeup smeared. Her eyes were bruised with shadow. Her crotch was visible under her dress, a wedge of white cotton underwear.

"I fell asleep?" Margaret pulled absently at her dress. Her nose wrinkled. "Why are you all wet?"

"I went swimming."

"In the pool?" Margaret looked out the window. "But it's raining."

Alex put on underwear with her towel still wrapped around her. A black shirt and a pair of cutoffs that Simon had hated.

"Sorry," Alex said, buttoning her shorts briskly. "Can I just check if my friend wrote back?"

Margaret had slept with her phone beside her: the mention of it perked her up. She sat up and typed in the passcode.

"Did my friend write back?" Alex was jiggling her leg: she made herself stop.

When Margaret handed her phone over, the phone background, Alex saw, had already been changed to the photo of Margaret and Alex. She regretted letting herself be photographed: why did the thought of existing on this girl's phone conjure up so much dread?

A text from Jack.

What time is good later?

Alex could tell Margaret was watching her. She typed quickly.

> *Can u come get me?*
> *Like asap. Sorry don't have car right now.*

Alex waited. Three dots appeared.

> Right now?
> I kinda said id have dinner w my dad tho.
> So maybe later like 9ish
> or ten idk

The hours that would have to pass before it was nine seemed interminable.

> *No chance u could come before?*

Did she sound too desperate?

> I can skip dinner

> *Really?*

> Yah I don't wanna go anyway

Before she could respond, more texts from Jack arrived.

> is fine
> where do I get u?

"What's the address here?" Alex said.

"Are you inviting someone over?" Margaret got to her knees. "You can definitely invite someone over."

"My friend is picking me up."

"You're leaving?" Margaret looked suddenly forlorn. "Karen can make dinner. For your friend, too. Or you wanna go out? We can go out?"

Was there some scenario where Alex stayed here for a night, or even a few nights, waiting out this last weekend before Simon's party, sharing a bed with Margaret, going to the tennis club and the beach club and eating sliced turkey under white awnings? But people's unhappiness could so quickly infect you.

"Sorry." Alex tried to smile. "I kinda already had these plans."

"You can invite your friend over," Margaret said. "I'm sure it's fine. We can all hang out."

Alex was barely listening. She texted him the address: Jack sent back a thumbs-up.

There in twenty.

"Sorry," Alex said, again. She wished Jack were coming earlier. She didn't want to spend any longer than necessary in this house—didn't want to interact with Karen, marinate in the slack air of Margaret's bedroom. She handed the phone back to Margaret. As Alex unplugged her own phone and wound the cord, she pretended not to notice Margaret watching with a lipsticked frown.

Alex went into Margaret's bathroom and shut the door.

At least the light in here was pink and flattering: even so, Alex looked sunburnt, unkempt. She combed her hair with her fingers, then clipped in the silver barrette from the woman's bag. The barrette already felt like it had belonged to Alex for a long time.

She rubbed moisturizer on her cheeks and covered the redness around her nose, no time for the whole routine. She knelt on the tile to take everything out of her bag, laying her clothes out before refolding them tightly, rewrapping the little black animal in the lilac sweater from Margaret. She weighed Simon's watch in her hand before burying it under a pile of clothes.

Already she felt better. She'd be leaving soon. Any minute. Any minute now, Jack would arrive, and Alex would be safely settled in the passenger seat of his big car. Margaret would be tucked away in her bedroom. And even if Karen was posted at one of the first-floor windows, watching Alex leave, Alex would let the shame glance off her, become a feeling she considered from a distance, and the house would get smaller, the gate opening for Jack's car, and by the time Jack turned out of the driveway and onto the street, the house and its occupants would disappear entirely behind a hedgerow.

8

JACK LOOKED YOUNGER THAN Alex remembered—
a child!—but maybe it was because his car was so oversized.
Or maybe it was his outfit. Sheepskin slippers with shiny
basketball shorts, a too-big T-shirt.

"Watch your head," Jack said as Alex climbed in the
passenger seat. Just settling in, buckling her seatbelt, Alex
felt the thrill of escape, relief at leaving misery behind.

The air-conditioning was on full blast. She hefted her
bag into the sandy backseat, alongside a striped beach towel
and a cobalt blue copy of *Siddhartha*.

Jack backed down the driveway.

"Is this your place?" he said.

"I was just staying for a bit. My friend's house." She resisted the urge to glance at the windows and see if anyone
was watching. "Sorry," Alex said, and made herself smile,
angled herself in his direction. "I'm out of it."

He shrugged. "No worries." The hair on his forearms
was blond against his tan.

"Thanks for picking me up," Alex said. "I don't have a car right now."

"'Sfine," he said. "It was close, anyway."

Jack was, Alex discovered, more talkative after drinking, but now he was almost courtly. He rubbed the back of his neck out of anxiety, patted his phone in his shorts pocket. Most of the time, he did not look her in the eyes when he spoke. The most animated he got was when he turned up the music, the volume maxed out and Jack bouncing in his seat with all the windows rolled down.

"This guy," Jack said, over the song, "he's, like, my favorite. I made my dad get this car 'cause it's the same one he drives."

"Mm." Alex was only half listening to what the boy was actually saying; she was trying to parse his accent. Did he have one, or was she imagining it, a pinched, almost Euro twinge to his sentences?

"Want to see something weird?" Jack messed with his phone, only half watching the road. He started a video, aiming the screen in her direction. It was security camera footage, the sickly green X-ray of night vision—a vast, landscaped backyard. And then an animal, a big cat, circling a pool—was this a mountain lion? Alex had never seen one before.

"Wow." It looked like death, slinking around the pool. A nauseous feeling rose up. But maybe it was just the day drinking, the sugar and the beer.

Jack restarted the video. The mountain lion's eyes glowed crackly green, everything in the video shades of green and black. "It's from my dad's house in L.A.," he said, eyes dart-

ing between the phone and the road. "A mountain lion in
the backyard. Freaky, right?"

His father, Jack told her, was a producer. Alex could not
honestly say what a producer did. It was only after Jack
used his father's full name for the third time that she understood that his father must be very successful. She could
tell by the way Jack said the father's name in a squeezed
rush.

That made sense, explained this mix of shyness and confidence. People always paid attention to Jack, probably, but
only in a secondhand way. Their interest was forever re-
flected off someone else, forever mediated by another aim.
She'd met people like Jack before, children of the rich or
famous, their personalities distorted by a false reality. No
one ever responded to them honestly, no one ever gave
them meaningful social feedback, so they'd never cultivated
a proper self. They told flabby, long-winded anecdotes
without any thought that they might be boring—and why
would they ever imagine they were boring? Didn't people
always seem rapt, eager to hear whatever they had to say?

Jack's phone vibrated. His face went instantly dark.

"My dad's calling," he said, "shit, hold on."

Alex looked out the window and tried to appear as
though she wasn't listening.

"God," Jack was saying. "Sorry."

Muffled noise through the speaker.

"I said sorry." A pause. "Well, stuff came up," he said.
"Okay?"

Sorry, he mouthed to Alex.

He held the phone to his chest: she could hear the voice on the other end continuing to talk. "Sorry," he said. "I'm supposed to have dinner with him. You wanna come with me? To dinner?"

"Oh. Really?"

"Please?"

The dad was still talking.

"Sure," she said. "Okay. Sure."

"I said fine," Jack said into the phone. "Jeez. Yes. See you." He dropped the phone on the console. "Sorry," he said, and turned the music back up.

THE RESTAURANT WAS RIGHT on the highway. Jack parked haphazardly, taking up two spots—he didn't seem to notice. The air was flickering with bugs, Friday night music leaking out of a bar next door.

"Are you sure you want me to come?" Alex could busy herself for a few hours. Though she didn't want to, particularly, and maybe he picked up on that.

Jack nodded, vigorously. "Come," he said. "Seriously."

The room was dark, candles on the bar and on the tables. White tablecloths, warm wood—she was underdressed, but so was Jack, so underdressed that he seemed totally at ease, his casual stride the ultimate sign of belonging.

"The French fries are good," Jack said, then his face fell. "Ugh, he's already here."

The dad was sitting at a table in a pink button-up. He was in good shape, in the manner of the West Coast wealthy: likely he played tennis and ran, or at least used to until his knees started to go. Definitely a trainer a few times a week. He raised his hand at Jack, then squinted when he saw Alex trailing behind. The table, she noticed, was set for two.

The father stood. "Hello," he said. "Who's your friend?"

When Jack didn't move to introduce her, Alex held out her hand.

"Hi, I'm Alex." A firm handshake, polite eye contact.

"Robert."

Alex kept an apology in her face, trying to indicate, however subtly, that she was sympathetic to the father, though she couldn't let Jack see. "Sorry," she said, "I think I'm a late addition."

"We can squeeze in another place, no problem," Robert said, and signaled to a waiter. He would be accommodating, she understood, smoothly shifting course so any irritation was barely noticeable, though Alex saw his jaw tighten. He was probably always like this, ferociously easygoing, adapting to whatever was thrown at him. It could be its own form of aggression.

Jack sat down hard. He grabbed a breadstick from the basket. Alex watched the father notice Jack chewing with an open mouth and watched him pointedly keep smiling.

"And how do you know each other?"

Alex waited to see what Jack would say.

Jack shrugged, still chewing. "From around."

"We were both at the beach," Alex said, pleasantly, the waiter placing a plate in front of her, utensils, a heavy napkin.

"Haven't been out as much as I'd like to," the father said. "I used to surf. We'd go out most every day in the summer, hmm?"

Jack grunted. His rudeness was so theatrical—was this for Alex's benefit? The father took it in stride, plowing forward with conversation.

"But it's been a while," he went on.

Alex had to work to keep the right tone with the father—it was too easy to accidentally slip flirtatious. Girl Scout cheer, she reminded herself.

"And you live in L.A.?" she said.

"During the year, yes. Mostly. I guess I could surf there but it gets pretty cold."

"Right," she said, and they shared a low-key smile. It was almost as though she and the father were on a date, Jack so absent, so insistently juvenile.

The waiter came with another cocktail for the father. "Anything to drink?"

"Can I have a beer?" Jack said.

The father cleared his throat. "I think water is fine for you."

"Water's good for me, too," Alex chirped. Like a good sport.

"Jack's mother and I were actually married in this restaurant," the father said. "It was fun. Very easy, a nice night. Lots of friends. A million years ago."

Jack smirked. His rudeness had crossed a line into the truly ridiculous, which made it harmless, the father's eyes skittering over his son's face without pausing. Like he and Alex had been interrupted by a commercial, a minor annoyance they had to sit through so they could return to the real conversation.

Alex kept up a smile, nodding every so often as the father spoke, but her attention was bouncing around the restaurant. Birds-of-paradise and other flowers with muscular stems soared out of an oversized vase. Menus in leather binders, like miniature briefcases, people shoulder to shoulder at the bar.

Did Simon ever come here? Did Jack's father know Simon? It wasn't impossible.

There were mostly couples in the restaurant, older couples, though she noticed a pair of bare legs—young legs. A woman with a curtain of glossy chestnut hair and a dress that was a little too flashy, sitting across from a white-haired man. Out of habit, Alex averted her eyes.

"We actually end up shooting a lot in Long Island City," the father was saying. "Lots of lots out there. Lots of lots, ha."

Alex smiled.

Something made Alex look at the woman in the dress again, some energy drawing Alex's attention, the woman's red mouth on the rim of her wineglass.

A glance at her empty plate, a glance back—and yes, Alex thought, it was Dana. It had to be.

It was a surprise how quickly she came into focus. Dana was nodding at the man she was with, and she was smiling, a coy smile. Had Dana recognized her, too?

Dana looked good. Alex assumed the man with white hair was not an actual boyfriend, though who knew where Dana's life had ended up. It amused her to imagine what

Dana might think of Alex, what Dana might make of the threesome at the table. She would probably assume Alex was with Jack's father.

Alex shot another look at Dana's table. She was sharing a piece of chocolate cake with the man, Dana taking a prim bite. Would she and Dana acknowledge each other? Sometimes she wanted someone to compare notes with. See if she was remembering things correctly, talk with someone who could fill in the blanks. When she saw Dana excuse herself, saw Dana dab prettily and needlessly at her lips, Alex got up, too.

THEY'D BOTH BEEN TWENTY, back then. Alex new to the city. Though, it occurred to Alex now, Dana had probably been futzing her age a bit, had probably been older.

Dana had shown Alex how to spot the others in public: vivid, pigmented lipstick. Usually red, even if a different color would have been more flattering. High heels they'd probably just put on outside the restaurant. A short dress that was too formal, either in jewel tones or a faded black. Dresses with some of the same sad reach for elegance as a prom dress. Girls clutching a purse with both hands. Girls in drag as girls.

Alex remembered one particular night. She and Dana dancing in a club with their eyes closed and their hands in fists. Alex wore a dress borrowed from Dana that was too tight under her arms. They sat on fake-velvet bench seats, part of a grotto area, nursing their drinks while a woman in a gold outfit wiped down the table. It had been some man's birthday, Mylar balloons spelling out *JASON*, balloons vibrating from the bass. The *J* was already starting to deflate, riding lower than the others.

Alex watched the *J* fold in on itself completely, then go limp.

ASON

A man sat down at their table. He told Alex he believed in God but laughed like a girl after he said so. The man leaned in to say something else. Alex smiled, automatically, assuming he was telling her a joke of some kind. When she realized the man was saying something about her nipples, she kept smiling, the smile buckling only for a second.

The girl in the gold dress came by with a bill.

"We need a credit card," Dana announced, hands on her hips. She waited for a beat, until the man understood: he fumbled in his pockets and handed over a credit card.

Neither of them said thank you. The man didn't seem bothered by this.

The night ended in a limo—Dana had made someone get a limo, so fucking cheesy. Alex and Dana sprawled out on the black leather, Dana making quick work of a bottle of bad champagne nestled in a trough of ice. The men in the car—different men—talked mostly to each other. A bald man who breathed through his mouth with alarming, audible effort, the other one with a glassy stare who kept up a constant nod at nothing.

A band of LED lights snaked around the upholstery. Every few seconds, the color bled into a different color, tropical purple and teal and blue.

"Tell the driver to change the music," Dana said. "This sucks."

The men barely looked over.

"Hey," Dana called, "hey, driver, change the music, okay? We want to dance."

The driver didn't seem put out. If anything, he was caught up in the fact of the girls, glancing in the rearview and grinning.

"How's the temperature for you ladies?"

"Too cold," Dana said, in a whine. "I wanna listen to my music," she said, scrambling across the seats to hand her phone through the divider, her dress rising so Alex could see a beige thong squeezed between her ass cheeks.

When the music filled the car, Dana pulled down her dress and took a deep inhale, like finally she could relax, the music offering her some necessary sustenance.

At some point, Dana and the bald man had disappeared, dropped off somewhere, and Alex was alone with the other man. Something was wrong, she'd done something or said something: the man made the driver pull over and let Alex out on the bridge—you're a bitch, he'd said, and Alex had thoroughly blanked on what she'd done, why the man was so angry. Sorry miss, sorry miss, sorry miss—the driver had felt bad for her, anyway.

So many nights she remembered only as a sour feeling, a bartender's cold look, strangers trying not to stare as a man squeezed her knee. The men always wanted people to be aware that they were with Alex, wanted eyes to follow them as they headed toward the elevators. Did they imagine that they looked like anything other than what they were? As if anyone would have done the math and come up with a different explanation.

Some party Dana had brought her to, a party on a terrace with blue inflatable plastic furniture, oversized couches and armchairs. It had been laughable, like the furniture in a teenage girl's bedroom. There were tables cluttered with fruit, grapes and half-green bananas and oversized strawberries, all the fruit flat with unnatural color. The fruit would go to waste, Alex was certain—nobody touched it. Young women drank flutes of champagne with grim intention and pulled their dresses up with one hand so their breasts flattened. They had vacated some major part of themselves, ready to be moved in any suggested direction; it didn't matter, really, who approached them. Inside, a small man was being cajoled into playing the piano. People kept going up and down a glass staircase. On his way up, a man stopped Alex to ask if she knew what the art on the wall was.

"Vaginas," the man said, "those are molds of vaginas." He watched to see how she would react.

As in other moments, Alex found herself smiling for no reason.

THE RESTAURANT BATHROOM WAS warm with more of the fine-grained wood, and a jumpy amber light from the wall sconces summoned a sort of maritime effect. Only one stall was occupied: Dana. The stall doors were the type that went floor to ceiling. Useful, in the old days, for drug taking, Dana crowded in with Alex, sitting on the closed lid of the toilet with her slip dress riding up her thighs, Dana's warm animal breath in Alex's face and a sharp inhale off the back of her hand. There had been a few times they'd been caught out, some attendant or security guard waiting when they emerged, but it had never been frightening, only funny.

Alex ran the faucet, then actually washed her hands. She made a quick mirror check, bared her teeth: everything was fine. A small cough from the stall, Dana clearing her throat. Then a muffled flush. Alex stayed at the sink.

The last time Alex had seen Dana, she had been living in that brand-new building, an apartment whose windows didn't open. A man in Houston had put down the security deposit in exchange for breathy phone conversations about who Dana had fucked that day and just how big their cock had been. There was a purple neon light on the wall that spelled out LOVE and a poster of Audrey Hepburn taped up above the couch. A metal sign on the bathroom door said *Les Toilettes* in scrolly cursive.

Why had Dana stopped talking to Alex?

The details were vague.

Here she was, Dana opening the stall door, going to the other sink. Dana in the flesh. In one brisk motion, Dana gathered her hair and let it drop down her back. She studied her reflection as she did so: she seemed satisfied with whatever she saw. She started to wash her hands.

Alex eyed Dana sideways: her dress was a degree too revealing, the cleavage too forced—didn't Dana know better? Hadn't she always caught those things?

Dana had pinned a mild, leave-me-alone smile on her

face, and she barely glanced at Alex in the mirror before she went back to washing her hands. Then she looked again.

"Jesus."

"Hey," Alex said.

"Ha," Dana said, more of an exhale than an actual laugh, and she kept washing her hands.

"What's up?" Alex said. The question seemed especially meager.

Dana used her forearm to shut off the faucet, then took up a folded cloth towel with dripping hands.

"I kinda wondered if I'd see you," Dana said. "You know how I could always kinda tell things were gonna happen before they happened?"

"See me?"

"Out here." Dana dropped the hand towel in a wicker hamper. She ran a finger under each eye, still watching her own reflection. "I hadn't talked to that guy in forever. Dom. He said you were out here."

Alex tried to appear calm.

"You know he's freaking out. He's been hitting up everyone." Dana studied her fingertips. "Asking about you."

"Well," Alex said. "You know how Dom is."

"I don't, really." Dana looked at Alex full-on. "I don't really know him."

Alex attempted to smile: warmly, she thought, a warm smile that might remind Dana that they had been close. Close enough.

"Maybe," Alex said, "if he's in touch again—maybe you could just not mention that you saw me? I'm going back to the city soon."

"I really don't want to be involved, Alex." Dana eyed her again. What did she see in Alex's face? She softened slightly. "I mean, anyway, he said he's already coming out here. I didn't really get details."

Alex made herself take a breath. Kept her voice steady.

"What exactly did he say?"

"That's all, okay? That's all he said. I really don't care to be involved in your shit anymore." She was already tired of Alex, tired of this conversation. She snapped open her purse, a tiny thing barely able to contain the phone inside. She checked the screen, made a slight hum.

"Well." A bright false smile in Alex's general direction. "We're heading out," Dana said. "Have a good night."

The door closed behind Dana. Music from the dining room bleeding in, then growing faint.

Alex had the impulse to follow Dana. To insist that Dana recount the conversation with Dom again, tell Alex exactly what he had said.

Alex didn't move.

She licked her lips. She tried to get on top of the paranoia, head it off before it got too bad: it would be unbearable otherwise, she wouldn't be able to get through dinner. She tried not to notice whether her hands were shaking.

Maybe Dom wasn't actually out here, maybe he was just bluffing. That was more likely, wasn't it? He wouldn't actually try to track her down, would he?

A jolt, the bathroom door opening: it was an older woman, in slacks and an old-fashioned blouse, who seemed just as startled as Alex, her hand flying up to her throat.

———

ALEX HAD ALREADY BEEN away from the table too long. She forced herself to walk back at a steady, normal pace. One step and then another. She made a quick scan of the people sitting at the bar, the faces in the dining room. Of course none of them were Dom; of course he wasn't here. Dana's table was already empty, a waiter scraping the tablecloth clean in swift strokes.

Talking to Dana had been a bad idea. Alex was missing the mark so often, lately. Everything was jarred from its proper place, or maybe the problem was Alex. Maybe she should cool it with the pills. Even as she told herself she would try to be better, she was aware that she would not.

Alex wished very badly for a drink. Could she order something at the bar, finish it quickly without anyone noticing?

But the father had already spotted Alex, and she smiled and took her seat.

Alex made herself tune back in to the frequency of dinner: Jack's father, Jack sitting beside her. Could they tell that anything was wrong? She shifted in her seat as the beaming waiter rattled off the specials. She tried to appear engaged even as she kept an eye on the front door.

Jack ordered a vegetable pasta, fries, mozzarella sticks. Alex got salmon. A slight wince from Jack—Alex remembered his *Siddhartha* moment, his vegetarian spiel. She ordered the pasta instead.

"The salmon sounds good," the father said. "Healthy. I should have that."

But, after asking the waiter multiple questions about the salmon, he ordered the steak. As he had probably always planned to do.

"I'm a red meat guy," he said. "I try hard not to be. But I'm a Midwesterner," he said, "hard to unlearn that."

"Your parents moved to Bel-Air when you were, like, two," Jack said.

Robert acted like he hadn't heard this.

When the food arrived, Jack made a point of watching his father cut into his steak. As soon as he took a bite, Jack pulled a face.

"They basically torture cows," Jack said. "They're so crammed together that they get all deformed. There's a million videos."

"Unfortunately," Robert said, "this steak tastes very good." He gave Alex a pleasant smile. She assumed he had been subject to this line of thinking before.

"And where are you from, Alex?"

"Upstate." Another vague gesture with her hands.

"We had a place," the father said, "when Jack was young. Like, seven, eight. You probably don't remember much of it," he said to Jack. "Near Millbrook. Very nice area."

"You hated it," Jack said. "You said it was a shithole up there."

"That's not true." His father seemed to have to work to relax. Jack looked triumphant—he'd forced his father to drop, if even for a moment, the veneer of pleasantness, his eternal Los Angeles sunniness.

Did the father dislike his son? Did his features seize for the briefest second?

Maybe. Or maybe Alex saw hatred everywhere, imagined it where it didn't exist, and that was her problem, not theirs.

WHEN HIS FATHER WENT to the bathroom, Jack reached across the table for his cocktail. He drained most of it in one go, then held out the remainder to Alex.

She took the last sip. A vodka soda. It had an ascetic taste, like water gone sick. All the girls had ordered this, the drink of the female martyr.

"Mom doesn't care if I have a drink with dinner," Jack said. "He's so annoying about that stuff. He doesn't actually care but he cares about seeming like he cares. Which is so much more hypocritical."

"He's not so terrible," Alex said. "It could be worse."

"Sorry. He's trying to suck up to you. He does it to everyone."

"It's fine," Alex said. "Really. I don't mind."

"I had to basically spend forever living with him," Jack said. "I'm just over it."

"In L.A.?"

"I mean, I just, like, was over the whole school thing." Jack looked up at her through his big fringy lashes. "You know?"

He told her that he had taken the last year off from school. "Just seemed like a good idea," he said, rubbing his neck. "A gap year, you know. Before college."

Alex wondered, because of the way he brought it up,

because of the way he plowed through the French fries as he talked, whether it had not been Jack's idea to take time off. Had he been asked to leave school? Suspended? Or whatever euphemism they used.

What might this mean? She didn't know yet, but it was more interesting information, tucked away for future use.

Jack should annoy Alex: these flashes of bravado, whatever he had done or not done to be asked to take a year off. But somehow he didn't. The effort he was making was too visible, defaulting young and anxious, his voice straining for praise. It made it easy to be nice to him.

Jack took another handful of fries, scattering salt on the table.

"Try one," he said. "Good, right?"

THE DINNER WENT DOWNHILL from there. Robert left the table at least twice more to take phone calls. As soon as he sat down the final time, his phone lit up again—"Just a sec," he said into the phone. "Sorry," he said to Alex and Jack. "We're in preproduction and there's a million fires to put out."

"Lots of important work," Jack said, smirking. "Big fucking surprise."

The father had started to stand—he stopped. "Enough," he said to Jack. "Enough." His voice changed. "Let me call you right back," he almost sang into the phone.

"You," he said to Jack, stabbing the air with his finger. "Let's step outside for a minute."

Jack darted a look at Alex.

"Come on," the father said. "Let's chat." He shot Alex a dazzling smile. "Alex will excuse us, won't she?"

"Of course." Alex kept her eyes down. She was used to this, the politeness of pretending that things that were happening were not, in fact, happening.

THROUGH THE RESTAURANT WINDOWS, Alex could see Jack flail his arms, then cross them in front of his chest. The dad's face was stony.

Now that she was alone, Alex took a larger interest in her own plate. Ripped more bread to chase the pasta down, no lag time between bites. The father had barely made a dent in his steak. She took a slice with her fork. Then another. Everything spread into a purity of satiation, of being fed. She kept going. The slight nausea wasn't actually unpleasant. It made her feel more solid to herself.

There's no way Dom would drag himself out here, that was dumb. She told herself this and it seemed true.

"Any dessert?" the waiter said.

"I think we're fine." Alex patted her mouth with her napkin, ran a fingernail between her teeth.

Only Jack returned. He pulled the chair out roughly, dropped his phone on the table.

"Sorry." He was upset, a new energy in his limbs, his smile too wide.

"All okay?"

"Yeah, totally. Nothing," he said, "just bullshit."

"Where's your dad?"

"On the phone." He pushed his curls out of his eyes. "So," he said, "what's up tonight?" His leg was jiggling. "You wanna get out of here?"

THE PARTY WAS ANOTHER thirty minutes down the highway, toward the tip of the island. Alex hadn't been out this far. Simon kept saying he wanted to bring her to the lighthouse, but it had never happened. Or hadn't happened yet, she told herself.

Jack's phone shivered—he ignored the call.

"What's this party?" Alex said.

"My buddy's house. It'll be a bunch of people, probably," he said, "I dunno if you'll know any of them. I texted Max to meet us there."

"How do you know them?"

"School, I dunno," Jack said. "Some from out here."

"High school friends?"

"Elementary school, too."

That continuity seemed nearly impossible to Alex: imagine the thread staying the same, the world remaining static. Would it be stifling, punishing, or was it the reason why all these people had this peculiar certainty about who they were, confidence that their identity had a context? In her hometown, there was context, but the context was negative, a vortex. The arc of your life was already determined, its limits already visible. This was something else.

———

ALEX COULDN'T TELL, UNTIL they were inside looking out, that the house was on a bluff, that the ocean was directly below. It was rougher out here, the coastline more rocky.

"Jack?"

The boy who came over was tall, Germanic looking, with features that seemed approximate, like they had been drawn from memory. He was talking very fast and kept one eye on the door. A conscientious host. He shook Alex's hand. Introduced himself by his full name: like all of them, the boy could be instantly and impeccably polite. He hugged Jack.

"It's been fucking forever, man," the boy said. "You're doing okay?" He slapped Jack's shoulder. "Good to see you out and about, man."

Alex caught some quick shame in Jack's expression—curious.

"Can you walk to the beach from here?" Alex said.

"No," the boy said. "No fucking way. It's, like, a cliff straight down. And it's all rocks down there, anyway. No sand."

There were twenty or so others inside the house. Alex recognized the rat-faced boy from the beach, wearing a pastel tie-dye hoodie and track pants. There were girls here, too, girls in silver hoop earrings with center-parted hair, girls who wore T-shirts and thick American blue jeans and penny loafers. They had already absorbed whatever information existed about how they should be in the world, what was correct. They looked so at ease, so casually pretty. Was their skin naturally good, or was it medical intervention, mothers who steered them to dermatologists' offices at any sign of imperfection? She assumed they were Jack's age, but how did the girls seem this much older, this confident? This was another strata than Margaret's, several degrees closer to cultural power.

She poured herself red wine from the fridge. When Alex took a sip, she found, to her surprise, that it was carbonated.

"Good with pizza, right?" Jack said.

There were pizza boxes on the kitchen counter. A few unopened clamshells of humid-looking salads, feta pressed against the plastic. Alex sat on a kitchen stool to pick at a pizza slice.

"What's his deal?" she said. "The guy who lives here."

"Noah?" Jack said. "I dunno, we've known each other forever. We used to ride dirt bikes out here."

"Mm. And you guys just haven't hung out for a while?"

Jack shrugged. Had he already finished his wine? "Yeah, I dunno. I've been busy. They all were in school last year."

He looked uncomfortable enough that she dropped it. Alex downed the last of her own wine.

"Bathroom?"

THE WHOLE BATHROOM WAS tiled—floor, ceiling, walls—in the same black hex. Nothing in any of the drawers except more toilet paper. Was the host smart enough to preemptively strip the place of things that could be stolen?

But what did any of these kids need that they didn't already have? Relaxing in here, this soothing cocoon of nothingness. Alex opened the window and pushed, freeing a wedge of air. Enough to stick her hand through. Her shirt was getting wet under her arms, the seam darkening. She plucked the fabric away. Already too late—there would be a stain.

She wanted to check her phone but knew it was pointless. Still broken, and anyway, she hadn't had Dana's number in years.

Did her left eye look a little pink in the mirror, could her stye be coming back? She told herself she was imagining it. But she wasn't imagining that faint wrinkle between her brows, the ghostly coin slot. She pressed it hard with a finger. Another glance at the mirror and the wrinkle jumped out at her, unavoidable, and so she kept her gaze vague and the wrinkle disappeared.

BACK IN THE LIVING ROOM, a girl in a striped T-shirt and jean shorts was talking to Jack. Her right ear was pierced up and down the ridge.

"Do not cut your hair," the girl said, ruffling Jack's curls. "Seriously."

Alex couldn't make out Jack's reply. Was he blushing?

Alex settled on the couch. She didn't notice the rat-faced boy until he sat beside her.

"What's up?" he said. "You good? You need anything?"

He was being solicitous but his energy was aggressive.

"I'm good," Alex said. "Thanks."

He was peering at her face. Too closely.

"What," he said, "is your name again?"

"Alex."

"Yeah. I'm Max." He smiled, his arm on the back of the couch. "How do you know Jack?"

"Just from the beach. Same day I met you."

"Oh shit, really? I thought you guys knew each other from before."

"Nope. Just from out here." Alex had crossed her arms without noticing: she uncrossed them.

"But you're not from the city, right? I can tell." He grinned. A little unkindly.

She didn't respond but it didn't slow him down.

"Neither am I. I'm from here. Like, actually live out here. Not like them," he said, nodding at the scrum in the kitchen. "They all grew up in basically a five-block radius from each other."

With this new information, Max clicked a few more degrees into focus. He did seem different from the others, his presence edgy and unsettled. Curious that he had identified her as another outsider—she didn't like it.

Before Alex could say anything, Jack joined them, the cracks in his lips already red from wine.

"My friend," Max said. "I was just hearing your love story."

Jack winced. "Come on."

"I'm teasing," Max said. "You should have texted earlier, I would've driven with you. I thought you were on lockdown."

"I wasn't sure what we were doing yet," Jack said.

"Your dad's fine with you being out?" Max said. "Daddy Robert doesn't mind?"

Jack squirmed away from Max. "It's fine."

Max shrugged, looking amused, glancing between Alex and Jack.

A small dog was scrambling around the house, nails clicking along the hardwood. A girl bent to pick up the dog, to hold the animal to her cheek. She made kissing noises in the air and the dog licked her on the lips. The girl didn't appear to care.

"I'm going to get a cigarette," Alex said.

Jack and Max were lost in their own talk: neither of them responded.

Alex pushed open the sliding doors. Around the side of the house, she found the pool. Smaller than she'd expected, looking out over blackness, the jagged line of the cliff and the sky choked with stars. It took a second before she saw the pool was occupied: a girl in underwear and no bra sitting on the edge, a boy leaning back in the water and sipping a glass of wine.

Alex turned in the other direction.

A slope of lawn, a wooden fence, the ocean beyond, which you could see only if you got close to the fence. Some kids had gone to the other side and sat on the ground with their legs dangling. She could hear them talking, the darkness punctuated with their laughter. One of the boys called out to Alex, something she didn't catch.

"Sorry?"

"I said, do you want help getting over the fence?"

"I'm good back here," Alex said. "Can I bum one of those?"

Even getting close enough to accept a cigarette and a book of matches made Alex dizzy: the drop was sudden, the silent shapes of rocks below. So many possible avenues for bad luck. For unhappy endings. No one else looked frightened at all, the danger barely seeming to register. They kicked their legs in the air, the backs of their sneakers scuffing against the cliff face.

She didn't even want a cigarette, but now she was glad for it, something concrete to do with her hands. A time-waster, perfectly contained. When she exhaled, the breeze carried the smoke away, and if she didn't look down, she felt better.

There was a joke rippling through the group: Alex only heard the tail end of it.

"And why," the boy was saying, "do we even like Max?" Alex handed the matches back and he accepted them without acknowledging her.

There was a burst of laughter, quickly controlled.

"Seriously." The boy looked around, earnest. "I mean, someone tell me. I mean, I just want to be reminded."

"Oh, come on," a girl said. "Be nice."

"I'm just teasing. Jesus fucking Christ," the boy said, peacefully. He lit a match and flicked it over the edge of the cliff: it burned out almost instantly.

"Stop," a girl said, but her voice was flat.

The boy did it again, a quick flare snapping to darkness. And again. Alex got the sense he would do this all night.

———

BACK INSIDE, ONE OF the girls was lying on the floor of the living room with the tiny dog up on her stomach. She lifted one of his front paws, as if they were dancing, while smoking from a vape she held with her other hand. After an inhale, she reared up on her elbows to blow the smoke in the dog's face.

Another girl filmed the whole thing on her phone.

"Wait," she said, "wait, do it again."

The other girl obliged, a fresh exhale of smoke shrouding the dog's tiny head.

"Where'd you go?" Jack said. He put his arm around Alex, just for a moment. Surprising, the gesture, but he seemed like he was already drunk, his eyes going unfocused, his smile taking a minute to catch up. "I missed you."

"Just had a cigarette," Alex said.

The party had doubled in size. A boy wearing a captain's hat was filling a row of glasses. The tall Germanic boy clicked a remote at a TV screen and cycled through movie titles. He tried to enter letters manually with the remote, then finally pressed a button and spoke:

"Scarface."

The screen registered words—the boy seemed unhappy with the results.

"SCAR-FACE!" he shouted into the remote. "Scar-FACE." He threw the remote on the couch. "Piece of shit."

The rat-faced boy, Max, was on the other side of the room, talking to a blond girl, but he spotted Alex and Jack and looked like he was heading toward them.

"Your friend's coming over," Alex said.

Jack darkened.

"I kinda can't handle him right now. He's being so an-noying tonight. He already pissed a bunch of people off."

"Is there someplace quieter?" Alex said. "Wanna go up-stairs or something?"

Jack raised his eyebrows. Starting to smile but stopping himself.

"Sure. Yeah, it's too loud." He drained his glass. How many glasses was that? "You want more wine or anything?"

"I'm good."

And she was good: one cigarette, one glass of wine, the house full of people. The Dana interlude already seemed like a hallucination. Jack was chewing his wine-soaked lips: he was a nice boy. Not nice, that was the wrong word. But there was nothing in him that meant any harm.

THEY SAT ON A bed in the room upstairs where people had stashed their bags. A few backpacks humped on the floor, a pair of swim trunks drying on the desk chair. If Alex was alone, she would have looked through the bags. But that impulse suddenly lacked urgency, didn't make sense here—because everything was fine. Being around Jack calmed certain urges, or deadened them, anyway. What bad things could ever befall him, this blond son?

"You having fun?" Jack's eyes were heavy. Up close, she could smell the baking soda of his deodorant.

"Yeah," Alex said. "Lots."

Probably they could spend the night here, in some bed

in this house. Probably they would wake up in the morning to breakfast. You assumed kids like these, kids like the host, didn't know how to cook, but, strangely, they usually did, trained by parents who fetishized the lifestyle of Europeans. Alex lay back, aware that Jack noticed how her shirt had ridden up to show her stomach. She put her arms behind her head, which exposed more skin.

"Come here." She patted the bed.

Jack lay down awkwardly. He seemed to not know what to do with his hands, finally folding them on his chest.

"Hi," Alex said.

He stayed still, only his eyes sliding to hers.

"Hi," he said. He smiled, involuntarily, the glint of his braces flashing on his bottom teeth before he covered his mouth with his hand.

"Why do you do that?" she said. "Put your hand up when you smile?"

"My braces."

"You can barely see them," Alex said. "It's just your bottom teeth."

She reached out to touch his lips with a finger—he froze.

"When you do that, cover something up, it makes people look harder," she said. "It makes it obvious you're hiding something. And you shouldn't worry. You're cute."

He smiled again. This time he didn't cover his mouth. "You're really nice."

"Nice." She smirked a little.

"Seriously. I like you."

"I like you, too," she said.

"Really?"

"Of course," Alex said. "Do you think I'd hang out with you if I didn't like you?"

His mouth opened, an exhale escaping when she tilted his chin toward hers.

"I'm gonna kiss you," Alex said. "Yeah?"

He blinked, nodding, and she felt some thrill, the boy prone beneath her, waiting for her to act.

When Alex kissed Jack, his lips were slack. But then she felt his tongue, a tiny peep darting onto hers, and the metal of his braces behind that. She rolled on top, his mouth tasting like the wine, hers, she realized, like cigarettes. He didn't seem to mind.

When Alex pulled away, Jack was breathing hard.

She smiled but felt that the smile wasn't reaching her eyes.

He held one of her hands. His palm was sweaty, sliding around hers. He closed his eyes and moved toward her, and she kissed him back, idly. His hips strained up. She could see the shape of his dick through his basketball shorts. She put a hand on his crotch, barely applying any pressure, but even so, his eyes flew open. He made a noise deep in his throat. He was looking at the ceiling. She had started to pull down his waistband, sat up on her knees to work his shorts down farther, but the music from the living room cut out and in its abrupt absence there were raised voices. Alex and Jack both paused.

The voices kept going, gaining volume.

"What the fuck," Jack muttered, but only stopped kissing her when there was a knock on the door. A girl hesitated in the door frame, her eyes darting between Jack and Alex before studiously staring up at the ceiling fan.

"Um, Jack?" the girl said. "Your friend? Is, like, freaking out? You better come?"

She glanced at Alex again, then snapped her attention back up to the fan.

DOWNSTAIRS THE CROWD HAD gathered in a flustered pack in the kitchen, the energy fractured and jittery. Only Max sat on the floor, his head leaned back against the island.

"What happened?"

The boy, Noah, had, they said, punched Max, but why? Something about the sister: Alex guessed the sister was the one presently crying on the broad white couch, being comforted by a cluster of girls.

"Why did you call the cops," the girl kept incanting. "Why did you call the cops."

"Someone called the cops?" Alex said.

"No way did anyone call the cops," Jack said.

She was sure they hadn't: these kids were too smart for that. Certainly. They would not believe in an authority beyond their own families, would not have any allegiance to a higher power—and probably they were correct.

Noah was pacing, his hands in fists, aiming some unintelligible vitriol at Max. Nobody bothered to step in. Were they waiting for Jack to do it?

"This is sort of dark," Alex said. Jack didn't respond. "Do you wanna check on your friend?"

Jack seemed reluctant, but made his way over and squatted by Max. Jack had a hand on Max's shoulder, whispering in his ear. Max appeared to ignore him. Then handed Jack something in a closed fist—Jack pocketed it in his sweatshirt. Finally, Max looked up, eyes locking on Jack for a second. Whatever he said made Jack visibly recoil. Jack returned to Alex with a hard expression.

"Forget it," he said. "Let's go."

"What just happened?"

"I didn't even fucking invite him," Noah said. He was addressing his tirade to Jack now. "Would I ever fucking invite him anywhere?"

Jack's hands were up. "Sorry," he said. "Sorry."

"I didn't actually think you would even come," Noah said. "And you bring this fuck. Aren't you not supposed to drink and shit?"

"It's fine," Jack said.

"It's not fucking fine," Noah said. "That guy's fucking psycho. Lily's fourteen."

"He didn't mean it," Jack said.

"He's not a good guy. Everyone hates him but you."

"Noah," the crying girl was saying. "Stop."

"Seriously!" Noah said. "He just doesn't get it," he said to Jack, "do you? You really are fucking crazy, aren't you?"

The other guests watched this exchange as if from a great distance.

Jack looked blinkered and young.

"Let's go," Alex said, pulling Jack's arm.

———

FOR A MOMENT, ALEX had not understood how to get off the property and back to where they had parked. The gate was automatic, triggered by cars but not by Alex and Jack, and she considered the problem. Could they climb over, or squeeze through the sides? Maybe someone from the house was watching their departure: the gate suddenly swung open.

Jack's face was set in a grimace, his gait unsteady.

"What was that about?" Alex said

"Nothing," he said. "People hate Max. I don't know. He got drugs for Lily but she asked him to, so it's not really his fault. Noah's being a dick."

She followed him to the car. Alex had assumed they would sleep here, at this party.

"Is there a place we can go?" she said. "Maybe we can sleep at yours?"

Jack looked genuinely distressed by this suggestion, genuinely disoriented.

"My dad's home. My dad and my stepmom. I don't wanna go there."

"Okay," Alex said. "So. Is there a place that's not your dad's house? Like, somewhere else?"

He had to lean back against the car for support. "What about your friend's house?" he said. "Where I picked you up?"

"I can't stay there," Alex said. "I'm kind of fighting," she said. "With my friend."

He was too drunk to ask any follow-up questions.

"Let me just think," he said. "I dunno, there's probably, like, a hotel?"

"There's a hotel around here?"

It was not an area where there were many hotels: this was not a place for visitors, as had been made abundantly clear.

"I'm not fucking going to my dad's house," Jack said, suddenly incensed.

"Relax," Alex said, "relax, I didn't say we had to go there. Why don't I drive?" she said. "I'll just drive us in that direction."

She had to adjust the driver's seat. It was like driving a tank, being up this high. When she turned on the ignition, the music was on so loud that she startled, but Jack didn't react: his sweatshirt hood was up, his body slumped in the passenger seat. He opened a pill bottle and deposited a small plastic bag inside—the drugs from Max—and now he was turning the pill bottle around in his hands, picking at the label with a fingernail, his feet braced against the dashboard.

"Maybe I know a place," he finally said.

"I'm just gonna drive, okay?" Alex said. "You tell me where to go."

ALEX HAD TO TURN the car around twice, Jack forgetting to tell her when to veer left, Jack not knowing the actual names of roads.

"I'll know it when I see it," Jack said. "There's a house on the corner before the turn."

When Alex reversed, the backup camera came to life, showing video feed of the asphalt. It was disorienting.

She drove back the way they'd come.

"How come you don't tell me anything?" Jack said suddenly.

Alex focused on the road. "What kind of things?"

"Anything. Like, I don't know where you're from. That's weird, right?"

"I don't know," she said. "It's boring." They had already gone down this stretch of road once: she strained to see whether the gas station was familiar or not, the shuttered farm stand and a field cut into rows, covered with plastic netting.

"Not weird like bad," Jack said. "I just wanna know. Where you're from."

"Oh. Upstate." She had said this at dinner, hadn't she? She glanced at him—would he be too drunk to even remember this conversation in the morning?

"And now," he said, "you live in the city. And you went to college—"

"In the city, too. I'm boring," she said.

"No." He sat up straighter in the passenger seat. "You're not." He burped softly, swallowed it.

They could park at the beach, she was thinking, if it came down to it, and sleep in the back of the car. That would be fine, and she had resigned herself to this when Jack suddenly tapped his window.

"Here," he said, "take a right here. Turn there."

They glided down a residential road. "Where are we going?"

"This one," Jack said, in front of a black gate, hedges on either side. "Yeah, turn in here."

"There's a gate."

"Yeah, I know the code."

Alex rolled down the window.

"Pound one-nine-seven-one."

The intercom beeped atonally, the light flashing red.

"Try again," he said.

It still didn't work.

"Now try without the pound?"

Nothing.

"I guess they changed it," Jack said. "Hold on."

He got out but left the passenger door open, the alarm dinging at regular intervals. In the LED glare of the headlights, she watched Jack crouch to shimmy an arm and shoulder between the hedge and the gate. When the gate began to creak open, he jumped to his feet and pulled himself back in the car. He grinned. "There's a button," he said, "on the other side. Easy."

9

THERE WERE NO LIGHTS on the property, no lights anywhere, just the cut of their headlights on the driveway.
Then the faint outline of a house, darker than the sky. As
they pulled up, Alex saw there were two houses, really—
a small gray-shingled house, like a perfect rectangular block
dropped onto the land, and a bigger house, half covered
with a tarp that made a heavy ripping noise in the wind.

"Good?" Jack said, turning to her.

She smiled but didn't say anything, and noticed how
that made him perk up, her withholding.

Alex followed him out of the car, but left her bag inside
until she saw how this shook out.

The house, Jack told her, belonged to the family of his
high school girlfriend.

"They're really nice," he said. "The whole family." She
gathered that they had been close, that the family had been
kind to Jack. Still, Jack only spoke about the parents, how

great they were. He didn't mention anything specific about the girlfriend. Was that strange? The parents took Jack along on family trips. Talked to his dad when things got bad. They stood up for him, Jack said.

"Where are they now?"

"They're usually here all summer but the house is getting renovated." He gestured at the tarp. "See all that shit?"

"So people are gonna be here in the morning? Construction guys?"

"Nah," he said. "It's, like, historic, so the town made them stop construction. They're suing or something. My dad says it's insane to buy an older house. It's nothing but problems. The pool house," he said, pointing to the smaller building.

"Why don't they just stay there?"

Jack shrugged. Maybe their summer was a rarefied commodity, one that couldn't tolerate any interruption, any downsizing.

THEY CIRCLED THE POOL house twice, Alex following Jack. All the doors were locked. Jack tried the sliding glass door without success.

Jack looked flustered. "Shit." He kicked the ground. "Fuck." He sat cross-legged in the driveway. "I'm sorry."

Alex circled the pool house again, checking for any windows that might be open. Nothing.

Jack was still sitting on the ground, wearing those sheepskin slippers. His head was in his hands, his hood up.

"Did they keep a key anywhere?"

"I dunno," Jack said. "It was just always open when I was here."

Alex lifted a few rocks by the pool house door. Then went to the back door. She pressed her fingers in the dirt of a few potted trees until she found it—a set of keys, a red plastic tag on the ring.

"Shit," he said, when Alex handed the keys over. "How'd you know how to do that?"

"I don't know," she said. "People are pretty much the same, you know? If you think, where would I hide a key, then probably other people think that, too."

The front door stuck a little, Jack leaning his full weight against it before it opened. A dark living room, the air stale and the curtains closed. When Jack flicked on the light, a galley kitchen was visible through a doorway. A hallway with a carpeted staircase that led, Alex assumed, to the bedrooms.

She checked the bathroom first—no medication, just unopened aspirin, some natural toothpaste. Alex put some on her finger, mashed the grainy paste against the roof of her mouth with her tongue. As she peed, she checked her phone. It turned on, for a minute, long enough to see the scrap of a new message from Dom—*do you want me to come out there*—then the screen rippled gray.

She studied the print on the wall: a black-and-white photo of a giant wave about to crest.

JACK WAS LYING ON the living room couch. His shoes were still on and his sweatshirt hood was pulled up.

"You okay?"

"My head hurts." He'd emptied his sweatshirt pocket—there was the pill bottle on the coffee table next to his phone.

"You want some water?"

He didn't move.

The kitchen floor was tiled in black and white squares. Inside the pantry were many varieties of unopened water crackers. Sparkling apple cider (nonalcoholic), a giant plastic tub of waxy chocolate almonds. Party food. The refrigerator was empty except for an orange box of baking soda. A few bags of frost-struck pineapple and a microwave pizza in the freezer, a cloudy bottle of tequila. She ripped open a sleeve of water crackers and ate a handful of the thin discs, powdery with black pepper, until their dryness made her queasy. She filled a glass with tap water and brought it to the living room.

Jack was snoring, curled into a ball, his body half wedged between the couch cushions. She left the glass on the coffee table. She glanced at the pill bottle. Pills inside, and the little baggie from Max. The prescription label was in Jack's name. She didn't recognize the name of the medication. She knew she wouldn't google it. Did she already sense it could only confirm something she did not exactly want to confirm?

ALEX WALKED THROUGH THE other rooms. You could get a sense of the absent family. How they made the detritus of living tidy, legible, even in these non-spaces. Even in a pool house, there was an impulse toward order. The manuals for the electronics in one drawer, organized and labeled. All the systems in place, all the uncertainties accounted for.

What was the old girlfriend like? Alex imagined a quiet girl who kept a journal and was nationally ranked in tennis and studied hard for every exam. Had they been in love, Jack and the girl?

There were clothes in the hall closet, but they weren't nice—they seemed like extra clothes, sweaters and a raincoat, rain boots, a basket of flip-flops. No money in the pockets of any of the coats, none in any of the drawers. A few quarters, a twenty in a cabinet of the laundry room that looked like it had gone through the wash, the bill leached of color. It was torn almost in half; she folded it in her pocket. Out the window, she could see the light was still on in Jack's car. It gave off a strange aquatic cast, like the car was filled with water. She went out to get her bag. Closed the car doors hard so the light flicked off.

Jack was still asleep.

"Good night," Alex said, her hand resting on his shoulder for a brief second. He turned over, his face squished from the cushions, pink looking and damp.

"Love you," he mumbled, reflexively, lips smacking together, his legs stretching out. He was still wearing his sheepskin slippers.

"Wanna come to the bed?"

"Stay with me," he said, nestling to the side to make room for her, his eyes closed, and even though she had seen the bedroom, the clean room with clean sheets on the bed, she slipped off her own shoes, her cutoffs, and lay next to him on the couch.

Good, she thought, good. And like that, the pressure she'd felt all night crested into a steady hum of nothing. Another day was almost over. A few more days till the party. Basically two days. And even though Dom knew she was out east, he didn't know where she was, exactly. What was he going to do, wander the streets looking for her? She didn't need to be afraid. Not out here, anyway. Not right this minute.

"Mm," Jack mumbled, reaching out for her. "Baby," he said, pulling her close.

She would just lie here for a second, she thought, that's what she told herself, but when she opened her eyes next, the room was bright and Jack was still sleeping soundly beside her, the untouched glass of water on the coffee table filling with sunlight.

ALEX UNLOCKED THE SLIDING doors to get to the pool, which had a gray plastic cover stretched tight over the surface. The day was already hot. Alex was in her underwear and bare feet, a T-shirt she tied in a knot, exposing her stomach. Two and a half painkillers, this morning—this seemed abstemious, responsible, though she'd taken less mostly because there were fewer and fewer pills remaining. Simon's party was in two days. She'd take the other half this afternoon, another pill in the evening, though better if she could hold off till tomorrow, and if she resisted the urge to double up, she'd have enough to get through the party.

She didn't want to think about what she'd do when the pills were gone. By that time, anyway, she'd be back with Simon. So it would be a solvable problem.

The pool situation, through the stolen sunglasses, looked promising. There was a covered hot tub sunk into the ground. A few patio chairs without their cushions, just spidery black iron frames. She circled the pool and bent at regular intervals to unhook the cover. Her optimism faltered when she got the cover off. The water was dirty. Biscuit-colored foam floated on the surface, visible grit settled on the pool's bottom. She crouched down: the water was freezing.

The garden shed was padlocked, but the way certain numbers had faded made it obvious what the code was. She just had to experiment with the last wheel, trying the next number and then the number before. The padlock dropped open. There was an automatic pool cleaner in the shed, its hose coiled neatly and hung from a pegboard, but she didn't know how to work it. Easy enough to use the blue net.

Soothing to dip the net in the water, to begin to gather the mess, collect the wet slop of leaves. The pills had their desired effect, produced a pleasant tightening in her chest. She could fall into a nice sort of rhythm, skimming the net along the surface, trying not to disturb the pockets of debris. Even after a steady run of work, the pool wasn't getting any cleaner, a gauzy cast to the water. Too gross to swim. And too cold, anyway. Oh well. Oh well.

She abandoned the net. She lay back in the sun.

It had been less than a week since she'd left Simon's house—was that possible? Could she even count how many days had passed? Not without effort. She'd left Simon's on

Tuesday. Today was Saturday. Time had started to feel a little slurred, a little unreal.

It was intolerable, in a way. Unbearable. But then, it *had* been tolerable, hadn't it? Because here she was. A familiar feeling, a dim feeling she could conjure too easily. The times she knew, with certainty, that she did not exist. It had been terrifying, at first. Certain days in the city that passed without anything imprinting on her. Heavy summer thunderstorms outside. Alex picking at her legs until they bled, eating bags of carrots until she was sick—she kept eating anyway. The nausea compacted in on itself, eventually. Certain hours of the night where doom made a terrible sense, where it seemed like the only possible outcome.

It was less frightening to feel that way now. Here, by this cold pool. Maybe she was the ghost she had always imagined herself to be. Maybe it was a relief.

SHE TOOK A QUICK SHOWER, then dried herself with one of the big beach towels. Combed her hair and parted it straight down the middle. Too hot to put on anything but underwear and another T-shirt. Jack was still asleep. In her absence, he had starfished over the couch, limbs bent at what looked like an uncomfortable angle. It was almost noon.

There was a coffee maker in the kitchen but no coffee. She boiled water for tea, the tea bags crunchy and dry. The tea tasted fine, still potent enough for a hit of caffeine.

Alex put on shoes to check out the main house. The scale was so overlarge, almost institutional. All these manor

houses, out here, summer palaces. Inside the house, she assumed, would be better things: better clothes, better meds,
but the doors, of course, were locked, and the tarp was
pulled tight across half the roof, a hot electric blue, everything else gray and beige and green. She walked around the
exterior. The curtains and shades were drawn, but through
a crack she could see what looked like the living room:
nothing on the walls. So they'd put the nice things in storage, she assumed. A few bulky pieces of furniture covered
with sheets, cardboard taped on the floors to make a walk-
way. From what she could tell, they'd demolished half the
roof before construction stopped. And here, through the
crack, she could see the regular beep of a red light coming
from a panel by the door. The main house, naturally, had a
security system.

Jack would be awake soon, and he would probably start
making moves toward getting the day started, going back
to his parents' house. Asking Alex where he should drop
her off. What would Alex do then?

It rushed at her, all the scrambling she would have to do
between now and the party. She let herself imagine giving
up. Imagined getting Jack to drop her off at the station,
imagined going back to the city. She pretended this was an
option. She knew it wasn't.

Why couldn't she stay here, on this empty property, in
this unused pool house? Just until the party. Two days:
barely any time at all. The owners didn't even care enough
about the pool house to install a security system. Wouldn't
it just be an efficient allocation of resources, matter rushing
in to fill a void?

So: figure out some interim spot where Jack could drop her off, and then make her way back here. She reminded herself to note the address before they left. Make sure she understood how to open the gate. Logistics were already crowding in, making her tired—this is what people like Simon got to avoid, the constant churn of anxieties somehow both punishingly urgent and punishingly boring.

JACK WASN'T IN THE living room. Wasn't in the kitchen. She found him outside by the pool, sitting on one of the patio chairs without cushions. He was wearing those sheepskin slippers.

"I thought maybe you left," Jack said.

"Nope," Alex said. "Still here."

He smiled. Made a tentative gesture for her to come over.

Another possibility—Jack could stay here, with her. Wouldn't that be the safest arrangement? Or could she go with him and stay at his father's house?

She got close enough to see the sleep in his eyes.

"What's your day like?" Alex said. "Can you hang for a bit?"

Before he could respond, Alex sat on his lap, still in her underwear and shirt. When she kissed him, his breath was actively unpleasant—but somehow his youth neutralized it, so she didn't mind as much. His mouth was too urgent but his hands were limp by his side. She had to grab a hand and place it, physically, on her breast.

"God," Jack said, his face going soft.

———

THE BOY HAD A birthmark on his shoulder—it was something Alex could sense bothered him, Jack tracking where her eyes went as she pulled his shirt off. He was, surprisingly, uncircumcised. His dick was the same even tan as the rest of him—how?—his golden curled pubic hair that went down his thighs, his slim calves. He cupped his dick and looked at her. He was embarrassed, she understood, but it was easy to make him not embarrassed, easy to smile, to show that nothing, absolutely nothing, would faze her in any way.

That's what they all wanted, wasn't it? To see, in the face of another, pure acceptance. Simple, really, but still rare enough that people didn't get it from their families, didn't get it from their partners, had to seek it out from someone like Alex.

He was grateful, overly grateful, when Alex kneeled in front of him and took off her own shirt.

"Oh god," he said.

His forehead was sweating. The power she felt was almost distressing, an awareness of each tick of Jack's insecurities, his needs. Like when she'd first moved to the city, and the men's humanness had been overwhelming to her, psychically exhausting. But then some veil had dropped, or Alex had adapted. The men had stopped being specific. It made things easier.

Jack looked continuously shocked at what was happening, at how his body was sweeping him along.

"Does this feel good?" she said.

He nodded.

"Here," she said, spreading out his abandoned T-shirt on the patio. The concrete was warm from the sun.

"Should we go in the house?"

"Nah." She patted the ground beside her. "Come here."

He was mostly silent. Whenever she spoke, it seemed to inflame him more, no matter how banal the phrases were, how rote.

"You feel good," she said in his ear. He shuddered.

She had to use her hand to guide him: he kept jabbing at her in a way that made her think he didn't have much experience. He played through only the most obvious motions, the basic moves. Still. She was wet, enough that she felt it on her thighs, on his spread-out shirt.

"God," he kept repeating. His face was flushed. "God."

When he was finished, he looked shocked, ill.

"Thank you," he said, his eyes unfocused, wheezing as he looked up at the sky. "Fuck."

THEY WATCHED A MOVIE on cable. A cop had his face surgically replaced with the face of a famous criminal, but then the criminal used the cop's face as his own and somehow this made sense in the universe of the movie, where faces could easily be unzipped from bodies, float in petri dishes until they were useful.

"The effects are so cheesy," Jack said. "Look, it doesn't even look like him, you can tell it's just a stuntman."

Jack's hair was damp, Jack in his boxers and shirt, taking periodic pulls from his vape. Alex was in her underwear and nothing else, her head on Jack's shoulder. They ate chocolate-covered almonds from the plastic tub—she couldn't stop, handful after handful, the cheap chocolate melting in her palm, going into a trance of sugar.

Jack was in some ways so shockingly confident. He giggled without self-consciousness at the movie. "Face off," he said to himself. Laughing. "Face. Off." He assumed her attention when he spoke. He had his insecurities, his anxieties, but underlying it all was the certainty that the world would be generous in its orientation toward him.

"Why don't you ever text anyone?" Jack said, during a commercial. "You, like, never check your phone."

"It's sort of broken."

"Don't you have to tell anyone where you are?"

Alex laughed, keeping her voice light. "Not really."

"That's weird."

"Weird?"

"I don't know, you just do what you want?"

Jack made this sound nice. Alex shrugged. "Mostly. And, I mean. It's summer, right?" It was already September—she tried not to think about this.

"You're lucky." He shoved more chocolate almonds in his mouth with one hand, the other arm around her shoulder. "I wish I lived on my own."

"You'll be in school pretty soon," she said. "Right?"

"Yeah," he said, darting a look at her. "Yeah, totally. But now, I mean. I wish I had my own place now. Like, I wish we could just stay here and I never had to go home."

She kept her eyes on the TV—better that way, more casual.

"Couldn't you?" She inspected her fingernails.

"Stay here?" Jack said.

"But I guess your parents . . . ," she offered.

"My dad would be happy if I was gone. They don't care."

"I'm sure they do," Alex said, "I'm sure they care," though, as she said it, she didn't believe it was true. Even for people like Jack, with parents like his. Or the kids at the party the night before. Hundreds of years ago, their parents might have abandoned their babies in the woods. Instead, the neglect was stretched out over many years, a slow-motion withering. The kids were still abandoned, still neglected in the woods, but the forest was lovely.

And anyway, most people didn't feel the way they were supposed to feel. Love as a sort of catch-all term whose mere invocation was enough, a way to avoid having to acknowledge how you actually felt. It would be easier for Jack if he didn't expect so much, if he understood these words were just gestures at meaning, not meaning itself.

"It's basically just my dad," Jack said. "And he's a psycho. I should just stay here. Fuck it."

She laughed like Jack was joking. It had to seem like his idea, had to feel like something he was making happen. He changed the channel. They watched commercials, then part of a show where two men stuffed caviar in their faces while a laugh track played. Their hands were gritty with it, their chins covered, the caviar glinting like tiny black diamonds.

DOING A LOAD OF laundry was gratifyingly domestic. As if this house were Alex's and not a stranger's.

"Why'd you have all this stuff with you?" Jack said. "All these clothes." He sat on top of the dryer with a sleeve of crackers. He chewed with his mouth open, that one recurring lapse in his manners.

"Just in case." She pressed the Start button, the water rushing in. She closed the lid.

"Should we swim?" he said.

"The pool's gross," Alex said. "Beach? How close are we?"

"Let's ride bikes," he said, suddenly energized.

There was a fleet of bicycles in the garage, bicycles and folding chairs and a rack of new-looking surfboards, and all of the missing patio cushions stacked and covered with a tarp. Though it took some effort, cobwebs catching in her hair, they rolled out two bikes onto the gravel of the driveway. He filled the flat tires with a dusty bike pump. Spiders had made homes in the pedals, across the handlebars—Alex used a stick to collect the webs, twirling until the end was cottony. A spider skittered toward her: she flung the stick into the hydrangeas.

They packed an old tote bag they'd found in the closet with towels, her book, Jack's vape. Another sleeve of water crackers. A thermos she'd filled with tequila and seltzer and a handful of frozen pineapple, why not. The pineapple struck Jack as an act of great ingenuity. He took a sip before she screwed on the cap.

"So good," he announced. Jack wore a white bucket hat, also unearthed from the closet, and sunglasses that appeared to belong to a woman.

It was a ten-minute ride to the beach—Alex pedaled hard enough that her hair lifted, the lawns and hedges passing at a good clip but never so quickly that she couldn't make them out in detail. Jack pedaled his bike fast, all at once, like a very young kid, then stood up on his pedals and coasted, looking over his shoulder to see if she was following.

"You're going so slow," he said, pedaling around her in wide, lazy circles.

He navigated confidently, turning down one shadowy lane, then following the curve of road along a grassy pasture. When cars came up behind him, he didn't rush to move out of their way.

SIMON HAD ONLY EVER come to the beach with Alex that first time: she had gotten used to spending days at the beach alone. It was more fun with another person.

Jack was a strong swimmer, puppyish in the water, pulling her under a wave so they both came up sputtering. She had her arms around his neck, her legs around his waist. He was shy about kissing her, at first, though she could tell he wanted to. When he did, his lips were chilled and salty.

They got out of the water only after their fingers started to wrinkle. It made it obvious that Jack bit his fingernails— the skin there was shock white, gnawed ragged. It hurt to look at.

The sun was strong today, her skin drying almost instantly, the towel big enough that they could lie side by side. They passed the thermos back and forth, ice knocking around, both of them in their sunglasses. She was dimly aware that she was keeping an eye out for Dom. But after a while, she stopped. It was dumb. A woman walked past, worrying a phone in one hand, and she glanced over at Alex and Jack. Alex tensed up, out of habit. But Alex was being crazy. There was nothing hidden in the woman's gaze, no submerged question—Alex and Jack made sense.

JACK WAS BODYSURFING, GAMELY throwing himself in the waves over and over. He was pretty good, actually. Alex closed her eyes, just for a minute. All this sun made her drowsy. Something wet touched her leg: she jerked up. A dog, black and shaggy, was nosing at her ankles. She scooted away and pulled the tote onto her lap.

"Go on," Alex said. She looked around, expecting the dog's owner.

Nothing.

By now, the beach had gotten more crowded, and there were a few other dogs trotting around, though you weren't supposed to let them off leash. Still, it didn't seem like anyone was looking for this dog—no one whistling, no one stalking the rows of towels.

Alex patted the dog's head. The tag on his collar was printed with a phone number. So there was an owner, and they'd be along any minute. She kept up a scan of the beach. No one came. Nothing else for her to do—it wasn't her problem. The dog would eventually make his way back to whoever he belonged to. For now, the dog was mellow enough, happy to curl up on the end of her towel, his tail heavy across her feet. Alex lay down again, a hand falling over her eyes, and drifted into a sun-splotched half-dream.

Shouting broke through her sleep. It took a moment to realize the shouting was aimed at her.

"You," the voice was saying, "you, striped towel."

She blinked and sat up. The shouting was coming from the woman on a nearby blanket, one hand gripping the black dog's collar. The man beside her was trying to protect the contents of a wicker basket: from the looks of it, the dog had already gotten into the food and left a scattering of lentil salad.

"Your dog," the woman said, up on her knees. "Can you call your dog?"

Alex looked around. "It's not mine."

"What?"

"I don't know whose dog it is."

The woman gave a harsh laugh. "We saw it with you."

"I didn't—he's not mine."

The woman was exasperated now, her fake good cheer wearing thin. "Can you just please control your dog?"

Alex could feel other people noticing the exchange. She tried to arrange her face to broadcast ease.

"I mean, I'll help but—"

Alex got up, making her way to their blanket. The woman thrust the dog at her by the collar.

"It's really not mine," Alex said. For once, she was not lying. That seemed important.

The woman wiped the seat of her white shorts, tucked her hair behind her ears.

"Okay," the woman said, casting a look at the man. "Sure. Okay."

———

JACK WAS DRIPPING WET. His nose glowed with sun-burn.

"Whose dog?"

"Mine," she said, "apparently. He just showed up."

Jack bent to scratch the dog's ears. "Good boy," he said. "You're a good boy."

He studied the tag on the collar.

"Should we call?" Alex said.

Jack shrugged. "I don't get service here. And I'm sure someone will come looking." He wrapped a towel around himself, then sat down and pulled the dog toward him. "He's just a baby, isn't he? You're a baby."

Jack let the dog lick his mouth. "He likes me," he said, hugging the dog with his still-dripping arms.

Another hour on the sand, the thermos long empty, the sun dropping, and neither of them said anything about calling the phone number on the dog's collar. No one stopped at their towel, no one claimed the dog. And then it was dusk, the air speckled with almost invisible gnats, and Jack yawned. He dumped the last crumbs from the sleeve of water crackers into his mouth, then balled up the plastic.

"I want real food," he said.

"What about the dog?" Alex said.

He shrugged. "If his owners took good care of him, wouldn't someone be looking? Let's just keep him."

She raised her eyebrows.

"For the night. We'll call in the morning. It'll be fun," he said.

She studied the dog, the almost-empty beach. What did it matter to her, either way? She'd be at Simon's by the time any real decision would have to be made.

THEY WALKED THE BICYCLES back, both of them a little tipsy, the dog trailing behind. The sun was low enough that they didn't need their sunglasses. The faint haze of mosquitoes hummed along the tree line; porch lights went on, car headlights, too, though the sky was still blue.

"I know where we are," Alex said, suddenly. They were not so far from Simon's house. The walled property, the driveway laid with smooth gray stones. Simon hidden somewhere inside, the rooms of the house cool and empty. He'd be happy to see her. At the party. Wouldn't he? "My friend lives around here."

"Who?"

Jack was studying her face. Why had she brought up Simon? She avoided Jack's eyes.

"Just someone I knew. A while ago. A long time ago."

The dog stared up at both of them.

"He needs water," Alex said. "What are we gonna feed him?"

"I'll handle it." The dog was sniffing Jack's outstretched hand, nuzzling against him. "He likes us," Jack announced. "He could just run away if he wanted to, but he's not."

Jack got on his bike and pedaled, the dog trotting alongside.

"See?" he called over his shoulder.

Alex climbed on her own bike, trying to catch up. Jack

was breathing hard, almost laughing. Alex felt it, too. How the farther they got from the beach, the more it seemed funny, the sudden fact of the dog, this animal loping at their side like an emissary from another, better world.

"THIS IS YOUR NEW HOME," Jack said, as the dog studied each corner of the pool house. The couch. The kitchen trash. "He likes it here. I can tell," Jack said. "Siddhartha says that meditating gets you in an animal state. He said he was like a jackal. In the book. That's kind of like a dog, right?"

"Let's get him water." Alex filled a cereal bowl—the moment she put it on the floor, the dog crashed into it, knocking it all over. Alex dropped a paper towel over the spill. Refilled the bowl.

Jack looked through the cabinet. "What does he wanna eat? Hmm, doggo? What do you want for your dinner?" Frozen pizza, Jack decided. "Dogs can eat pizza, right?"

While Alex turned on the oven, unearthed a sheet pan scabbed with burnt food, Jack poured two glasses of tequila, dropping a handful of ice in each.

"Thirty minutes," he read off the pizza box. He handed her a glass. The dog watched from the floor, perched on his front legs like a sphinx. Jack had insisted on trying to fix Alex's phone—it was presently nestled in a bag of old-smelling rice.

Jack drank, wiped his mouth. "I really," he said, "don't want to go back to the city."

"Doesn't school start pretty soon?" She took a sip.

"Maybe it'll be fun. After the time off." She couldn't tell, from his face, whether this break from school was a sore subject.

"Yeah, maybe."

"I bet it was weird. Not being there," she said. "While everyone else was still there. All your friends."

"I kind of had to take the year off. He said I had to. My dad. And I guess the school, too."

"Why?"

"I don't know. I was having a bad time." Jack was staring up at the ceiling. "I didn't really mean to do anything," he said, "but everyone was really freaked out. I just was pretty upset about this girl."

"Your girlfriend?"

"Yeah. I dunno, we fought a lot. And she wouldn't answer my calls to even let me apologize. I got kinda mad, I guess. Annie was freaked. But it was mostly her parents that flipped out."

He checked her face sideways.

"But you can't be like, 'It wasn't serious, I didn't mean to.' They don't believe you. It wasn't a big deal, though."

Alex tried to keep her expression impassive.

"Is this freaking you out?" Jack said, sadly.

"No," she said, without knowing if it was.

But it did unsettle her. The idea of Jack unstable, vulnerable. What had he done to the girl? Or to himself. Jack in his oversized car and sheepskin slippers. Something not quite right. She was so bad at reading people, lately. Probably it had been a mistake to stay here with him. Another miscalculation.

———

SHE TOOK A SHOWER, scrubbing her scalp hard and keeping her eyes closed against the running water. She needed
to get back to Simon, and that was the point, and this thing
with the kid had just been an unfortunate error.

"Alex?"

Her eyes snapped open. It startled her, Jack standing in
the bathroom, already in a towel.

"Sorry," he said. "Can I come in, too?"

A sad pleading in his face. She wanted to be alone. But
easier to smile, to hold the shower curtain aside so he could
step in. She soaped his body, the light dusting of chest hair
and the two pink nipples and the flat ass that was pimpled
but somehow still appealing. Jack kissed her with his eyes
closed, the water hitting his face. If she closed her eyes, too,
she could pretend he was Simon. Fast-forward to when
this would all be over, Alex back in her proper place.

When Alex's finger starting nudging around his asshole,
like Simon liked, Jack's eyes opened and he moved out of
the way of the showerhead.

"What are you doing?" he said, partly laughing but also,
she understood, partly afraid.

"Doesn't this feel nice?"

He allowed that it felt okay. "Kind of weird."

"Just relax," Alex said.

You could get off on it, she saw—the moment when she
knew Jack did not want her to do this, and the fact, contained in the same moment, that she would do it anyway.
Her finger was inside him, now, his eyes closed.

"Alex," he said.

When he came, bracing himself against the wall of the shower and gasping, she felt a release, too, like now she could be nicer to him. Like this made it easier for both of them, the lines drawn more clearly. She'd be gone soon enough.

IT WAS DARK BY the time Alex finished getting dressed. Jack wasn't in the bedroom, wasn't in the kitchen, wasn't in the living room. The dog was gone, too. Jack had turned off the oven, anyway, the pizza cooling on the counter.

Maybe it had been too much for him and Alex had crossed a line. Of course she had. Another thing she had torched. Hard to know exactly what she was feeling, whether she wished he hadn't left or whether she was relieved to be alone.

It didn't matter, either way, because when she looked out the window, she saw his car was still in the driveway.

SHE WAS FOLDING THE clothes from the dryer when she heard scratching at the front door. Had Jack locked himself out? But it was the dog, the dog who jumped up her legs as soon as she opened the door. She squinted into the darkness beyond: Jack was a few paces behind, his steps coiled and tense. He said something into his phone before hanging up.

"We went for a walk," he said.

Once inside, Jack paced in a tight circle. "Fuck," he said, mostly to himself.

"Is everything okay?"

It seemed possible he didn't even notice she was in the room, he was so absorbed in his pacing.

"My dad," Jack said, "is a fucking prick."

Without warning, Jack punched the wall, hard. The drywall crumpled, a black triangle that opened inward. The dog flinched, and Alex tried to keep the animal close.

"Hey," she said, "hey. Let's sit down."

Jack looked on the brink of tears, his mouth set tight and his hands in fists, but he let Alex lead him to the couch.

Jack's dad had, apparently, texted all of Jack's friends, and Max said he was demanding to know where Jack had slept last night, and he was tired of his father keeping tabs on him like this, acting like he was a kid, and nobody asked his dad where he slept all those nights he'd been gone for so-called work, had they?

"Suffocating," Jack said. "He makes me feel like I'm suffocating."

"It's okay," Alex said. "Maybe you both just need a little space."

Jack nodded.

"Yeah," he said, "yeah, that's it. I'm not going home. Let's just stay here, who cares."

"And he's okay if you take a few days? You told him that?"

Another nod. "God," he said again, overtaken, throwing himself back against the cushions.

Good to make him sit down, to let the adrenaline burn itself off. She patted Jack's back, lightly, just to indicate her presence, though it didn't help. He barely seemed to notice she was there.

Only the dog, jumping up on Jack's knees, knocked him out of the trance.

Jack's face split in a sudden smile. "Doggo," he said. "You're a good boy, huh? Aren't you?"

ALEX CUT THE PIZZA into ragged squares with a bread knife. Jack shifted a square onto a paper towel. He took small bites.

He had calmed down: another drink, another square of pizza. He apologized for his outburst, at least. So he was aware enough to know he'd acted badly.

"I'll fix the wall," Jack said, a wholly unlikely possibility, but one that he seemed to believe. They both averted their eyes from the yawn of drywall.

Jack picked errant cheese off the paper towel, rolling it into a ball before putting it in his mouth. He ripped off another piece for the dog, who perked in anticipation. Even as Jack seemed to compose himself, his speech picked up speed again. A conversation he was having with himself.

"You met him," Jack said. "My dad. So you get it. Didn't you see it right away?"

Jack was talking so fast she could barely track it.

He started almost to cry, telling some story about the puppy his stepmom had made his dad get. The puppy was peeing everywhere, tearing up the furniture, and everyone, he said, was just getting mad at the dog.

The worst thing, he said, was that they could have just sent the puppy away, there were places you could send puppies and they came back in a month or so, perfectly well behaved, perfectly trained. They could have paid their way out of this. Why wouldn't his dad just admit that he actually hated dogs, that he didn't care what happened to them? Everyone would have been happier.

"He just yells at the puppy," Jack said, "and the puppy doesn't even know why the fuck he's yelling at her."

Jack believed that people should be fully transparent, that everyone could just tell the truth and in this way avoid pain.

"She's getting fat now, too," Jack said. "My stepmom. A thyroid condition, she says—this doctor comes to inject her twice a week. But she's just getting fat. Sorry," he said. His voice sounded as though the words were being forced out of him. "Sorry. I won't talk about it anymore. You're annoyed with me, aren't you?"

Alex shook her head. "I'm fine."

"Okay," he said, "just tell me if I'm being annoying. Okay?"

He studied her with visible anxiety. Could he sense that she had pulled away? Did that make her feel powerful, clocking how agitated she could make him, how closely he was tracking her attention?

Alex crumpled up her paper towel.

"If it's a big deal," Alex said, "if your dad's really so mad, maybe you should go home."

"It's fine," Jack said, his voice jumping an octave. "Really, I'm sorry, okay?"

"I don't know, maybe it's better to just go back."

"Seriously?"

She didn't respond, washing her hands in the sink. The energy had turned, curdled. His unease was palpable.

"Well, why don't you go home?" he said. His voice was approaching shrill. That was new.

When she didn't say anything, he seemed to understand he had upset her. She was normally better about hiding those things.

They stared at different places in the room. A noise in the driveway made her meet Jack's eye. He didn't look worried.

Then a knock on the front door. Then someone opening the door without waiting for a response.

The owners? She stood up, instantly braced for trouble, but Jack barely reacted.

"Hey," Jack called out. "We're in the kitchen."

THERE, AMBLING INTO THE kitchen, was Max, sucking a smoothie through a straw, the smoothie a muddy-looking purple. He sucked audibly, leaned against the stove with his thin hips jutting out.

"Hi, Alex."

"Hi." She wasn't smiling, but she knew that she should smile, that smiling would be normal. Max looked between her and Jack with an inscrutable expression.

"Where's the bathroom, man?" Max said.

"Just back that way."

When Max left the room, Alex straightened but kept her voice low.

"You invited your friend over?"

"Yeah? So what?" Jack said. "Are you mad?"

"I mean. I don't know. We're in someone else's house. It's not exactly ideal to start inviting more people over."

"It's just Max," Jack said.

She heard the toilet flush; she just shook her head.

When Max returned, he lifted a slice of pizza, took a sniff, then dropped it back on the pan.

"Just visiting the outlaw," Max said. "Our little runaway. And the new dog." He petted the dog with careless attention.

Alex glanced at Jack: he looked unconcerned by Max's tone. Was there pride on his face?

"He told you Robert called me?" Max said to Alex. "They're freaking out." Max sucked harder on the straw, then shook the plastic cup, trying to knock something loose. "I told them I was sure you were fine."

Jack shrugged. She could see that the mention of his father made him anxious.

"And you are fine," Max said. "They're pissed your phone's been off."

"It's been dead, mostly," Jack said. "Dunno."

"But didn't you check in with them?" Alex said. "Your dad?"

Jack shrugged again.

Max was addressing Alex now. "You've met Robert, I assume?"

"Yeah," she said. "Once." Jack, she noted, was not looking at her.

"Nice guy," Max said. "But not happy with our friend here." He slapped Jack on the back.

"He's not that nice," Jack said.

"I'm not gonna say anything," Max said. "You're my friend, not them. I told them I didn't know where you were. Which was basically true, wasn't it? Until, oh, a half hour ago."

"But wait," Alex said, "it's only been, what, a night?"

Another shrug.

"Didn't you tell him you were staying with a friend or something?"

Jack didn't answer.

"You really don't know Robert, do you?" Max said.

"He's just protective," Jack mumbled.

"Well, yeah," Max said. "They said you left your meds at home."

Jack blushed.

"I'm not saying anything." Max gave up on the straw, plucking the lid off the plastic cup and tipping the contents into his mouth.

Alex looked from Max to Jack. Jack winced, his eyes jumping away from hers.

The silence that fell was loaded, Max noticing, surely, that Alex and Jack had both gone quiet.

"Shit," Jack said, when the dog squatted to pee. He shooed the dog toward the door. "I'm gonna take him out," he said, "just a sec."

Alex busied herself by opening a fresh roll of paper towels. She dropped a sheet on the puddle of urine. What exactly did this mean for her, the parents looking for Jack? Jack with his meds, the meds he was or wasn't taking. He was definitely not supposed to be here, at this girl's family's house. At least Jack didn't know Alex's full name. That was comforting. Alex could feel Max watching her.

Max shrugged. "Seems like you're pretty set, huh?" he said. "With our friend."

"Sorry?"

"Nothing." Max emptied his cup. He wiped his mouth. "Just, not really sure what he's getting out of this. I mean, I know, but I don't really know, right?" He laughed a little.

Best not to respond. She bent to pick up the sodden paper towel with pinched fingers and drop it in the trash. She washed her hands, thoroughly, more thoroughly than she needed to.

"I just don't like it," he said, "if I think someone is using him."

Alex wiped her wet hands on her shorts. "Right."

"Like," Max said, "why are you guys here? He's not supposed to fuck with Annie anymore, and definitely not break into her fucking house. Why can't he just stay with you?"

She was off her game—her mind was blank, no answer floating up as it usually did. Alex made herself shrug.

"Do you even have a car? You know he's seventeen, right?" Alex didn't move. Max's eyebrows rose. "Oh shit," he murmured, smiling.

Before she could respond, Jack came back to the kitchen.

"Hey," Jack said. He went to touch her; she felt Max watching.

"I'm tired," she heard herself say. Her voice was faint. "I'm just gonna lie down."

Max studied her as she got to her feet, and Jack looked anxious, too, all his feelings right there on the surface, and she didn't want to see it.

Max wiggled his fingers at her. "Sleep tight."

ANOTHER FIFTEEN MINUTES BEFORE Alex heard the sound of Max's car in the driveway. Jack appeared in the doorway of the bedroom. The room was dark. The dog was breathing audibly, curled around himself on the carpet.

"He's gone," Jack said. "Are you mad or something?"

What was this feeling? It was, what, feeling stupid?

It took a moment for her eyes to adjust to Jack's face. She had to look away: he looked especially young, in that moment, the babyish fat in his cheeks.

"Are you mad?" Jack said.

"I'm"—she stopped. She didn't know. He was seventeen. But better not to know, not to ask. The less information, the easier things would go. She should probably convince Jack he needed to go home. Because, no matter how she arranged things in her mind, they should probably not stay here. Definitely not together, and maybe she couldn't even stay alone, now that Max had seen her here, now that Jack would likely have to account for the missing day. Or days? It was already Saturday, she thought, how had that happened?

"Please," Jack said, his words spilling into each other, "don't be mad."

"I'm sure he's worried. Your dad." She spoke in a faraway tone. "We shouldn't be here."

Jack opened his mouth, then closed it.

"Sorry," he said finally. "I didn't know he'd be so mad. Can't we just stay one more night? He's mad already, he's not gonna be that much more mad."

She should insist. She was already implicated.

Could he could tell what she was about to say? He chose that moment to pull her phone from his pocket. He held it out to her, an offering. "I think it's working," he said.

"Seriously?"

When Alex turned on the phone, there was no stutter, no jar: her home screen appeared, bright and clear, and it was as if nothing had ever happened.

"Is it okay?" he said, but he knew by Alex's face that it was: he was obviously pleased.

Alex clicked through the phone, checked the browser. Everything was fine.

"Damn," she said.

"I told you," he said, but it was sweet.

Alex palmed the phone. She tried to imagine the night ahead. It was easier not to insist, easier to stay here—where would she go, anyway? She'd figure it out tomorrow.

10

ALEX STOPPED THE BIKE in the same beach parking lot, ringed by the same dunes. She left the bike leaning against the wooden fence, the dog at her side. Jack had still been asleep when she'd left. It was early enough, even on a holiday weekend, that the beach was mostly empty. A few surfers dragging their boards in the sand, an old man in a wetsuit and hood swimming ferocious lengths. No lifeguard posted up yet, no families staking claims with their tents and buckets. The dog ran to the water, then ran back to Alex, his fur wet and particular. When she scratched under the dog's chin, his tongue shot out, showing its crinkled black ridges.

The ocean was rough. The waves were high enough to scare Alex. But she'd come all this way. She waited until a set was over, then forced herself to get a running start. She had not timed it right: when she surfaced, a wave crashed into her, hitting with enough force that she was pinned to the sand. She sputtered underwater until she saw the white froth overhead dissipate.

"You okay?"

The man in the wetsuit was bobbing nearby with his wetsuit hood pulled back, his nostrils pinched shut with a piece of plastic.

She nodded, catching her breath. There was sand everywhere: she could feel it in her scalp, in her swimsuit bottoms.

"That last one really knocked you over, didn't it?" he said.

Alex smiled, tightly, gave a nod. "I'm fine," she said, "thanks."

He paused, as if he might say something more. Offer some further warning. Then he pulled his hood back over his head, disappearing under the water.

She forced herself to stay in the water a while longer, to keep bracing for the next wave. Conditioning herself to wait out the fear. To wear herself out. Even when she got knocked over again, it was thrilling this time, her head clear, the world winnowed to this immediate moment.

The water was the warmest it had been all summer. What did it mean that the waves had a milky cast? She tried to remember if that was a sign of something, some indication of favorable or unfavorable conditions. She didn't know, either way. So it didn't matter.

She kicked to stay in place.

She needed to get rid of the kid. That was the main thing. She'd already fucked up, spending so much time with him. And there were things she would have to think over before tomorrow. Certain things she would need to figure out how to explain to Simon, details she might need to soft-pedal. Dom still had to be dealt with. She didn't let herself dwell on whether she had caused new problems in the interim. The painting at George's. Whether this thing with Jack would end cleanly—how to tell the boy that she was leaving, that their temporary world was over. She would get herself to Simon's, and Jack would take care of himself. Return to his own home, his own family.

She ducked under the water. When she surfaced, she was farther out. Her body was moving her along. Moving her along as it always had. Water streamed into her eyes, pressurized her ears. She wiped her nose.

At some point, she knew, she would tire herself out. How far out could she get before that happened? A mile? More? She couldn't even start to guess, though; at this moment, it didn't feel impossible that she could swim forever, that she would never get tired.

Nothing terrible had happened, she told herself, nothing insurmountable—this had just been a brief dream, a rip in the ordinary fabric, and now it was explained, justified. She had continued on, persevered, because, in some part of herself, she knew this could all go back to the way it had been before, and that she had only to outlast it.

WHEN ALEX FINALLY GOT out and made her way to the shore, she saw the blood. A cut on her knee that glowed white when she wiped it clean, then pooled immediately with blood. The red looked too bright, like the bad special effects in that movie they had watched. The cut didn't hurt, just felt sparkly from the salt water. She sat with the towel pressed to her knee. Eventually, the bleeding stopped.

She ate a cold slice of pizza she'd brought in tinfoil, and then a second piece. That was the last of it. Dinner tonight—they'd figure something out. One more night to get through—that was nothing. Her phone was fixed. The party was tomorrow. The end was in sight.

In this state—her mind whirring—it took a while for Alex to notice the dog was gone. It didn't seem possible. She stood on the sand, scanning the beach. Her eyes skipped along but never landed on the thing she wanted to see. She walked one way. Then the other. She called out for the dog. She climbed to the top of a dune, shading her eyes. She jogged back to her towel. Expecting to find the dog waiting for her. The dog wasn't there.

The search was obviously futile. Still, she set out again in the other direction, whistling for the dog. She couldn't go back to Jack without the dog. The absence of the dog made her looming defection worse. If she could just give Jack the dog, then she could go to Simon's and all would be well. There was a cleanliness to that exchange. It made things fair, somehow.

Seagulls bombed a garbage can. Then scattered just as quickly.

Another fruitless scan of the beach.

Nothing. The dog had disappeared.

The dog was gone, truly gone. The sadness was instant, piercing—her eyes watered. But then, almost as quickly, the fact of the dog's absence seemed, all at once, like just a fact, another thing that she could not change, a thing she could not help.

"SHIT," JACK SAID, WHEN she walked in the house. "Are you okay?"

It took a second to understand: her knee.

"It looks worse than it actually is." She let her hand drift over the cut without actually touching it. A pause. "The dog ran away."

Jack didn't respond. Like if he kept waiting, she might say something different.

"It's my fault. I wasn't watching him."

"I don't get it," Jack said. "Did you look for him? Did you look?"

"Yeah," she said. "But at a certain point, it was, I don't know. There was nothing to do. I looked. A lot. He's gone."

It made it worse, how Jack tried to appease her.

"I'm sure it wasn't your fault," he said.

But wasn't it?

"We can look tomorrow," she offered. Though she would not be here tomorrow. "But I mean, maybe he was going home. Right? Back to his actual owners."

That prospect seemed to comfort Jack.

"Sorry," he kept saying, "sorry."

"Why are you apologizing? It's my fault, not yours."

She was speaking too briskly. Was it obvious, how little energy she had for him anymore? Even one more night felt interminable. She was too impatient for her new life to begin.

When he reached out to hug her, did he notice that she

stiffened? He didn't deserve her sudden coolness toward him—it wasn't his fault.

"Hey, I have an idea." He was trying to sound excited, trying to recruit her back. Close the distance between them. "You want to do molly?"

"Now?"

He brightened, seeing her interest.

"I have some," he said. Pleased he had something to offer. "Max gave it to me."

"You really want to do it today?"

"Don't you? It'll be fun."

She could sense the urgency behind his smile. Panic on a low-grade simmer. A not unfamiliar feeling, only Alex knew how to hide it.

Alex could give him another night. She owed him. A last go. Now that he didn't even have the dog. Alex would wait until the morning to tell him she was leaving.

Then she'd get herself to Simon's party. It was all moving forward.

WHEN IT STARTED TO get dark, Jack rattled his pill container in Alex's direction.

"Ready?"

Inside were a few pills she didn't recognize—his meds?—and a little glassine envelope printed with stars. It was full of a dun-colored powder, biggish crystals that Jack broke up by hitting the bag with the bottom of a drinking glass.

"We have to just eyeball it, I guess," he said.

Jack separated the powder into two piles: people were

never more focused and professional as when they were splitting drugs, suddenly fastidious. He licked a finger and dipped the tip into the pile before sucking the powder into his mouth. She did the same. The powder was bitter, coating her mouth and throat. She drank water but it didn't help.

"Ugh." She wiped at her tongue with the back of her hand.

"How long do we have to wait?" Jack said.

"Half an hour? Less? I dunno."

"Let's go in the hot tub."

"It's cold," she said. "The heater's off."

"So we'll turn it on."

THEY GOT INTO THE bed while they waited for the hot tub to warm up. Alex let Jack kiss her. Getting into the pure physical sensation of it. Which wasn't unpleasant. And who cared at this point? Why resist, why make too much of it? It was all nearly over.

Jack was on his stomach on the bed, Alex fingering the bumps on his back, the gaudy pimples that pushed out of his skin.

"Don't look at those," Jack said, twisting away.

"Come on."

He rolled over. "No, god, you're being weird."

"Please?"

"It's weird," he said.

"I want to."

"Why?" he said.

"It's fun. Let me."

He lay back on the bed. She straddled his ass.

It was quick, anyway: Alex finding the tight spots, pressing his skin until it suddenly erupted. She wiped her fingers on the sheets.

"I'm gross." Jack pushed his face into the mattress.

She rolled over so they were lying side by side.

"Oh," he said. His eyes squeezed shut.

The rush came on all at once. Alex's jaw was clenched—she forced herself to relax. Jack's hands were flexing, his toes too.

"I wish the dog was here," he said. "That'd be nice, right?"

Neither of them moved.

When she went to the bathroom, her face, in the mirror, was flushed. She didn't like seeing her eyes—there was almost no color, just pure black. As if there was no humanness in her.

All this adrenaline could go either way, good or bad. She tried to keep it tilting toward good. Telling herself the story: things were looking up, soon she'd be with Simon. A single night to get through, that was it. All this would wrap itself up.

"Look what I found," she said, coming back to the bedroom. There was a nightgown hanging on a hook in the bathroom: old-fashioned, white with a pink ribbon around the neckline. "I'm putting it on."

She took off her shirt to slip the nightgown over her head.

"You look pretty."

"It's just a joke." She glanced in the mirror on the dresser.

There they were, her black-hole eyes. She avoided her reflection.

"I'm so pink," she said, coming back to the bed. "My
face. I look crazy."

"You look pretty," Jack said, gazing at her. "You're really
pretty."

There was warmth in her chest. She looked around the
room. Where was her phone? Had she left it in the bathroom?

"My hands are really sweaty," he said.

"That's okay." Her hands were sweating, too. She was
chewing the inside of her mouth.

"I thought you were pretty when I first saw you," Jack
said, his voice almost a whisper. "And then I was so happy
when you talked to me."

"That's nice." She kept repeating this to herself, that everything was nice. Jack's eyes looked wet.

"You know the opening of *Siddhartha*?" he said. "Have
you read it? Should I read it?"

"If you want."

"Okay, just stay here. I'm gonna go grab it. It'll be like
one second. Are you gonna stay?" Did he know this was
their last night? Something in his urgent tone made her
think he could sense it, sense how she had already absented
herself.

IN THE SHADE OF *the house, in the sunshine on the river
bank by the boats, in the shade of the sallow wood and the fig
tree.*

Alex tuned out, listening to Jack's voice as he read without consciously tracking each word. Her eyes were closed. The moments smeared together, his voice coursing along.

Love touched the hearts of the Brahmans' young daughters when Siddhartha walked through the lanes of the town with the luminous forehead, with the eye of a king, with his slim hips.

Soothing, being read to. It offered just enough of a frame for her brain to relax into, like Jack's words short-circuited her own thoughts. She couldn't hold on to any details of what he read. Just a sense of forward motion, a journey. A man in search of something.

Siddhartha had started to nurse discontent in himself, he had started to feel that the love of his father and the love of his mother, and also the love of his friend, Govinda, would not bring him joy for ever and ever, would not nurse him, feed him, satisfy him.

Was the dog in the room? Alex could sense its presence. But no, the dog was gone. Gone where? Jack kept reading. His voice hit a steady rhythm, an incantatory hum.

The vessel was not full, the spirit was not content, the soul was not calm, the heart was not satisfied. The ablutions were good, but they were water, they did not wash off the sin, they did not heal the spirit's thirst, they did not relieve the fear in his heart. The sacrifices and the invocation of the gods were excellent—but was that all? Did the sacrifices give a happy fortune?

Alex couldn't tell how long Jack had been reading when he finally stopped. The room seemed changed somehow. In the silence. Like he'd shifted the atmosphere.

"Cool, right?" Jack said.

"Mm."

"Alex?"

She didn't want to open her eyes. As if it would upset this new balance. But she knew she had to. When she finally did, she saw Jack had put the book down.

"I think this is crazy to say," Jack said. "But I kind of love you. Is it crazy?"

"Sort of. Yeah. I've only known you a few days."

"But I feel that way."

"Are you crying?" She reached out to touch his wet face. "I think that's crying." She was trying to joke but it came out sounding serious.

He pushed his head against her chest. She ran her hands through his hair, his scalp hot and damp. She had done this for Simon, scratching his scalp with her nails.

Simon. Simon had not loved her. That seemed obvious. But it had been close enough. And close enough was fine.

It was coming on so fast. Her new life. Surging toward her.

"I really feel close to you," Jack said. "Really."

"It's the drug," she said, but her voice was faint—he couldn't hear her, or was pretending not to.

She sat back so she didn't see his face.

"Where are you?" he said. His voice wavering in the room. "How come I'm all alone?"

ALEX THOUGHT IT WAS Jack's phone, both of them jumping at the sudden ring—it didn't make sense, for a second, where the phone was located, because the ringing was coming from under them, coming from inside the sheets.

Jack groped around until he found the phone, Jack confidently answering, though right as he held the phone to his face, she understood that it was her phone. Even her urgency felt distant, packed in cotton.

"Hello," Jack said, in a half laugh.

"Stop," she said, reaching for her phone. "Give it."

She was laughing, too, but when she saw the name on the screen, she was suddenly, horribly sober.

Dom. On the call timer, the numbers were already ticking along.

14 seconds.

19 seconds.

Could she just hang up? She should just hang up.

24 seconds.

But she didn't. She tried to marshal herself. Force herself to focus on this situation. It was a struggle to hold on to what was happening.

Hang up, why not?

But another feeling, pushing its way to the light—maybe she could just explain things to him, Dom, just tell him the truth.

Alex brought the phone to her ear.

"Hello?"

A pause. What sounded like the universe whistling through the phone, though it was just static.

"Who is it?" Jack was saying. "Who's calling?"

Alex got up from the bed without looking at Jack and went into the bathroom. She closed the door behind her.

"Hi." Did her voice sound normal? The grid of tiles under her feet seemed especially stark. Was he in the city? Or was he out here somewhere? She didn't want to ask.

"Well," Dom said. "I've called you a hundred fucking times."

"My phone was broken," she said.

Alex sat on the edge of the bathtub. Her phone was broken, she was telling the truth. Why had she never tried that before, tried just telling the truth?

"Listen," Alex went on. "I can't pay you back."

He didn't say anything. Which was worse.

Another lag.

"Alex?"

"I can't. I thought I could, and I really tried to figure out how to. Like, fix this. But I can't." It was a relief to say it.

Silence. She kept going.

"I should have told you. Before."

"Alex."

Why did he keep saying her name like that?

The air rushed through the phone.

"You're fucking with me," he said, evenly.

"It's gone," she said. "All of it."

And she wished that wasn't true, she truly did. Didn't that count for something?

"Alex," Dom said again. But shouldn't he sound more angry? There was an unsettling note of triumph in his voice. Like this information wasn't new.

She blinked. The phone warmed her cheek.

The truth hadn't helped anything. Why had she thought it would?

"You think people get away with this shit?" Dom murmured. Something like a smile in the words. "I know you're staying with that guy. That Simon guy."

Alex stopped breathing.

Dom seemed to take her silence as a victory. "See?" he said. He was very calm. "I told you. That you couldn't just make this disappear."

Had he followed her? Or had he just wormed into her brain somehow, taken up residence there? Did he know what she thought before she thought it? Nothing seemed totally impossible, nothing beyond his purview.

"He seems like a nice guy," Dom said. "Seems like he probably doesn't know too much about you, right?"

She was quiet.

"Am I right, Alex?" He sounded like he was enjoying himself. "Am I right that he might be surprised by a few things?"

A solution. She'd come up with a solution. Something to say. She'd buy some time. But her mind was blank.

She watched the screen. The numbers sped ahead, second by second. Dom hadn't hung up either.

She pressed the red button, and the numbers stopped, her home screen appearing.

Dom was gone, the portal had closed.

"WHO CALLED?" JACK SAID. He was squeezing Alex's thigh. "Who was it?" It was easy to grab his hand. To ignore the question.

"Let's go outside," Alex said. This felt urgent. "Come on."

"I don't know. I like it in here."

"Let's just put our feet in the pool." She was holding his hand too tightly, smiling too broadly. "Okay?"

The hot tub was still cold. The heater wasn't working—it had been hours and the water was the same temperature. Another broken thing. Alex sat on the patio with her knees up inside the nightgown.

There were things that you actually could not fix.

Still. There must be a moment where this goes away, she told herself. A moment when the fear burns up all the psychic fuel that keeps it going and then, out of pure exhaustion, it will have to fall away.

But it wouldn't ever stop. She knew this. There was a hollow, alien sensation in her temples. No getting away. No correcting this error. She would never be able to relax, not really. She'd lost the thread.

JACK CAME BACK OUTSIDE with a bottle of room-temperature sparkling cider. They took turns drinking from the bottle. The cheap sweet bubbles. She couldn't sit still. The drug wasn't wearing off yet, but she knew it was going to, soon, the edges of her thoughts fraying.

All this effort. All this effort for nothing.

Jack reached out for her. His hand didn't quite make contact with her shoulder. "What's wrong?"

"The guy on the phone." Her shrug took extraordinary energy.

"Something happened?"

She didn't respond. She was aware her silence was inflaming, in Jack's mind, into all varieties of crisis. But that wasn't exactly incorrect.

"What's this guy's name?"

"You wouldn't know him. Doesn't matter." She didn't consciously decide to tell Jack something true. But what did it matter anymore? "I owe him money. Like, a lot of money."

Jack sat up. "Who is he?"

"This guy. He used to be a friend. Or whatever. He's really fucked up. I don't know what to do." She made an abbreviated attempt at a laugh. "I'm scared. Like, really scared." It was the truth. Another true thing.

His brow furrowed.

"How much money exactly?"

THE SAFE WAS IN his dad's closet. The combination was his dad's wedding anniversary—from his first marriage. There was cash in there—who knew how much, exactly, but enough. Jack had seen inside the safe once, when his father showed him where it was. Ran him through the whole thing. In case of emergencies. A gun, in the safe. A supply of antibiotics. Some gold coins, because that was the only trustworthy investment. If the world went to shit.

Jack presented this information like this was a perfectly reasonable solution. Like nothing had ever been more obvious.

"Come on," Alex said. "Stop."

But Jack didn't drop it. The more he talked, the more excited he got, swept up in the drama. Maybe this situation was something he could understand—Alex needed money. Jack had money. What was complicated?

It was ridiculous enough, at first, that it seemed like a joke. A dumb scheme, the fantasies of a teenager. Jack wanted to pretend he'd been kidnapped, then demand his dad provide ransom.

"Like that kid," he said, "with the ear. He kidnapped himself."

"How would that even work?"

"I'm sure I could figure it out," he said.

"That's crazy."

Jack was excited by the chance to force his father to prove exactly how much he loved him. The blunt emotional calculations that would have to be made. Then he was briefly concerned it could go the wrong way.

"Like, what if he doesn't pay?" Jack frowned. "No, he'd pay. He'd be too embarrassed if people found out he wouldn't pay."

"Come on." It still seemed fake. A game he was playing. "And you'd just, what, grab the money from the mailbox?"

"Yeah, I guess he'd, like, call the cops or whatever. Don't they, like, trace the money or something anyway?"

"It's not your problem," Alex said. "I'll figure something out."

But even as she said this, she could hear that she didn't sound very convincing. That some part of her was still allowing space for someone else to solve her problem.

And then he just suggested walking into the house and taking the money.

The simplest option.

The dad wouldn't even notice anything was gone. Why would he even check? And by the time he did, it wouldn't matter anyway.

"But that's crazy," Alex said. "Won't he be home? Won't your stepmom be there, or whoever?"

He shrugged. "Yeah, but not tomorrow. It's Labor Day. They go out on this boat. Every year. We'll just go in. It's my house, anyway. And he owes me."

THE LAST NIGHT.

Alex was especially loving to the boy. Attentive. She squeezed his hand. She kissed him with her eyes closed, with full focus. He looked drugged with happiness—so responsive to any tick of affection.

All the problems had disappeared. All the worries dropping away.

Her imminent departure made it easy to be kind. To pet his hair over and over. To say, when he said I love you, "I love you, too" and let him hug her more tightly. And she did love him, in a way—he had solved everything.

She would pay Dom back.

She would return to Simon.

All the wrongs would be corrected.

Already Alex was saying goodbye in her mind. Goodbye to the boy. Goodbye to the bed. Goodbye to the little house.

Jack spoke of places he wanted to take her in the city. Of a future that included both of them. She let him keep talking. Let him lull himself into a stupor, his words all slurred together. His eyes flashed in the dark. They could get a place together, he said. Figure out some way to make all this work.

"Sure," she kept saying. "Yeah. That sounds good." She scratched her fingers along his scalp. The way Simon liked. Jack made a moan of pleasure.

He groaned when she got up. "Don't go."

"I'm just getting a sweater."

When she unrolled the lilac sweater from her bag, the little onyx animal fell on the floor.

"Shit."

"I got it." Jack hung over the side to sweep an arm under the bed. He sat up, splaying his hand to reveal the animal in his palm. "I like this," he said. He held it out to her. The weight of the little animal surprised her. The stone felt cool, charged. Before she could think too hard about it, she handed it back.

"Keep it," she said. "It's yours."

"Really?"

She felt a pang, watching his hand close around the object. But then, like all feelings, it passed.

"I love you," he said. Drunk off his own solemnity. He probably believed life would always feel like this. This heightened, this vivid. A constant state of emotional inebriation.

Alex said it back.

I.

Love.

You.

Convincingly, she said it convincingly. Though she felt the familiar throb of a scowl on her face. Jack rested a finger on the furrow between her brows.

"You frown so much," he said. "Even while you sleep."

"Yeah," she said, flinching his finger away. She rubbed the spot like she could erase the wrinkle.

He fell asleep before she did. Mushed into the pillow, his mouth open. She could smell his breath. His lips were chapped. He looked like the teenager he was.

She would miss him, she told herself. He was a sweet boy. In the end. Wasn't he? And it was better this way. For both of them.

11

LABOR DAY. FINALLY.

Bad, anxious dreams, a bubble of dread in her chest when Alex woke up. But she could barely remember any specifics of the dreams, only a submerged sense of urgency, the knowledge that there was a task that she was failing at, that she would always fail at. By the time she got out of bed, the feeling was gone. Not even a memory.

The morning was overcast, the bushes outside seeming to hold dampness, a chilly breath emanating from the windows. Patchy clouds. Would it rain for the party? Simon's lawn wet and swampy and his guests huddled under a humid, dripping tent. She'd imagined a perfect day, a blue-sky reunion. But the rain would probably clear up by the time the party started, anyway. Simon usually got the things he wanted.

Jack wasn't in bed. Easier that way—she had some time alone. Each thought that appeared in her brain was smoothed to a psychotic polish. She played through the next steps, then played them through again.

A detour to Jack's house. Jack would get the money. She'd meet up with Dom, deal with that problem. Then she'd go to the party.

Dom had agreed to meet her at the train station. A public place, a comforting enough place. She'd have the money.

No fucking around, Dom had texted. And sent a screen-shot of Simon's company website.

Alex spent a long time in front of the bathroom mirror upstairs. Brushed her teeth hard enough that her gums bled, scrubbed her tongue with the toothbrush. She wanted to be clean, immaculate. She combed her hair, redid her part twice so that a white line of scalp showed. Lined her lashes with minute dashes of an eyeliner pencil. This labor all felt freighted, meaningful. It was like a meditation, proof of her piety, her good intentions.

Her last three pills.

She swallowed them, one after the other, with a scoop of water from the faucet. It made her clench up, the sight of the empty pill bottle. She filed the feeling away. Because soon she would be back at Simon's. Today. In a few hours. No more grasping, no more scrabbling.

Alex moved slowly. Gathering her things. Folding her clothes with care before putting them in the bag. Preparing for her exit. She would be on best behavior this time. She would never drop the ball again, not for a second. She would appreciate what she had.

Jack had agreed that it would make sense for them to

split up, for him to go home afterward, act like everything was normal. She'd pretended that they would meet up again in a few days. And what would Jack do when that didn't happen? When he realized she had disappeared? Jack would take care of himself. He'd be returned to his own home, his loving parents. Or good-enough parents. He didn't know her full name. So what could he even do to her, how would he even find her again?

Soon she would be with Simon. Dom would cease to exist. All of this would be funny, in retrospect. She would see it as an amusing break from the correct order, a sojourn into the wilderness that had always been just that: a detour, something temporary.

WHEN ALEX CAME DOWN the steps, Jack was stretched out on the couch in his satin basketball shorts and his big T-shirt. His forehead was dazzled with sweat. When he turned to look at her, he seemed concerned—what did he catch in her face?

She'd been grimacing. She made herself smile.

"You missed it," he said. "It was raining." He blinked out the window. "But it'll clear up," he went on. "Don't you think?"

"Sure."

He looked up at her again. A crooked smile. "They'll be leaving for the boat in like an hour."

The waiting made her antsy. She redid her eye makeup. Kept drinking half a glass of water, then forgetting where she'd left it.

Preparations for Simon's party would be gearing up. The caterers would be backing up their truck in Simon's service entrance. Emerging in pressed white shirts and dark pants, setting up burners and long folding tables. Extension cords in the grass, umbrellas blooming in the yard.

What was Lori doing right now? Scrambling around, running the show, trying to keep the dog away from the bartenders.

And Simon? Harder to picture what exactly he'd be doing. She let herself imagine him in the pool, cutting through the water. Laps always relaxed him.

She took an anxious little shit in the upstairs bathroom. Put in earrings, the earrings Simon had given her. They jittered in her lobes.

It had been Jack's idea, hadn't it? She hadn't asked him, hadn't forced him. He wanted to. And what if it went wrong? Would she have to account for herself, explain things? The most important point to make clear was that the boy had offered. And really, what seemed the more salient point was that, for a while, that brief stretch of days, everything had been good. Hadn't it? The boy slept late. The boy was happy and they swam in the ocean and returned with salt in their hair. They'd both gotten something out of this. A fair exchange, in the end.

THEY GOT INTO THE car in silence. Jack adjusted the mirrors. He took a big raggedy breath. "Ready?"

"Only if you're sure," Alex said. As if she didn't care either way, as if he might actually change his mind.

He drove with uncharacteristic focus—not fucking with his phone, not chattering away, not playing music.

Everything was okay, Alex told herself. Like there was a momentum that she could relax into. And it wasn't raining. Just a fine mist in the air, the sun already cracking through the clouds.

All the signs were good.

Maybe the first guests would already be arriving at Simon's. The older couples and parents with children, the foreigners who came promptly at the start time. There would be food in silver warming trays and sauces burping away on burners and sautéed shrimp flashing in pans. Bottles sweating in buckets of ice.

Better for Alex to show up when things were already in full swing. When the party had its own logic, its own inevitable unfolding. The Dom problem would be over and done with. She let herself watch the green world blurring past the windows, spacing out in a pleasant trance—here it was, nearly returned to her.

AT A STOPLIGHT, JACK kissed her with urgent attention, Alex feeling his lips, his tongue. He stared into her eyes with intensity. An unsettling intensity. A stranger, she thought to herself, this person is a stranger. But before the thought could bother her too much, the light turned green. Still, Jack kept gazing into her eyes. The car behind them honked, then swerved suddenly around them before speeding off.

Alex squeezed his knee. "Thank you."

Did she love him, in that moment? Something like it.

———

WHAT HAPPENED NEXT:

Jack slipped into his big white house, emerging with the money in a casual, easy way, like he'd dropped by for a glass of milk.

Alex gave the money to Dom. He was deleted from her life.

Alex went to the party.

Simon was happy to see her. Simon cleaved across the grass to meet her, taking her hands in his. He kissed her.

All was well.

OR THAT'S WHAT ALEX wished had happened. She could see it all so easily, each click of the frame advancing, so that it already felt real—of course she had solved all her problems. Of course it had all worked out.

What actually happened: Jack cleared his throat. He appeared to be driving down a street they had already been down.

Did she know, already? Was it obvious in his tone?

"Listen," he said.

The silence between them opened up—that's when she understood.

"There's no safe," the boy said. He kept looking at the road. "I don't know why I said there was."

Alex was quiet.

So it was over. So she would not be saved.

Ha. Ha ha.

He darted a glance at her. His cheeks were red. "I'm sorry, okay? I'm sorry."

Fine. Fine. A gag of rage appeared, then disappeared. Her mind was racing. A manic urgency was already overtaking her, a hilarity that teetered close to panic. All wasn't lost. It couldn't be. There were still things she could do. She'd do something. Do what? She couldn't meet Dom. But she could go to the party. She'd go to the party and she and Simon would make up. And so she'd explain. Lay it all out. And he'd help her. It would still work out.

Alex forced a neutral expression.

"Can you drop me off?" she said.

A flicker in Jack's face, a downshift. "Drop you off? Where?"

"A friend's house."

"What friend?" His voice was edgy. He had expected some reaction, surely, but not this one.

"A friend. But we can hang out again." The lie was obvious. Her words were limp, her performance half-hearted. She should have been more reassuring. Should act like she didn't care about his lie, didn't care about the money. She should be spinning out a vision of the future to soothe him, a game she knew how to play. But she didn't. She couldn't summon the proper energy to massage this situation.

"Now?" he said.

"Can you actually just drop me off," she said, "at the intersection before town? Where the market is?"

"But, like, right now? Right this second?" Jack looked

frightened and young. It was painful how young he was. A baby, a child. He pleaded with her, silently, for guidance. He reached for her hand.

She stopped herself from recoiling, but he still noticed.

"Come on, Alex, I said I was sorry. I was just high. It sounded true when I was saying it. I'm dumb. I'm sorry."

"It's fine," she said. "Really. Let's talk later, okay?"

"I do want to help you. We can figure something out. I love you," he said, and hadn't that been enough of a warning sign, how quickly he said that, his feelings flailing around for any place to land?

"You're a sweet boy, okay?"

"Fuck," he whispered, "fuck," and he turned to Alex with a ragged, wild face. "Can you just wait? Why do you have to leave right now?"

It was sudden and startling, the way he crumpled.

"I'm sorry," Jack said, his shoulders heaving, wiping his nose with his forearm. "Okay, I'm really sorry. Don't leave, please. Please."

She should comfort him. But she was frozen.

"I'm not in a good place." His voice was nasally. "I'm really not doing good, okay?"

"I'm sorry." She did feel bad, did feel sorry, but when she spoke she sounded sober and faint and bloodless.

"Alex," he said. "Please. Come on." Jack was still crying. Unbelievable, this flood of tears. Why, really, did it surprise her? He was a kid.

He switched tactics. "Where are you going? Tell me. Okay? You have to tell me."

Her head was pounding: already she was steeling herself

for a series of wearying logistics. She spoke very clearly and slowly. "You need to go home," she said. "Just drop me off at the beach, okay?"

It was good he kept driving, that they were putting distance between themselves and the house, but, she thought, this wasn't any road she recognized, the houses thinning, the dunes getting scrubbier and more forested, the car picking up speed.

"We have to talk," Jack said, hands white-knuckling the wheel. "You can't just leave, it's not fair."

Alex held her bag more tightly on her lap.

There was something she could say, some way to convince him to let this go—she had always been good at maneuvering disappointment—she just had to think for a moment, and how could she think with him crying like this?

"Just talk to me," Jack said. "Please. I love you."

His face was anguished, churning with pure misery. He wept and pawed at his eyes. Saying her name over and over.

"Jack." She tried to speak calmly. Her voice rasped as if she'd been yelling: had she been yelling?

"I'm sorry," Jack said, his shoulders heaving. "Okay, I'm really sorry. Don't leave, please. Please." His words squeezed together. "I don't know what I'll do. I might do something bad. If you leave."

Was he telling the truth?

"Did you hear me? Don't you even care?"

Alex told herself the boy wouldn't actually do anything. That he would be fine.

"Jack." What was she going to say next? She didn't know.

She was watching the boy's face, not the road, and she saw the boy flinch, his features seizing up, and then she saw it, too.

A deer in the road. Teetering on its legs, the soft cupped ears in high alert. Standing right in their path. Why didn't the animal move, Alex thought, why wasn't it afraid?

The trees rushing at the windshield.

Then, a tremendous sound.

ALEX COULD NOT, FOR a moment, move. Curious, was her first thought, curious. The boy. The question of the boy appeared in her brain. The prickles began at her spine.

Had she grabbed the wheel? No. The boy had swerved, hadn't he? Like anyone would.

Move, she thought, her eyes rolling around in her skull. Move.

Jack coughed. He blinked in a strange, sleepy way. His head swiveled slowly toward her.

"Jesus," he said. His voice was spaced out, wobbly. "Are you okay?"

"Yeah. Are you?"

"Did we hit it?"

Alex's door stuck, then opened. It took a moment to realize that the window wasn't rolled down: the glass was all over the road. She stood there, outside the car, her knees locking.

The boy had gotten out, too. Standing by the driver's door. He looked fine.

"You look fine," she said.

They had not hit the deer. But they'd hit the guardrail. The front bumper was smashed, but not the hood. No glass in any of the car windows on her side. The windshield was intact.

"Fuck," he said softly. "Fuck. My dad's gonna be so mad."

He looked at the car, looked at the ground. He pushed a fist hard into his forehead. "Fuck," he said again, more quietly. "Should we call someone?"

He was waiting for Alex to say something. Waiting for her to have the answer.

But she'd been thinking the same thing: how long before someone else deals with this?

Alex was holding her breath—she realized when she started to feel light-headed.

"Yeah," she said. "Yeah. Let's call. I'll do it." Her phone was in her bag, which had migrated, somehow, to the backseat. When she found it, the screen seemed crisp, unusually clear, words and messages hovering there in unbelievable detail. Dom had texted, Dom had called. Where was she, Dom wanted to know. He was waiting. She ignored it all.

She dialed the number.

She said there had been an accident. A small accident.

She said that the driver was okay. In the moment, she could not remember his name.

She said she did not know where they were.

A street address, the man on the phone said, look around, but there were only trees.

"Where are we," she said to Jack.

"Detrick Road. Say Detrick Road by the highway."

Are you hurt, the man said.

Was she? She didn't answer.

"Thanks," she said, ending the call.

ALEX SHOULD STAY WITH the boy, wait there with him by the side of the road until someone arrived. That's what she should do. But what good would it do? If she stayed or didn't stay. It didn't change what had already happened. It could only make things worse. For her. Maybe for both of them.

"I'm just gonna see if there's a house or something," she said, not exactly making eye contact. "I'll come back and get you, okay?"

Goodbye, she was saying in her mind.

"Should I come with?"

She shrugged.

"You stay here."

Did the boy know she was lying? Surely he noticed that Alex brought her bag with her. Still, he smiled anyway. Maybe he was good at pretending, too—she had never considered that possibility.

GET TO SIMON'S. THAT'S all Alex had to do.

Don't pause, just keep walking, even though she could feel something wasn't right, her neck too tight, something off in her gait. But she was fine if she kept her eyes forward, if she did not stop or slow.

Alex saw things without really seeing them: the bicyclists passing in a line with their flashing red safety lights, the fork where the highway split in two.

All was good.

All was well.

Lovely, even.

Look at the hydrangeas. The white flowers with the slightest tint of yellow. The glossy leaves with their serrated edges, like little animal teeth. Look at the houses, gray-scaled with shingles, a flag hung over the door filling and slackening in the breeze.

Alex cut down the first lane she saw. She passed more houses with their fences and gates, cars parked in their driveways, and the sight of these things comforted her, the evidence of other lives that existed and would continue to exist. A dog in the distance started to bark unevenly.

She could smell the ocean. Didn't the roads feel familiar? This pasture, this wooden fence. Hadn't she and Simon driven these roads once? Everything looked starkly outlined and seemed to hover a little in her field of vision.

Her hands were shaking. She worried she was going crazy. At the same time, she knew she would never actually go crazy.

Her phone rang. Jack was calling. She ignored the call.

A text from Jack:

When u coming back?

Her left eye seemed to throb. She wanted to scratch it. But, she told herself, she was just imagining the pain. She willed this to be true. And the feeling went away.

She only had to get to the party. That was the only thing left to do. After so much effort. She could do that.

ALEX WALKED UNTIL SHE hit a beach parking lot. The beach air was indistinct, hazy. A lifeguard was atop the tower, his chin slumped in his hand. His face was hidden in the shade of his hat. A few families were on the sand and an older couple in white clothes meandered along the shoreline. The woman glanced at Alex as they passed: it looked like the woman had been crying. Did the man's expression darken when he saw Alex?

Was everything rising from the place she thought it was hidden?

No, she told herself, no. Everything was fine.

She looked up directions on her phone. Simon's house was some distance away. But no matter. All this energy coursing through her. She could walk forever.

This was all drawing to a close. This mess. Everything would go back to how it was.

She changed in the beach bathroom. A coppery party dress with thin straps: another dress that Simon had bought for her. She took off her underwear so there wouldn't be any lines. The fabric of the dress was wrinkled. Silk was unforgiving that way. She told herself it wouldn't be noticeable. The bathroom mirror was warped metal, not glass. So she couldn't actually see her reflection. Alex took a photo of herself on her phone. She studied the image. She looked fine. Her eye wasn't pink, she told herself. She was only imagining it. She blinked hard.

Another ding:

> Where r u?
> R u coming back?
> Alex?
> Alex?

Jack would be fine. Surely. Surely he was already guzzling water and figuring out how to get his father's car towed and soon he'd be back at home. Safe and sound.

Maybe everyone would walk away from this unscathed.

And Simon?

She could picture him. Simon standing there at his party in his fresh white shirt. Simon's face breaking into a smile when he saw Alex arrive. He would hold his hand up in a wave, Simon, and he would beckon her over.

Even his shape would be comforting. It was the shape of her life.

All she had to do was get herself there.

That was it.

Easy. Just a brisk walk.

She was a lucky girl. Wasn't she?

Jack called again.

She ignored it.

More texts from Jack:

> Alex.
> I might do something bad.
> Im not kidding.

She could forget the boy. She could forget Dom, waiting for her at the train station. She'd forget it all, with a little effort.

But maybe some things could never be erased. Maybe they tinted some cellular level of your experience, and even if you scraped away whatever part was on the surface, the rot had already gotten beneath.

The scratch on the painting, the itch in her eye.

If that was true—if it had all counted.

But maybe it didn't.

The phone rang again. Dom, now.

THIS NEXT PART WAS EASY:

Alex stared at the phone. The phone that was still ringing.

Alex turned the phone off.

Alex dropped the phone cleanly into the bathroom trash can.

THE AIR WAS HEAVY by the time Alex arrived at Simon's. But the sky was blue, the morning rain just a memory. He had gotten his perfect day. As she had always known he would. She was happy for him.

So many cars parked along the gravel driveway. So many guests, already here. It was all happening.

Alex made her way to the entrance of the walled property. Her body carrying her along with the fluid quality of a dream.

Did she expect some resistance? There was none. The big wooden door was wide open. As if everything was working in concert to allow for Alex's arrival. To urge her forward. Already she had forgotten the walk there: couldn't say how long it had taken, what roads she'd passed. The slate was wiped clean.

HERE IT WAS. THE world. Just as she had left it.

Alex crossed the threshold.

Instantly she was handed a glass of pink wine.

She didn't recognize anyone at the party. Any of these strangers who gathered in chatty nebulas in the yard, coming together, coming apart. But why should she know these people? Simon had all kinds of friends. Of course she wouldn't have met all of them. Not yet.

Alex cut across the lawn. A group of women seemed to stop talking as she walked by. But she was imagining it, surely. She raised her glass in their direction.

A sip of wine. Her hand was sweating around the stem.

She turned at a run of chatter from the deck, a sudden bawling laugh that sounded especially loud—had the music stopped, had music ever been playing?

Alex stood there. She kept a smile on her face. The grass was wet, she could feel her sandals getting damp. The roses had exploded in the last week—was that possible, would they bloom all at once like this, this late in the summer? So many soft blowsy colors crawling up the wall. It was a beautiful house. A warmth was spreading through her. An expansive, generous feeling, and when Simon's dog came lurching toward her, she was happy to see him. When Alex held out her fingers, the dog sniffed. Then did a funny slouching turn and loped back the way he'd come. Abruptly, he'd left so abruptly. But no matter. Because there was Lori, bustling around in her familiar way. Lori, who kept it all together. Alex felt some affection for Lori. For all of this.

She waved at Lori. Lori's nose crinkled, almost invisibly. Alex waved again, and crossed over to Lori.

"Hi."

What was Alex expecting? Some reaction. Even a negative one. But Lori barely acknowledged her. Her face was a mask.

"Glad you could make it," Lori said. Rather stiffly. Maybe she was just surprised to see Alex. Or concerned, like Alex might make a scene. But she didn't need to worry. Alex would behave this time. She'd be no trouble at all.

Alex smiled wider.

"The lawn," Alex said. "It looks great. You filled in the holes."

"Sorry?"

"The grass," she said. "It looks nice."

A silence fell. Lori didn't exactly return Alex's smile. Alex blinked. Sweat starting to prick around her hairline.

"Well." Lori wiped her hands on her pants. "Well, excuse me."

Then Lori disappeared. Leaving Alex standing alone.

Oh well. Not a problem. Nothing could bother her. Not now.

Alex joined a line for the food. The coins of beef marinated in vinegar and blood, a silver pan of green beans and purple onions, a pasta salad that she didn't touch. A square of salmon that looked overcooked, charred lemon slices stuck to the surface. The guy tending to accordioned cuts of pork loin under the murderous red glow of a warming lamp.

Alex took a plateful of watermelon and mint. She ate with her fingers—the wet pink cubes softening, dissolving on her tongue. All this sweetness in the world. She set down the plate for a moment, to go back for a napkin. When she returned, her plate was gone.

Alex brushed her hair out of her eyes. She let herself survey the scene. The surface of the pool was a little choppy in the breeze, the water a murky gunmetal. Hadn't there been a lip, before? Around the water's rim? Was it safe, a pool that dropped so abruptly into the ground? Wouldn't it be easy to fall in?

Alex needed to make her way to the house and leave her bag inside. Better to be unencumbered when she finally saw Simon.

"Excuse me," Alex said, trying to squeeze past a man. He didn't move, lost in conversation with a couple. "Excuse me," she said again. He glanced at her, then turned away. Showing his broad slab of back in his blue shirt. Why did the couple he was talking to look familiar? The thin woman, the short, unhappy-looking man.

George—the name bubbled up in her brain. George and his thin wife and the painting she had ruined.

Did George know about the ruined painting?

No, she told herself, no.

And maybe this wasn't George.

No way to be sure.

It probably wasn't. Of course it wasn't.

Everything was fine. She kept smiling.

She made herself look away from the couple, made herself keep moving. The body with its own momentum. Carrying her forward.

Simon was here, surely. She just had to find him.

He wasn't near the bar. Wasn't on the lawn, wasn't near the food.

It didn't worry her. There was no rush. It was all going so well.

IT WAS QUIET INSIDE the house. Familiar. The entryway was as Alex had left it. The mirror looming at her from the wall, the vase of flowers from the cutting garden. She avoided her reflection. The chill of the concrete floor penetrated her sandals as she walked down the hall. Here was the kitchen. Looking as it had always looked. She opened a cabinet door—there they were, the pale green glasses all in a row, just as she remembered.

"Can I help you?" a waiter said. His tone was unfriendly. "If you need a drink, I'm happy to bring you one outside."

Would he stand there until she left? It seemed so. She smiled a tight smile. It wasn't the man's fault. He didn't know that she belonged here. Her dress was sticking to her damp skin. Was the silk dark with sweat? Just a little. Her eye stung: she ignored it. She had the urge to check her phone, but her hands were empty. She'd thrown the phone away. The phone was gone.

If Jack was calling, she didn't know about it. If Dom was calling, she didn't know about it. So it was the same as if they weren't calling.

ALEX WANDERED THROUGH THE other realms of the party. Passing through other people's conversations—the briefest wash of their chatter, of their lives, falling on her, like light from a door being opened. Strange to see the stark yard suddenly populated. So many people with open, gnashing mouths and glasses in their hands, their private moons of alcohol. The moon was going to wobble soon: this fact came to her unbidden, then dropped away. There was a man in transition lenses that made it impossible to gauge where he was looking, though it seemed to be right at Alex. Did he look a little like Dom? Did the woman pulling a thin sweater across her bony shoulders look familiar, too, some memory rising up, then dissipating?

A child darted past, narrowly missing Alex, and she'd barely recovered before another kid ran by, giving chase to the first, and this kid knocked into her hip. Alex stumbled a little. But didn't fall—she didn't fall. She smiled in case anyone was watching her. She swallowed hard. The wine coated her throat unpleasantly.

Alex blinked. The sun like a sodium flash.

And then she saw him.

Simon.

Alex had somehow known it was going to happen before it happened. Seeing Simon. Everything started to feel inevitable. Moved along by some larger force.

Simon.

He was standing on the wooden deck outside the kitchen. Chatting to a couple sitting at the wrought iron table. Was it George and his wife? She pushed down the question before she answered it. And it didn't matter—because here he was.

Simon.

He had one foot up on a chair and was leaning forward slightly, resting his weight on his knee. He gestured with his glass. There was something in the languid way his hand moved that felt very intimate, like he was sending her a message. Scrawling a sign in the air.

Maybe they were both thinking the same things, she and him. Their minds syncing. Maybe he was feeling it, too. The way the seconds were churning past. How close this was to being over.

How innocent her past mistakes seemed. The world was suddenly benevolent, instantly absorbing her errors and showing her how good everything actually was, how absolutely fine.

Here, he was right here. Simon, at last. Looking as he had always looked. As if nothing had changed. As if the past week had been deleted.

Only a lawn separated them.

Some glitch, some stutter, a murmur from the couple, and Simon was turning to look at her.

Simon.

The breeze whipped his shirt. His body was aimed at her body.

She smiled again. Everything had turned out fine. She felt herself smiling out to the universe, the sun catching sharply on the water of the pool, dancing along her vision.

But this was all wrong—why was Simon making that face? Why did his eyes seem to look at something beyond her?

Was it possible that Simon didn't recognize her?

Alex held her hand up in a wave. The smallest wave.

She could hear her breath in her ears, the heartbeat that kept coming, beat after beat.

Would he come to her?

Simon didn't move.

Okay. Her smile cracked wider.

Okay. Simon had been waiting for her. She would go to him. He was waiting for Alex, and all she had to do was walk over.

Now, she told herself, willing her limbs to work. She didn't move.

Now.

EMMA CLINE is the author of the *New York Times* bestselling novel *The Girls* and the short story collection *Daddy*. The winner of the Plimpton Prize, she has been a finalist for the National Book Critics Circle Award, the First Novel Prize, the *Los Angeles Times* Book Prize, and the *Sunday Times* Story Award. She is the recipient of an O. Henry Prize and was named one of *Granta*'s Best Young American Novelists.

This book was set in Caslon, a typeface first designed in 1722 by William Caslon (1692–1766). Its widespread use by most English printers in the early eighteenth century soon supplanted the Dutch typefaces that had formerly prevailed. The roman is considered a "workhorse" typeface due to its pleasant, open appearance, while the italic is exceedingly decorative.